Nari

Sharath Komarraju began his professional life as a software engineer, but has renounced it all in favour of a writing desk and a word processor. His first book, *Murder in Amaravati*, was longlisted for the Commonwealth Book Prize 2013. His best known work is *The Winds of Hastinapur*, the first in a series that attempts to tell the story of Mahabharata from the perspective of its prominent women characters. *Nari* is his fifth novel. He may be contacted at www.sharathkomarraju.com

Also by Sharath Komarraju

Fiction

Murder in Amaravati

Banquet on the Dead

The Winds of Hastinapur

The Puppeteers of Palem

Non-Fiction

Money Wise:
The Aadmi's Guide to Wealth and Financial Freedom

NARI

– a novel –

Sharath Komarraju

PAN

First published in the Indian subcontinent 2015 by Pan
an imprint of Pan Macmillan India,
a division of Macmillan Publishers India Private Limited
Pan Macmillan India, 707, Kailash Building
26 KG Marg, New Delhi – 110 001
www.panmacmillan.co.in

Pan Macmillan, 20 New Wharf Road, London N1 9RR
Basingstoke and Oxford
Associated companies throughout the world
www.panmacmillan.com

ISBN 978-93-82616-57-3

1 3 5 7 9 8 6 4 2

Typeset by G.S. Print Line
Printed and bound in India by Shree Maitrey Printech Pvt. Ltd., Noida

To Kanishka, for telling me that my books suck,
and for pitching them to publishers anyway
(probably out of pity). Keep doing it, Kan.

PROLOGUE

Stop Press: News Flash

Abhilash Tirthankar, retired army officer, was found dead at home in Banjara Hills.

His wife, Ramya Tirthankar, has accused their manservant, Narayana, of the murder.

Narayana has been taken into custody.

There are reports of rape as well.

Testimonies have been recorded.

Trial awaits.

TESTIMONY I

ONE

One of the first things I noticed about Narayana was the strength he had in his fingers. On the third day or so after Captain had brought him home, I saw him remove the husk of two coconuts with his bare hands. This was six months ago, and he had just turned seventeen. But he had tight blue veins sticking out on his forearms, even then. His fingers resembled the dead roots of an uprooted tree, and I often felt that if he were to close his fist, he would be able to touch his wrist easily.

In all other respects he was a boy. In the months with us, we fed him well, so he has filled out a little now, but back then he had that thin, snake-like build you see in villagers. Captain often joked that if Nari held his hands straight over his head, he could be rolled up inside a carpet. He had the legs of a stork, and when he walked it seemed that he could topple over at any moment, much like those kids swinging on tightropes on the street.

Whenever I say that he was – and is – just a boy, people ask me if it is not fair that his punishment be made lighter owing to that fact. To that I only say that the law exists for a reason. I am an army man's wife; I have full faith in our country's policies. I will abide by them without complaint.

But I will also say that not all parts of Nari are boyish. Certain organs of his body belong to a larger, stronger man. And I do not refer just to his arms and hands.

I have a friend who remembers the way the rain had slapped on her window pane the night she gave birth. Another man I know swears he can hear the wind coo in his ears every time he thinks of that winter morning on which his wife breathed her last. I am not like that. I am not a weather watcher. If you ask me about the evening when Captain first told me about Nari, I could tell you nothing about whether the roses in the flower pots on the terrace were in full bloom or were wilting, whether the guava tree on the street corner swelled with fruit or stood shorn of leaves, whether the smell in the air came from bees or from mosquitoes.

I do know, though, that I sat on the cane swing in the living room with my hands stretched over my head, holding the upper frame. The tips of my toes touched the marble floor. Through the thinning cushions the chair pricked my back and shoulders. The long shadows of late evening filled the room. Natural light came in only through the cream curtains on the windows at the front of the house. All the other windows were draped in black – my choice, much to Captain's displeasure.

He entered the room in his grey overcoat and blue track pants. He had his pipe in his mouth, his stick in his right hand. At the doorway, he tapped the floor with its rubber tip. It was his way of knocking.

Kicking off his walking shoes, he sat on the sofa, folded his legs and stretched his toes. It reminded me of Sridhar's toes, the way they curled when he climaxed. In spite of the sweat and stuffiness in the room I found myself aroused at the mere thought. He had not said anything about the darkness yet. A white line of smoke exited his pipe and dissolved into the air.

'Do you remember Shankar, the farmer in Singavaram?'

I turned the swing with my feet so I could face him, and nodded. The previous summer Captain had gone to Singavaram to see to a library, and had been bitten by a snake. This man, Shankar, had then sucked out the poison. I had not been there, but I had heard the tale often enough.

'He asked me if we could keep his son as house help,' said Captain.

The first thought that came to my mind at his words was how I was going to keep meeting Sridhar. Now whenever Captain left for his camps, I had the house to myself, and as long as I took care to stay out of sight of the neighbours, I could do as I wished. Once or twice the Sikh truck driver who lived in the ground floor of the apartment complex across the road had given me the shifty eye, and I had wondered if he had seen Sridhar come and go. For a while after that, I made him come only long after nightfall, after all the lights in the street's houses had been dimmed.

'Do we need house help?' I asked Captain. 'I manage quite well without one.'

'Quite. But it's Shankar. I could not say no.'

'If you wish to repay Shankar, give him money.'

'I did. He wouldn't take it.'

'Put his son in a hostel. Give him work in your army canteen somewhere.'

'He wants us to take care of him, Ramya.'

I could tell from the way his foot had begun to shake that he was getting agitated. Pushing it further would make him suspicious too, and once doubt entered Captain's mind, he did not rest until he got to the bottom of it. If he knew about Sridhar, he would kill him. Whether he would kill me as well or not, I did not know. A small part of him probably still loved me enough to leave me with my limbs and bones intact.

So I decided the matter should rest, for now. Sridhar and I would have to plan around this little mishap. Or perhaps I could concoct some situation which would get Captain to drive this kid out of the house. So I put on my best smile and said, 'Whatever you say, dear.'

Captain blew another puff out of his pipe, unsmiling.

After breakfast the next day, I set out on foot to my clinic. Captain had offered to drop me off on his way to the NGO, but I said no. Sridhar had begun to make little comments about my hips lately. A brisk early morning walk should fix whatever it was that he saw. I went to the end of the street and turned to the left, ignoring the grocer who I knew would be looking at me, hoping to catch my gaze so that he could flash his black teeth.

Once again I noticed how close together these 'independent' houses had been built. The eaves of one three-storied building scraped the outer wall of the house next to it. I thought of the sly way in which the woman next door looked at me every time she came out to speak to the milkman. Could she have heard me and Sridhar? We took care to bolt the windows and draw the curtains, but one could never tell. I should remember to stuff my mouth with a sock, and give him my finger to bite on. Captain and I were quiet in our lovemaking, a series of hoarse breaths – all his – leading up to a low guttural grunt or two, and then nothing. If I was lucky I would get a peck on the cheek before he rolled away to his side of the bed.

I opened the rusty black gate to the clinic and pushed open the door. Inside, Sridhar sat on the table, leaning on his hands and laughing with Ankita. He had told me that he never flirted with her, though it wouldn't matter to me all that much if he did. I did not expect him to lay down his life for me. As long as he was available, I would have him. If someone came into his life that made him leave, so be it. Someone would come into mine too, perhaps.

Both of them got to their feet when I entered. Ankita looked down, tucked a lock of her hair behind her ear, and murmured: 'Good morning, madam.'

Sridhar said, 'Hi, madam.'

I nodded at them and went into my chamber. I placed my bag on the glass table and adjusted the paper weight so that it sat in the centre. Leaning against the edge and running my hand over the glass, I examined my fingernails. There was a chip on the edge of the ring finger, which showed rather grotesquely against my black skin. Ankita always kept her nails painted; last week it was a light shade of silver, this week it was pink. She wore bright reds and blues too. She looked like one of those mannequins in apparel shops, white as sugar and lifeless as wood.

The clock on the wall said eight-thirty. My first appointment was not until half-past nine. One of these days I should look again at whether I really needed Ankita. It had been six months since she had been with me and I had not yet seen any ability, save for typing away on her computer. Even the details of my clients I remembered more than she did. If all she could do was chat with Sridhar and distract him from his work, she could do it on her own time, in her own place, with her own money.

I rang the bell. The door opened and Sridhar peeped in. 'Yes, madam?'

'Have you finished your report on the aphasia patient we had last week?'

'Yes, madam, would you like to see it?'

'Yes, please.' I cleared my throat and walked to the couch. I undid the first two buttons of my dress, and when he opened the door again, with a stapled bundle of papers in his hand, I was sitting with my left leg crossed over the right, my shoe dangling off my foot.

He swallowed, and locked the door behind him.

'I thought you said we should not use the office for – er – activities.' He stood in front of the couch and pulled up his pants. I lay sprawled, my dress still hiked up. While I waited for my breath to return, I looked at the morning light gleam in his hazel eyes. I had told him on our first meeting that he was the first hazel-eyed man I knew. He had blushed. The girls at the university had told him the same thing, he had said.

'We must from now on,' I said. 'The house is no longer empty during the day.'

'Relatives?' He pushed back his hair, revealing a row of red spots on the forehead.

'Servant. He arrived this morning.' With me lying down and him standing up he looked taller than his six-foot-one, and when I rubbed my thighs together they seemed to release his cologne into the air. 'Don't you think it's exciting to do it here?'

'I guess.' He looked in the direction of the window. 'I need your signature on the work certificate. Doctor Mane was asking for it last week.'

'I will give you your signature,' I said, sitting up. 'I know Mane quite well.'

'And the letter? You will give me a letter too, recommending me to the board?'

'Of course I will, darling.' He grimaced when I said 'darling'. I shouldn't have, I know. We had talked about that before. No terms of endearment, no gifts, no gestures of love other than those that we share through our bodies. These were my rules, but I broke them the most. In the warm glow of contentment it was hard not to slip, now and then.

'I wish we could go to your house. I don't want Ankita knowing about us.'

'Why?' I asked sharply. 'What if she does?'

'I – word can get out. People at the university may come to know.'

'What if they do?'

'They may say it is against the rules. Teacher-student relationships and so on. You know how it is.'

'I am not your teacher.'

He fidgeted, avoiding my gaze. 'But you're my supervisor. They may say that I traded favours for a good grade.'

'Well,' I said, 'aren't you?'

A little smile appeared on the edge of his lips. 'I guess.'

'And your favours are quite good, if I may say so. I can recommend them to any woman on the faculty. I think it will do them good.'

He pushed his hair back and chuckled. 'Ah, but you're biased.'

'Yes, happily so.' I looked up at the clock. There were still twenty minutes to go; too long for conversation and too short for sex. I looked up at him. 'Is your tongue too tired with all this talk?'

He shook his head, confused.

I lay back on the couch and pulled up my dress. He snickered, then kneeled between my legs and thumbed my thighs. My eyes closed. My fingers went into his hair. I threw my head back.

★

At Captain's funeral, I stood alone among the uniformed officers and the street kids and asked myself if I loved him. The answer was yes. If she had been present, my sister Vimla would have said that it was easy to love a dead man. Dead men do not change, they do not judge you, they do not ask for love, they do not need attention.

But even when he was alive, there were times when Captain and I had a certain warmth in our relationship that could be called love. I don't speak of the very first days of our courtship of course, that first flutter of excitement one feels at the first brush of male attention which too many young women mistake for love. I speak of the days long after our wedding, after we had come to Hyderabad and moved into this house. I remember the time when jaundice had consigned me to bed for three full weeks during which he would make tomato and corn soup for me every evening. Each night he would gather me in his arms and whisper tales into my ear until I fell asleep.

In the first year of marriage we kissed each other morning, afternoon and night. We made love three times a week. Messages of eternal love and longing would fly between our phones when he was gone for but a few hours. Now that I think back to that year, I smile at how foolish we were; I was nineteen, so perhaps I could be forgiven, but he was forty-two. He had been in the army, he had seen the world. He had known women before me. How did he persuade himself that our marriage could last?

When I first met him I was a seventeen-year-old girl who had grown up on the beaches of Goa. Living in a holiday spot fills your life with romance and cheer, all false and all borrowed, I now know, but back then I thought people lived their lives as they spent their holidays: with howls of laughter and wide toothy grins. It was an age at which one likes men in uniforms, hand-held walks, kisses in the moonlight, Wordsworth's poems. Captain Abhilash Tirthankar ticked all those boxes.

What is it about older men that makes teenaged girls go weak in the knees? I try now to see Captain through the eyes of my teenaged self. I look at our wedding photographs where he was younger and leaner, his arm circled around my shoulder. I am smiling like I had just been crowned an empress. I fail to see what attracted me to him, because his hair was already balding by then, and it did not take much longer for it to go grey.

Dad made no scene when I told him of Captain's proposal. He only sat down for an hour with his head over his hands. When he got up his eyes were red. 'He's old enough to be your father,' he said. 'Are you sure you know what you're doing?'

I did not tell Dad that I had had enough of him, that I wanted to run away from the house and this was my chance. It would have broken his heart. For all the things that he did to me and Vimla, he was a kind man. For all her snapping, Vimla knows it too, because at Dad's funeral she wept by his coffin and beat silently at its side with her small fists.

On the night of our first anniversary, Captain drank a bottle of Old Monk and beat me with his bare hands. That night he had sex with me. When I protested, he slapped me till I passed out with the pain. The next morning he bawled like a child and fell at my feet. I should have kicked him, but I didn't. I was too afraid.

He sent me to university, encouraged me to study further. He came to my graduation, and was present when they awarded me the doctorate. At the function I sat next to Satish Verma, my guide, and before I went up on stage, he gave me a hug. That night, after we got home, Captain came at me brandishing a cane. Vodka dripped onto the floor from his frothing mouth.

'How long have you been sleeping with him?' he asked me.

'With whom?' I said.

'That tall guy with the beard and earring.'

'Satish? He's my guide, Captain.'

He reached for a bottle and pulled out the cork with his teeth. He thrust it into his mouth and drank. Slamming it back on the table, he smiled at me. 'Guide, huh? Do you think I don't know what happens in these universities, with all you – you *young* people *guiding* each other?'

'Captain, you should sleep.' I must have shown fear in my eyes, because he pounced on me and held me by the shoulders. I shrank back from the whiff of alcohol in his breath, but he shook me until I looked him in the eye. 'Captain,' I said, my voice quivering.

'I am not good enough for you,' he said. 'I can see it in your eyes that you hate me. Don't you?' He pulled me close, our eyelashes almost touching. 'Don't you?'

'I don't, Captain. I love you.'

He roared in laughter. 'Bitch! Do you think I am blind? Huh? Do you think I can't see how your eyes perk up when you speak to that bastard guide of yours? Do you think I cannot read what he means by his impish smile?'

'Captain, I don't know what you're talking about. I love *you*.'

He threw me against the wall. I crawled to the corner and buried my face between my thighs, hugging my knees with my arms. I felt the first blow scathe the skin on my back but I did not budge, afraid that if I were to look up, he would strike my face. With each lash pain coursed through my limbs and arrested my body in a spasm. My jaws clamped together, my teeth chattered in pain and fear, and I whimpered. I felt his wet, warm breath on my neck, and I cried out, 'Don't hit me, Captain, please!'

'Will you ever think of another man but me?'

'No, I promise. I swear, Captain, I won't!'

'Will you remember this night every time you even think of someone else?'

'Yes, Captain, it hurts so much, please don't hit me.'

He stood up straight, holding himself steady against the wall with his left palm. He ordered me to shut up and kept bringing the cane down on my back. I bit my lower lip and shut my eyes tight, counting up to ten and down to one, up and down, trying to go someplace in my head where there would be no pain or smell of vodka, but his voice would bring me back each time and hold me in the present.

He only stopped that night because his arm began to ache, I think, and he stumbled off to ascend the stairs to the bedroom. I did not know when I fell asleep, but when I woke up, I realized with a start that he was sitting by my feet. When I tried to scamper away from him, he held my shins and pulled me toward him.

'I am sorry,' he said, and I just nodded.

'Do you hate me?' I shook my head.

'You're not lying, are you?' I shook my head more forcefully.

'You forgive me, don't you?' I nodded.

Later, I lay on my stomach on the bed and he rubbed coconut water into the wounds on my back. Each time I groaned he shed a tear, and covered my body with kisses. His moustache carried the stench of Bagpipers. Throughout the morning he went about the house mumbling to himself, and in the afternoon he cooked me a meal with chicken, rice, turmeric and cumin that was quite tasty.

When I first met Sridhar I was three months past my thirty-third birthday. My clinic – though Captain liked to call it office – had been running for three years, and it was the first year the university got in touch with me to ask if I would be willing to take in doctoral students as interns. I confess my first impulse was to refuse, but call it loneliness, curiosity or the pull of something novel; I said yes.

The interview went well, because I had seen and liked enough of him in the first few minutes to wish to keep him. I asked him some fairly simple stuff, and we signed a bond that morning itself that he would do twenty hours at my office every week, and that at the end of thirty weeks, I would give him a certificate of work and a letter of recommendation. With the university I had another arrangement of course, whereby I would give weekly feedback of his progress.

Now that was the fourteenth year of my marriage with Captain, and I would say that I had not had sex for about ten of those. For the first four years, in spite of his volcanic nature we still found time and mood for intimacy. But the fires burned out, and by the time Sridhar entered my life, I was little more than Captain's blow-up doll. Once every few nights, he would come up the stairs into my bedroom, ease himself onto the bed, and throw his arm over me. I would push it away and say no. He would mount me, push my legs apart and slide himself in. I would look away and count the spots on the ceiling or the number of times the fan creaked.

'Do you like that?' he would ask between strokes.

'No,' I would say. I would will my loins to dry up and burn his penis, but my body did not know what my mind did.

We never had children. We never spoke of them. Ever since he first beat me, I had decided I did not want kids, because that would mean a different kind of hell. I never did ask him what he thought of children and why he did not want them. I supposed that he had had a vasectomy during his earlier marriage that he forgot to tell me about.

Was I faithful all throughout the ten years? No. After I became a doctor I would get invited to conferences all over the country, and in some of those, one young man or the other would make his intentions plain. He would slip in the key to his room in my handbag just before dinner, and I would succumb.

I don't feel guilty about these incidents, because due to them I realized I had the ability to please a man. For all the intellectual stimulation and contentment that my PhD gave me, it was this boost to the biological ego that I hold dearest to my heart. There had been a few fleeting experiences with patients too; when you're cooped up with an attractive man for hours on end in a room with a couch, things are bound to happen, sooner or later.

That being said, there could not have been more than eight such incidents over the last five years, so it would be fair to say that by the time Sridhar entered, I was ripe for the picking. So was he, as I found out later, because he had been celibate for two years. Don't ask me why; all I will say is that if I had him for a classmate, I would never have graduated from college.

About a week after Sridhar came to work for me, Captain went to Singavaram. His NGO was building a library there, and they needed someone influential to travel to all the headmen in nearby villages and procure funds. It was a three-day trip, he told me, and I waited a day, just to make sure he didn't come back unexpectedly. On the second day, I invited Sridhar home for lunch.

'Shall we go back together from the clinic?' he asked on the phone.

'I am not coming to the clinic today,' I told him. 'I have a headache, and I hope to relieve it with you.'

Waiting for a long-awaited lover takes you back to your teenage years. The mirror and the make-up kit come out. Clothes and poses are tried. Lip-stick and nail polish are applied and erased and applied again. Whereas in your teens you're still nervous and shy about your beauty, now you're confident. Cocky, almost. But somewhere deep down in your heart you feel a little twinge of doubt. What if he doesn't like dark women? What if I am too short for him? Are my breasts his size?

I took a long bath that morning and wore a sleeveless silver nightie with straps running down the back. I left my hair loose, because I had seen him glance at me guiltily at the clinic when I undid my hair to tie it into a bun. I had met men who liked women's hair tied, but not enough. Most of them liked something to run their fingers in. For my nails, I agonized over different colours before deciding to leave them clear. I covered myself in baby lotion, and made sure that a faint wisp of lime lingered in the air. Cherry-flavoured gloss on the lips, and black liner under the eyes. I left my lashes untouched.

He brought cake. We had it in the living room by the dining table, sitting in opposite chairs, talking. Twice he fed me a piece. When I tried to do the same he trapped my finger between his teeth. When I told him doing that to a supervisor was most inappropriate, he replied that all he wanted to do was relieve my headache.

'I've always had a thing for tall guys,' I said, getting up and starting toward the bedroom. I heard him push the chair back and follow me. 'I hope I can last as long as you can.' I have long learnt that nothing matters more to a man – nothing in the world – than an open admiration of his sexual prowess, real or not. I have tried it on every man I went to bed with, and some of them were nowhere near as good as I told them they were, and it worked every single time. You never cast doubts on a man's sexuality; unless, of course, you want to maim him for life.

Sridhar entered the bedroom and closed the door. I clapped a hand over my mouth, feigning indignation. 'What if the neighbours hear us?'

'I hope they do,' he said.

'Yeah? You think you can make me moan?'

'I know I can.' He came after me and pushed me on to the bed. I burned with the desire to pounce on him, but I have learnt to cede the first round to the man. Let him come, I thought. Let him have me the way Captain never would.

It was only three hours later, when I woke up and turned to see his naked sleeping form next to mine in the wall mirror, that I noticed how fair he was. I had stolen glimpses at the reflection of our twining bodies during the act (something I had never done with Captain), but I had not felt the contrast in our complexions as keenly. Now I placed my hand on his bare back. I let my hair fall over his neck. I ran my foot over his calf. He snorted softly and lines appeared on his forehead, but then the next moment he was back to peace.

I tried to find spots on his body, an ounce of fat, an inch of flab. On his right arm was a pink gash that ran from the shoulder to the elbow, about a quarter of an inch in thickness. I ran my finger along its length, and I felt desire kindle between my legs again. I slipped my leg between his thighs, and my fingers caressed his knuckles, squeezed his palms. I shook him awake. He seemed irritated at first, but when he saw me he smiled and opened his arm to pull me in. I placed my hand on his chest, then slid it slowly downward, pausing for a moment at the belly button, then moving down to his waist.

'What are you doing?' he asked, even as he responded to my touch.

'It is my turn now,' I said, and straddled him. My hands closing around the hair on his chest, I eased him into me.

TWO

Those first three days after he arrived at our house, Nari kept out of my way. I heard his squeaky voice and laughter often, but around me he stood in the corner, with his head bowed and hands held in front of him. He wore a light blue shirt with white buttons, a black rose printed on the left pocket. His shorts were navy-blue, and I told him on the day he ripped out the coconut husks that if he tucked in his shirt, he would look like a schoolboy. He coloured and stole away without meeting my eye, and Captain said that I should not scare him.

He belonged to a wandering tribe that earned their living as labourers in farms. The women cleaned porticos, drew water and looked after children at the big houses. Captain once said that some of them looked after the men in those houses too, but he had downed a few pegs by then. They sent some of their children to night school, apparently, and Nari was one of the lucky few. On the second day, he took from Captain a slate and a piece of chalk. After he had gone to sleep I glanced at what he had drawn. On one side there was an apple with a round hole, and on the other a crescent moon with a bunch of stars around it.

I could look at him without flinching when he slept. I never could look at his eyes for a length of time. Sometimes they looked like black holes punched into an empty gunny sack. Sometimes they reminded me of a dying tree's hollow. Even when he sat in front of the television and laughed at it, his eyes would come alive only for a few fleeting moments, during which they would turn into rich shades of green and white. I would sit up to look, because those eyes reminded me of Albert, but the next second they would retreat and become grey again.

Nari fell sick with a bout of viral that week, and I don't know why but I tended to him. I put him on a foam mattress in the guest room, gave him an old but unused cotton blanket with a print of yellow flowers and green creepers, and made him drink milk four times a day. He grimaced when I commanded him to gulp down the eggs I had boiled for him, but the bread he ate hungrily and with moans of agreement. Twice, on returning from the clinic I found him gorging on cake and cream biscuits, and on both occasions I made him go to bed after dinner without dessert.

I read for him stories from the *Panchatantra*, and each time he would slip into sleep before I had finished the tale. Tenali Raman and Maulvi Naseeruddin made him giggle. Akbar-Birbal made him thoughtful and grave. When I told him about the beginning of the *Ramayana*, he said he wanted three wives too.

His illness lasted a week. On the last night, the third after his skin had begun to cool and his throat begun to clear, after he had gone to sleep, I shut the book and got up to turn off the light. Just as I turned away from him, he gripped my wrist.

When I turned to look at him, his eyes were moist. He joined his hands and held them up to me. I held them and planted a kiss on his forehead.

That night I thought of Albert.

In my bedroom that night, by the light of the bed lamp, I saw dust on the glass surface of the Radha-Krishna painting on the side wall. After running a moist cloth over it and blowing upon it a little, I quietly got into bed, praying that the creaking bed would not bring Captain upstairs. He had not beaten me for a few months now. These calm days put me forever on edge, because it only meant that the day of the storm was drawing ever nearer. Often I picked fights with him just to puncture the bubble of anger, so that he would be a man again for a few days.

I thought of the eighteen-year-old girl who had once thought he was more of a man than Albert was. As I sank under my sheets and covered my ears, I heard his lilting voice in my ears. 'He is not the man for you, Ramya,' Albert had said on the eve of my engagement. We had been sitting on the beach, just out of reach of the waves. Behind us the waiters of Sammy's Shack were shutting up for the night. Sam called out from behind his counter to ask if we wanted anything. Albert half-turned and waved to say no.

He pulled his folded pants further up to his knees and buried his toes in the sand. His hands smelled of salmon and crab. 'I hope you're not doing this because of Vimla,' he said, and quite deftly averted his eyes when I looked up at him.

'Vimla can go to the dogs, for all I care,' I said. 'This is about me and my love, Albie.'

'Your love?'

'Yes, mine, not Vimla's or yours.'

'Tell me one thing you have in common with him.'

'We both like Wordsworth,' I said.

'So what are you going to talk about when you're sick of discussing poetry?'

'For all the common things that you and I have, what have we ever done, Albie?'

He smiled at the sea. 'If I say I wanted to marry you, will you call off your wedding to this man?'

'No,' I said. 'Don't be an idiot.'

'There's one idiot on this beach, Ramya, and it's not me.'

I had wanted to stuff a handful of sand in his mouth that night, and slap him, for all those times when he pretended to ignore my glances in his direction, for all those times when he pulled away his hand when it touched mine, for that time he took Vimla to the New Years' dance and left me at home alone, for kissing her and telling her that he loved her, for writing poems for me in cards and then claiming that he did it only to amuse me.

Albert had green eyes, and in those flash-like moments in which Nari sprang to life and laughed, he looked just like him.

I woke up in the middle of the night with Captain's hand massaging my left breast. I turned around and said, 'No.' He grunted and increased the pressure of his fingers. My nipple hardened. I tried to push him away. He moved closer and trapped both my legs with his. His hand moved down my waist.

'Captain, no.'

'I know you like it,' he said, and his hand slid into my underwear. I closed my eyes and willed my mind to flee. It went to the beach, and I saw in front of me Albert and Vimla, talking and laughing. I hovered above them like a ghost and laughed with them, but they did not see me. Albert's hand was on Vimla's crotch, and in no time she was moaning in my voice.

'I know you like it,' said Captain, and I was back in the bedroom. Both my hands were wrapped around his wrist, and his fingers prodded and plumbed. I whimpered and bit my lips because his fingernails hurt me, and of course he went faster because he thought I liked it. With his other hand he was stroking himself, I knew, and once again I closed my eyes, imagining the room in fresh white morning light with my legs wrapped around Sridhar's marble-like waist. I tried to buck my knees the same way I did with him, but Captain's fingers bruised my flesh and I cried out again.

'You're hurting me,' I said.

He pulled out his hand with such force that he scratched the inside of my thigh, and I turned away onto my side, watching the flute-bearer and the cowgirl entwined in an embrace amid bounding calves. A brown hand yanked me by the shoulder, and a big mass of fat and muscle enveloped me. Something familiar yet distant entered me, and I closed my eyes again. If I said no now, he would slap me until I bled from the lip. It was best to make the necessary sounds – I knew them all, by now – for as long as he held out. It would all end with a throaty whine from him and a contented sigh from me.

I thought of Sridhar but he morphed into Albert. Albert striding in this room naked, his chocolate-like skin made browner by the sunlight, his long feminine hands undressing me and propping me up on pillows, pushing my legs over my shoulders so that he could enter me, my hair thrown out around my head on the snowy white bed sheet, the air heavy with the stain of salmon and musk.

After a while, Captain rolled off me and slobbered over my cheek. I looked up at the ceiling, wiped my forehead clean of his sweat, lowered my nightgown, and waited for the throbbing to subside. I told myself that I would look up Albie the next time I went to Goa, but I also knew that the feeling would pass, that even if I were to run into him at Sammy's Shack, I would pretend that I did not know him.

The next morning, after Captain had left for the NGO, just as I was about to finish my cup of morning tea, Nari gave me a rose. I did not ask him where he got it from. I just took it and said thank you. As a child I gave roses to many of my teachers, and took great pleasure in watching them set the flowers in their hair. I did the same as Nari watched, and only when I turned back to see the look in his eye that I felt the first tug of fear. It lasted for only a moment, but it was there. I had not seen such a naked picture of lust in any man's eyes that Nari had in his that morning.

And yet the next moment the look on his face was that of compassion and deference. Looking back now, maybe I should have taken a stronger view of this little incident, but then hindsight is a wonderful thing, isn't it? If I had even an inkling of what was to come, would I not have driven him out of the house on the day Captain brought him home?

'You have a sister, don't you?' I asked him after the moment had passed. 'Tell me about her.'

'Her name is Raji,' he said. 'She is eight now. She goes to school in the village.' He did not smile when he spoke of her. He looked away, and folded the end of his shirt up and down as words tumbled out of him, in pairs and threes. 'She likes roses.' He looked up at me guiltily. 'She likes shiny paperclips.'

'And you? Does she love you?'

He smiled thinly at first, then it broadened to fill his face. His teeth were uneven and yellow, his incisors were flat, his canines big and rounded. 'Yes,' he said, nodding. 'She does not sleep unless I sing to her.'

'Your mother?'

'My father married a woman in our village after my mother died. She is not our mother.'

I thought of Mummy, whom I knew only from photographs, and I thought of Vimla's curly hair framing her long face in a triangle. I remember Dad hugging her and whispering in her ear that she had mother's eyes, and Vimla would just laugh and push him away.

'Does your father love you?' I asked.

'He said so, always. He would come and sleep next to us when the nights were cold. He would keep us warm by hugging us.'

I sat up in the chair. Call it practice, call it an ear for detail, call it whatever you wish, but I can hear the footfalls from quite afar. Perhaps I ought to call it Dad's loving gift to me and Vimla. I asked Nari how his father kept them warm.

'By hugging us. Sometimes he would slide his hands under our clothes. His hands were always so warm, so hard.'

'And did he do this before or after his second marriage?'

'Before,' said Nari, but he thought for a moment. 'Sometimes after too.'

I did not know the ways of his tribe, but I could guess. Men would earn and protect their women. They would drink and beat them, and at night they would crawl into their beds and have sex with them. The women would perhaps resist by a meek word here or a quiet gesture there, but they would not – could not – hold back sex from their husbands. Marriage gave the man full right to sex whenever he demanded it.

It was not just the uneducated, poor class that behaved this way. Captain, for all his suavity and panache, was merely Nari's father in a suit. If Nari's father drank arrack, Captain drank Glenfidditch.

'I would like you to tell me about your life in the tribe,' I told Nari. 'Will you?'

He nodded, but seemed uncertain. 'I – come from a poor family, madam.'

The anger in his eyes, the firm softness of his speech, the constant fiddling with his big brown fingers, that look of naked thirst for flesh; all these aroused my interest. Once again, looking back, I was perhaps playing with fire, but that morning, I remember being flushed with excitement.

When I stepped into my clinic, I heard Sridhar's machine croon in the voice of Jim Reeves. Even my musical tastes – though I was eight years older – are more modern than his. I paid no attention to Ankita, who had been in the process of laughing at something he said as I entered, and motioned Sridhar into my chamber.

When he came in, I told him we were not going to have sex that morning. His face fell.

'I have to recover from last night,' I said.

He understood. 'I don't know why you still stay married to him.'

A man slithers so naturally into the role of a protector. When there is a woman scorned, have no doubt that she will find a man with a suitable shoulder to lean on. That has been the way of the world, always, and that is how it shall be. Between Sridhar and me there had been nothing but physical pleasure, and yet whenever the topic of Captain came up, he bristled, adjusted his spectacles a bit too much, ran his fingers in his hair, licked his lips, sweated in the armpits.

'We've been over this, Sridhar,' I said. 'Let's not begin again.'

'You're beautiful. Don't shake your head, Ramya, you know you are.' When he realized he called me by name he looked at the door, to make sure it was locked. 'You're independent. You're a doctor, for god's sake! If you don't kick a bastard in the balls, who will?'

'Stop it, Sridhar.'

He came to the couch where I sat and knelt on one knee. He took my hand in his and looked earnestly into my eyes. 'Why do you not leave him?' he asked.

'Leave him and then what? Marry you?'

'Marry no one! You don't need to be married to be happy.'

'I know.'

'No one can mistreat you without your permission, Ramya. Isn't that what you tell all your clients?'

I nodded. My hands relaxed in his.

'Then why don't you practice what you preach?'

How could I tell him that giving advice and taking it were two different things? In fact, the giver and taker of *anything* have such differing world views that one can never understand the other. Could you blame the moneylender for losing sleep over a percentage point of interest? Could you expect a prostitute to see the world through her customer's eye? We never truly understand the other side, as much as we pretend that we do.

'I will think about it,' I said, and I could see that it made him angry, because it was not the first time he was hearing it from me.

'I wish you to be happy, that's all,' he said.

I did not tell him that Captain had said the same thing on our wedding night. In fact, he had said the same thing a few nights before, just after he had raped me. Vimla had said it countless times over the years, and even today her calls never ended without her declaring that she wished on me all the happiness in the world.

I nodded and said, 'I know.'

'You *don't* know. You're just afraid.'

'Of what?'

He left my hands and threw his arms out in despair. 'I don't know! You have nothing to be afraid of. You will have your dignity, you will have your self-respect –'

'Enough.'

He stopped and sighed helplessly. I placed my palm over his cheek. He reminded me of ripe summer mangoes. I took off his glasses and pulled him closer by the ear. 'I thought we were not having sex,' he said.

'We're not. But I want to see your nose go red.'

He stood up, and I unzipped him. Two strokes with my fingertips and he became hard. 'Can I sit down?' he said.

He sat next to me, and I bent over him, threw my hair over his thighs and waist. I gave him my finger to suck on. At the first touch of my lips he groaned. A thick, happy mist covered my mind, the kind that covered Captain's, perhaps, when he pulls me toward him under the covers.

Three minutes later, Sridhar's toes clicked under his dusty white socks as they curled inward, and his nose went red.

Fellatio gives me a headache. That evening, by the time I reached home and crashed on the couch, I felt as though someone had taken a sledgehammer to my head. On days when Captain forced himself into my mouth and commanded me to suck, the knocking would be light enough to be ignored, and my left eye would flicker every few minutes for the next two hours. Only with Sridhar my head would feel ready to split in two down the middle.

I sank into the couch with a hand lightly resting upon my brow. From underneath the palm I watched the polished silver surface of the refrigerator. How nice it would be to walk over and bang my head against it until my brain splattered out. Somewhere in the house an air-conditioning unit turned off, and into the sudden quietness came the clicking of the metallic cuckoo clock on the far wall, one that Vimla had given. I glanced at it and saw that the minutes hand was on nine. I breathed out in relief. If that red and white bird on spring wheels had come out now, I would have pulled it out and twisted its neck till it snapped.

To the light and navy blue smudge hovering in the corner, I said, 'Get me some coffee, Nari.' He disappeared.

Captain came out of the room, dressed in blue track pants and a tucked in red polo shirt. Captain always tucked in his shirts and always combed his hair. I used to tease him in the early days of our marriage when he came to bed in an ironed night suit and neatly parted hair. He picked up his cane from the iron quiver behind the corner table and strode to the middle of the room.

'What's wrong?' he said. 'Headache?'

I nodded.

He placed his cane on the table and went into the kitchen. After a few minutes he came out with a steel vessel covered with a plate in one hand and a white napkin in the other. 'I told you not to work so hard.' Sitting on the couch next to mine, he slid off the plate and dipped the napkin into the water. He squeezed it dry and lifted it up to my forehead. 'Remove your hand.'

'I will do it myself.'

'Remove your hand.' He squeezed my hand with his, the way Albert had once or twice when we went walking down to the corner of the beach in the middle of his shift. We would only get away for a few minutes before Sam called for him in his crusty voice. But it was enough for Albert to take my hand in his and run his fingertips over my palm in circles. I never told him it tickled me.

'Does that feel better?' asked Captain, looking at the smile on my face.

'Yes,' I told him.

'You work too hard sometimes, Ramya,' he said, his voice tender. 'What is the need for you to work? You can just stay in the house and look after it, keep yourself busy that way.'

'It was just a tough case today,' I said, thinking of Sridhar. Drops of water had accumulated on my forehead. One of them slipped down the side of my eye and made for my cheek. I wiped it off with my forefinger. 'I will manage.'

'Rape?'

I shook my head. 'Her appointment is tomorrow. Today, it was a banker with a conscience.'

'Oh, boy.' The napkin went into the vessel again. This time after he had squeezed it, Captain put it in my hand and I raised it up to my head. The hammering had subsided now, though a small thud hit my temples every minute or so. He patted my knuckles, ran his thumb on the back of my hand

'You were going somewhere.'

'Yes, I have a meeting with the fundraisers.'

'Then you should go. Don't let me hold you back. I will be fine.'

He looked into my eyes. 'Are you sure?'

I smiled. 'Go.'

He covered my cheeks with his palms. He had big brown hands, Captain, and I could feel my face disappearing into them. He leaned forward and kissed me on the forehead, then on both the cheeks. When he clutched me close to him I smelled rose perfume in his chest hair. I shut my eyes and wrapped my arms around him.

'I will be back before you know it.'

I nodded, and prayed that he would smell of only rose when he returned. Generally when he returned from these 'meetings', he carried on his breath and body the odour of something heady. It would make my headache worse. In the kitchen I heard a noisy scramble and wondered what was taking Nari so long with the coffee.

Captain left. I sat back on the couch and heard Sridhar's voice float in the air. The sun had just set outside. Nari had turned the kitchen light on. I watched his shadow move on the marble floor by the doorway, and squeezed the wet napkin into a ball. Sridhar had called me cowardly and needy. I would perhaps have called myself the same things if I had been one of my patients. The car's engine squeaked to life outside. As the drone of the engine faded away, the cuckoo came out of the clock and sang. My headache had subsided enough for me to just watch it, as though it were just another shadow.

Nari came out of the room bearing coffee.

If you have grown up with servants and maids like I have, you learn to take their presence in the house for granted. They always wear the same clothes, walk a certain way, speak when spoken to, and do what they are told. On days you feel good about yourself, you may utter an extra word of kindness, perhaps give them some of your old clothes, but you do not care for them as you would for another human being. If you did, you would not have them work for you in the first place.

I had looked after Nari when he fell sick, but I did that only because he reminded me of Albert. Even when he was drinking milk from the glass I held to his mouth, I saw him only as a fuzzy shape dressed in blue. If he had left our employ during those first two months, I daresay I would have forgotten him, and would now be unable to recall his appearance or his name.

But on this day, Nari became more than a servant. The fuzzy lines sharpened and grew in detail. I saw the brown ridge in the middle of his chin, the black spots on his cheek that resembled sprinkled pepper, the yellow tinge that covered his flat teeth, his glass-like lips and his rough tongue, his over-grown left canine, that pressed against the corner of his mouth when he smiled, his habit of ruffling his hair and making it stand up, the hint of Parachute coconut oil that he smeared himself with – all this and so much more.

On this day he had come to my clinic, unannounced. He peered in through the window and saw me and Sridhar sprawled on the couch. At that instant, Sridhar was on top of me, and my fingers gripped his arms. His pants were at his ankles, and he had just thrust into me and held me from sliding up toward the edge of the couch. For some reason he looked up at the window, and his face changed. 'What the hell?' he said.

I craned my neck backwards but could see nothing. 'What happened?' I asked.

'There was someone at the window,' said Sridhar, pulling his pants up. He hurried to the door and pulled it open, even as I scrambled to get behind it so that I could get my clothes on. Just as I reached behind my back and hooked my bra, I heard voices. I slipped my pants back on, tucked my shirt in and adjusted my hair.

'Who are you?' Sridhar said.

'I came to give madam her lunch,' said Nari's voice. If I could put my thumb down on one moment and say with certainty that yes, this was the starting point of all the mess, it would be this: when I stood behind the door of my chamber frantically clothing myself and heard the steady, squeaky clean voice of Nari outside.

'Did you tell her that you would be coming?' asked Sridhar, trying to make his tone stern, but I thought I heard a little tremor in it. 'Even if you did, why did you come and look through the window?'

'This is my first time here,' said Nari. 'I did not know where the front door was. I saw the window half open and thought I should see through it.'

I remembered that Ankita was outside, and though I could not see her, I could picture her listening to all this with rapt attention. If this questioning went on for longer, she would know too, slow as she was. So I cleared my throat and said, 'Sridhar, call Nari into the room.' There was a chance yet that he had not seen as much as we thought he had. Perhaps we could sit down and ascertain what he made of it all. Perhaps we could convince him that there was a perfectly innocent explanation for what he had seen.

When he entered the room, therefore, I beamed at him, took the lunch box off his hands and thanked him. I sat on the couch, folded my legs and looked up at him. 'When you come here next time, Nari, you come to the main door and ask to see me.'

'Yes, madam.'

A picture of decorum and deference, he was, though he had powdered his face – Ponds was his brand – so generously that he looked like a little devil straight from hell. 'And if I forget my lunch box again, do not come here without calling me.'

'Yes, madam.' He held his hands in front of him. He bowed his head.

Beside him Sridhar twisted his fingers, looking at him, at me, and then back at him. I motioned him to my seat and trained my eyes on Nari. I tried to see if he would give away anything, a touch of regret, a hint of embarrassment, anything for me to go on. But for an occasional swipe of his lips with his tongue, Nari did nothing. I weighed up my options; one, I could claim that I had done nothing wrong, and that Sridhar and I were conducting an experiment which involved us taking off our clothes. Two, I could tell him that this was a secret that should not get out come what may, and make it clear to him that I would be willing to give him what he wanted.

I do not know now what would have happened if I had denied the whole thing and drummed it into his uneducated head that this was what psychologists did for a living. Maybe he would have believed me, and even if he had repeated what he had seen to Captain, maybe I would have been able to brush it away as a duffer's ramblings. Either way, things would not have taken the turn they did, one thinks. Captain would not have died, Nari would not be in prison now, and I would not be sitting here, talking about it all.

Maybe because I had been taught to come clean when caught, maybe because I thought Nari to be too smart to buy my lies but at the same time dumb enough to allow me to bribe him with money, maybe because I thought I could win him over with my charm and kindness, I went for option number two.

I pulled out two hundred-rupee notes and held them out to him. When he looked at me I gave him my best smile. 'Take these, Nari,' I said, 'and go to a movie today. Make sure you're back before Captain returns home in the evening.'

He did not hesitate. His white lips spread out in a wide grin, exposing his canine. He snatched the money from my hands, joined his palms toward both of us, and exited the room. For a long time after that I remember that neither of us spoke. It was as if we were both waiting with bated breath for him to return. Only Ankita's ringing voice – 'Yes, madam is in today ... yes, twelve-thirty is open ... yes, I will book that for you' – broke the silence.

At length, Sridhar said, 'Hmm.'

'Hmm,' I agreed.

THREE

I have seen stories of blackmail in numerous movies, and in all of them the blackmailer, once he understands the amount of power he wields on his victim, becomes greedier and greedier with time. With Nari I did not see that. After the day I first gave him money, I anticipated that he would come to me with demands for more, but he didn't. Of course, he became more visible to me after this. Every time I spoke to Captain he seemed to be there or thereabouts, hovering, dusting this or arranging that, stealing a glance our way at just the right time so that he would catch me looking at him.

I first thought – in desperate hope, I suppose – that he did not understand why I was bribing him. Once or twice I questioned my judgement; did I stir up doubt in his mind by giving him money? By wearing my guilt so openly, did I invite him to take advantage of me? I decided to wait and watch, because for almost two weeks after that first day, he did not approach me. I was about to let the matter rest with great relief, and was mulling over giving the good news to Sridhar and resuming our trysts at the clinic, when on a hot Sunday afternoon he knocked on my bedroom door.

'Come in,' I said, knowing that it would be him. Captain had left town the night before, and was not expected until the morning after the next day. As he walked in, I thought he had acquired a swagger in his stride. He stood by the edge of the bed and pushed his hair back. I was leaning back on the bed, reading one of the early passages from *Wuthering Heights*. I would not say I was afraid yet – that would come later – but I was beginning to get wary of his presence. I should not have called him in, I thought. 'Yes, Nari? Everything all right?'

'Yes, madam.'

'Need some money?'

A smile lit up his face. Under his bushy eyebrows, his eyes twinkled. He folded his hands, and his fingers wrapped around his arms. His fingernails were large and round, pink and brown, scraped and flat. Each of his fingers would easily be as thick as two of mine. 'How much?' I asked.

'Same as last time?'

I reached for my purse on the side table. As I burrowed in it, I thought I should test him, see how much he knew, and how far he was willing to go. 'This is the last time I am giving you money, Nari. Okay?'

He did not respond. His eyes were fastened on my purse.

'I gave you enough money at the clinic. What did you do with it?'

He shrugged. 'I spent it.'

'On what?'

He looked down at the ground. 'I went to a movie.'

'With two hundred rupees?'

'I went to three movies.'

'Good,' I said. 'So you had your fun, didn't you?'

He nodded.

'I will give you some now too, just because you asked. But don't make this a habit.'

'Yes, madam.'

I thought of the few nights before. Captain had not tried touching me, which was welcome in many ways, but it was strange. I had seen Nari and Captain whispering to one another a few days back. I wondered whether I should let it rest and allow matters to take a course of their own, but it did not hurt to make sure that Nari had said nothing. He also needed to know that her refusal to give him money was not an invitation for him to go to Captain and bare all.

'Did you tell Captain about what you saw at the clinic?'

'No, madam.'

'Good boy.'

'I – I know what you were doing with that man.'

'You do?' I studied his dry, rough face. It showed no malice. 'What do you think we were doing?'

'You were fucking.'

That cleared it up. I felt glad for not having told him that we were doing research. Boys grew up fast, especially in these villages with huts which had only one room, where father and mother – or mistress – went behind the tattered sari after dinner every night. Children grew up hearing and smelling sex; it was naive of me to not have thought of that.

'Yes,' I said. 'We were fucking.'

'Captain sir will not be happy if he knows.'

His voice had risen from a squeak to a cold, steely note when he said these words. He was yet to acknowledge his power openly before me, but he was feeling me up, seeing how badly I wanted my secret to be hidden. 'He will not be that sad either,' I said, and his face shrank.

But immediately he said, 'Then I will tell him when he comes back.'

'Be my guest.'

He frowned, looked again at the purse and the half-drawn notes. For a moment he thought of taking the money. His hand wavered, and he almost reached for them. To entice him, I pulled them out and spread them on the bed. 'This,' I told him, 'is your price for being quiet. Either take it or go and tell Captain. I will tell him my version too, and between you and me, I think he will believe me.'

'He won't,' he said.

I smiled at him. 'Do you think he will believe the word of a servant over the word of his wife?'

'I am telling the truth.'

'What is the truth? It is my word against yours, Nari.'

Again he took a step forward and stared at the notes. He scratched his head, shifted on his legs, licked his lips. 'Come,' I said. 'Take this money, and we can both pretend that nothing has happened.'

'No,' he said, looking up at me. 'No.' He shook his head, and his mouth curved into a sly smile. 'I don't believe you.' He took two steps back. 'You're bluffing.' He walked back until he hit the closed door. He opened it while still facing me, and his grin broadened. 'Let us see whom the Captain will believe.' He shut the door behind him.

I gathered the notes in my hand, looked at them for a minute or two, returned them to my purse. I leaned back on the pillow and placed my hands on my chest. I looked up at the revolving ceiling fan.

Some say that rape is about power. Others say it is about lust. I have been to conferences where grey-haired professors claimed that it was about anger. Some married women speak of it as a means of control. Activists specializing in sexual abuse by family members point to misshapen psychologies, bent minds, twisted histories. For them it's a crime of helplessness. A rapist rapes, they say, because he cannot not rape.

All these groups fiercely fight one another on the subject. A man who believed that rape is about power will listen to no word spoken by one who thinks that it is driven by lust. Professors and women's rights activists participate in long-drawn debates aimed at concluding, once and for all, the motive for rape. They often do not stop to consider even the possibility that there could be more than one of them. After all, if other crimes like murder and robbery could have multiple motives, why should rape have only one?

I do not know what pushed Nari down that road. I do not know what made a man like Captain, who nursed and cared for me when I was sick, to take me against my will, to violate my body, to cane me when I disobeyed. I will know the answer to neither question, for Nari will not speak of it and Captain cannot. I am resigned, therefore, to guessing. Nari grew up in poverty and saw his father marry a woman after his mother died. Captain was impotent, and though he didn't tell me this explicitly, I am convinced his first wife left him because of it.

Some others talk of rape in human beings as merely an extension of coercive sex found in other animal species. Male grizzly bears, dolphins and spiders, besides many others, have been found to use harassment and aggression to force females of their species into mating with them. Human males are no different, this theory argues, and that the same instinct that bids men to court a female also drives him to rape.

I have taken to admitting to myself, therefore, that we will never eliminate rape from our societies. As long as we remain wedded to sex, we must remain so to rape, whether we like it or not. That does not mean I endorse rape – I do not, and that is why I think Nari should be given the full punishment of the law as if he was a full-grown adult – it just means that I have come to terms with reality.

'I do not understand,' said Mrs Krishnamurthy, tucking her hair behind her ear and clasping her hands about her knees. She wore a blue chiffon sari with white flowers printed on it. She did not wrap it around herself like women her age were wont to do; instead she let the end of her sari lie loosely on the armrest of the couch. A tear-drop shaped red sticker sat in between her eyebrows. The skin around her cheeks had begun to sag, but I could see that in her twenties, which would have been some while ago, she must have been a beautiful woman.

'I do not understand why I feel guilty,' she said, looking down at the floor. I sat in my chair opposite her, my notepad and pen on my thigh. 'I hope you don't write this down. I am ashamed at having to speak about this.'

Putting away the pad, I told her, 'You don't need to speak if you don't wish to.'

'Yes, yes, I know. I have come here to your office thrice in the last few months, you know?' Her eyes climbed to meet with mine for a flash, then lowered themselves again. 'Each time I would come to the main door, climb the steps, make to knock, and at the last moment my courage would fail me. But I am here now. Yes, I am here now.

'I don't understand why I feel guilty. I went to a convent. I kissed a boy when I was fourteen. I first had sex when I was sixteen. By the time I was twenty-one, I had had three partners.' She looked up again, and her cheeks coloured. 'I tell you this so that you know I am no prude. I knew what sex was. I knew what it meant.

'So I don't think it's my fault that he raped me. I am not that stupid. And it only happened once, and he was my friend, and it was at a party where all of us were drunk, and I have forgiven him. Yes, I have forgiven him. But I cannot forgive myself – I don't understand why. I think about him more than I think about my husband, doctor. I think of all the things that he did to me that night, and the number of times I said no, the whine in my voice when he hurt me, the dirty smell of his underpants, his beer-soaked breath on my neck – I remember everything.'

'And you feel angry?' I asked.

She began to nod, but her hand went to her head to squeeze it, as though she couldn't remember. 'I did,' she said, her voice breaking, 'but not anymore. Not anger, no.'

'Shame?'

'Yes, a lot of shame.' When she met my gaze I saw tears in her eyes. 'I feel I ought to have protected myself better. I feel that he has taken me – stolen me away from my body – you know?'

I nodded. Something in my nod made her frown at me.

'You too?' she asked.

'Yes.'

'Then you *do* know.' She reached into her black purse and brought out a yellow handkerchief with little blue kittens strewn all over it. Here one was resting its head on its paws. There another was playing with a ball of twine. Mrs Krishnamurthy swabbed her eyes with it, tapping under each lid twice. 'You know what the worst part is?'

I just listened.

'The worst part of it is that you remember how your body responded to his touch.' Mrs Krishnamurthy rolled the kerchief into a cylinder and squeezed it. The pink tips of her fingers went white with the pressure. 'I still remember how my thighs shivered when his fingers hovered over them. He didn't have to touch them, he just ran his hand over them, like this.' She demonstrated with her free hand. 'My lips trembled, even as I said no, and my breathing quickened. Each time he kissed me I bit his lips and drew blood. But I also moaned.

'It was like there were two of me. The rational part of me, the part of me that was *awake*, that hated him and wanted him off my body, and the other part, all body and no mind, which seemed to like it. My nipples were erect, and he whispered into my ears that he didn't believe me when I said I didn't like it. He flicked them with his forefinger, like this.' She again demonstrated with a wave of a dainty finger. 'And each time he flicked them, they grew harder. He laughed and said that I liked it.'

'But you didn't.'

She shook her head. 'I didn't. I wanted to push him off, but he was too strong. I scratched him, bit him, did what I could, but he only laughed and said that I liked it. He said I was feisty, and that he liked women who had spunk in bed.' She looked down at her handkerchief, at the picture of a cat about to spring at a goldfish inside a vessel. 'When he entered me that night, I had an orgasm.'

I remembered those long nights when Dad would visit Vimla first, then me. He did not ever go beyond sliding his hand down my pants (though I never spoke to Vimla about what he did with her), but when he would ask if it felt nice, I would shake my head and say no. But later, thinking back, I would hear a voice within me whisper, very softly, that it didn't feel as bad as all that. Long into adulthood I would dream of those nights, and when I woke up I would find my inner thighs sticky and wet.

'I had an orgasm,' said Mrs Krishnamurthy, looking straight at me. 'A man raped me and I came from it. I mean, *what the fuck*?'

I knew I had to say nothing, that I should let her speak, but I said, 'I understand that you're confused.'

'Confused is an understatement, my dear,' she said, lapsing back into her primness. 'I dare not say this to anyone but another woman who has gone through a similar thing –' she raised her hand to stop me from interrupting '– don't bother denying it. I see it in your eyes.'

I nodded, and kept the silence for a moment. Then I said, 'It is a lot like being tickled, Mrs Krishnamurthy. No matter how sad you may be feeling, if someone were to tickle you, you would still laugh.'

'Yes, well, that's rather unfortunate, isn't it? I can't help it if my body behaves a certain way when touched.'

'Yes, you can't,' I said. 'That is why you shouldn't feel guilty about it.'

'Ah, if it were only that simple, doctor. The more I think about it, the more I don't understand. Are our bodies really that far removed from our minds? As a specialist on minds I ask you this question.'

'I am hardly a specialist, Mrs Krishnamurthy, but evidence suggests –'

Mrs Krishnamurthy leaned forward in her seat and looked into my eyes thoughtfully. 'You know, doctor, I said I forgave him, but I am going to change my mind on that.' Her fingernails were clear pink and perfect circles. She smoothed the hem of her sari. 'I forgive him for raping me, for ignoring all my pleas, for using me as a plaything for his own pleasure. I forgive him for all that. But do you know the one thing that I can never forgive him for?'

I knew the answer, but chose to be quiet.

'I will never forgive him for making me think that I liked it.'

*

That evening on the way back I stopped by the library and picked up a copy of *The Psychology of Blackmail.* I have never believed that books contain all the information you ever need, but they do give you a good starting point. When, at seventeen, I took up squash at St Agnes, the first thing I did was to read a book on it to learn how to grip the racket, how to step across the court, basic strategy etc. Blackmail is similar to squash in some respects; the first player hits the ball, then the second, then back to the first – and so on until one of them gets exhausted.

That was the evening before Captain was due back in town. I read some of the first pages on the bus home. It began with the words: 'Blackmail is about power'. I paused there and wondered whether it wasn't man's obsession with power that made him see it in everything, everywhere. If we were to make a list of all things that were *not* about power, I thought, it would be a small one indeed.

Nevertheless, I appreciated that blackmail was perhaps more about power than rape was. Here, the power rested in the information that the blackmailer held. If I were to firmly decide that it was of no matter whether or not Nari told Captain about what he saw, he would have no hold over me. The afternoon before, I had spoken to him with a sense of bravado, knowing that Captain was not home and that Nari could not reach him. But now, with Captain's return mere hours away, I sensed my heart had quickened.

Even the bougainvillea that crowded over Miss Mehta's ceramic gate did not cheer me up. It had just stopped raining, and the smell of wet earth skulked in the breeze. A yellow and blue kite flew side by side in the sky, and just as I was about to turn into my gate, Blue turned a full circle around Yellow and pulled it a notch downward. A group of children hooted from atop a terrace.

I placed the book, open to the page I was reading, on the coffee table, away from the stain from the morning's cup. I scraped it with my nail and found that it had dried. Nari had not cleaned it. I began to call for him but decided to let the quiet remain for a while longer. Like they did every day, the glum shadows gathered. I thought of my bungalow in Goa, and my bedroom with its French window facing the sunrise. Vimla and I would go up to the terrace when we were children and watch the sun sink into the Western horizon. Here, if I had to catch a glimpse of the sun from the terrace, it had to be noon. There was nothing independent about an independent house in Hyderabad.

I thought of what Captain would do if he knew about me and Sridhar. I was not afraid that he would kill me; St Agnes had driven all belief of afterlife out of my head, so death did not scare me. I once had a friend who came to Sammy's Shack every Friday night, and whenever I sat with him, he would ask me the same question. He would lift up his empty bottle of Foster's and ask me: 'If you had the choice to be you or this bottle, what would you be?' He had already been forty-one then, and I was no more than nineteen. I would say I wanted to be me, and he would just chuckle, shake his head, and signal to the counter for a refill.

So death did not scare me, no, but the manner of it did. If Captain decided to kill me, he would plan the slowest, most painful way of doing so. Even if he chose not to kill me, even if he decided to drive me out of the house, could I stay by myself in this city? Sridhar said he would look after me, but men tended to say that when their loins were bursting with testosterone. Dad said it. Captain said it. Sridhar would find someone younger, and he would find another reason to give me – and to himself.

A blue smudge appeared at the kitchen door. Nari's dark fingers wrapped around the frame. I ignored him. Mrs Krishnamurthy was really me. Like her I saw no rational reason for staying with this man. I knew that I could fend for myself, that I could live alone. I could go back to Goa and see what Albert was doing. I could go to Chandigarh and ask Vimla if I could live with her for a while. She would not say no.

But I felt I was bound to Captain, the same way I once felt bound to Dad. Vimla got out of the house the first opportunity she got, and she never came back, until the day of Dad's funeral. But I stayed. I slept in the same room, dreading the moment the door would creak open and Dad's steps would come fumbling in. It never occurred to me that I could leave him and go, until Captain came and proposed marriage.

When Dad died, I did not cry, because in many ways Captain had taken his place already. Vimla broke down and wept, because she had thought she hated him, and she did, as did I, but I think she realized on that day that he would always leave a hole in her life. In the year following Dad's death Vimla would sleep with four of her natural history students, one of them a girl.

When you live your whole life in fear, when it becomes a part of who you are, take it away and your hands begin to tremble, your speech stutters, you gasp for breath, you struggle against invisible tubes fastened to your arms and punctured into your wrists. You become addicted to fear, and you become hopelessly dependent on the source of it. It was difficult living with Captain, I admit, but it would have been harder living without him.

I was looking at the open book on the table while I thought all this. I did not know if these were rationalizations of a victim or if they carried any scientific truth, but I did not care. The bottom line was that I would be lost without Captain. I would be depressed to the point of suicide. I knew this with as much clarity as I knew that I was a woman. This meant only one thing: Nari had to be given whatever he wanted.

'I saw you looking through Captain's library yesterday,' I said, beckoning him into the room. 'Turn on the light, please.' The sudden flood of white light made my eyes ache, and I closed them, massaging my eyelids with my fingertips. When I opened my eyes I saw Nari staring at the end of my sari, which had fallen to the side on the maroon cushion of the couch. I made no quick movements that would alarm him, but pointed at the coffee stain. He went into the kitchen and returned with a wet sponge. I used the interval to wrap my sari around me.

After he had cleaned the spot I repeated the question. He nodded.

'Would you like to go to a school? Study further?'

'No, madam.' His eyes were furtive, and something in his tone made me think that he was lying.

'Studying will make you a big man one day, like Captain.'

'Like you too?'

'Yes, like me too. You can work at things that need your mind. You do have a keen mind, don't you, Nari?'

'My father always said so.'

'I know so. If you go to school, I will give you two hundred rupees every week.'

His eyes lit up, but he said, 'What about the work here in the house?'

'I will manage, and you will help out after school, won't you?'

'Will you help me with – homework?'

I thought of the look in his eyes a few minutes ago, when he stared at my unfurled sari. But I pushed it aside, telling myself that I was being too much of a therapist. I nodded, and he beamed with such childlike innocence that I chided myself for doubting him. He was no more than seventeen, still a boy.

'Will Captain agree?' he said.

'I will talk to Captain, don't worry.' I frowned at him. 'You will not tell Captain what you saw at the clinic if I send you to school. Will you?'

'I will not, madam.'

'And whenever you need money or anything else, you can come to me with no fear. Understand?'

He nodded.

I leaned forward so that I could look into his eyes better. 'Anything at all, okay?'

He looked intently at the floor and nodded again.

Taking out a few notes from my purse, I held them out to him. 'Here,' I said. 'Take this and buy something to eat for yourself. Remember, Nari, it is our secret, and the longer you keep it, the more I will give you.'

'Yes, madam.' He took a step forward and extended his grubby hand. I placed the notes in it, and my fingers brushed his palm. I thought I detected a faint shiver in his wrist at that moment, and as I withdrew my hand, a pink shade filled his cheeks, and he mumbled something I could not quite catch.

I presumed he said thank you.

I waited for a week after Captain returned before I broached the topic. I did not want to play my hand first and realize later that Nari had changed his mind. So the first seven days, I sat back and watched for changes in Captain's face, in his voice when he spoke with me, in the way he touched me, anything that would hint that he knew. On the fourth night back, he forced himself into me, but that was par for the course. I even thought he was gentler than his usual self. On the sixth, he had one peg too many and advanced at me with a raised cane. He stopped when I removed my sari and showed him my blouse.

On the seventh day, I had decided that he knew nothing. I did not want to wait too long either, because that would make Nari fidgety. So on the eighth morning, before Captain left the house for the NGO, I handed him his coffee and said that Nari wanted to go to school. I timed it such that Nari had just awakened and was rolling up his mat and pillow in the living room, under the staircase. He had to be in earshot.

'How will you manage the house?' said Captain. 'Can you not teach him at home instead?'

'Let him go out, see the world,' I said vaguely. 'It will do him good.'

'It will be another expense. Once we start sending him to school, he will need a phone. He will need books. He cannot roam about in his blue shirt and shorts any more.'

'Yes, Captain. I will pay for all of those.'

He looked at me, amused. 'He has asked you to speak with me on his behalf, hasn't he?' He craned his neck toward the kitchen. 'Nari! Come here.' The boy scrambled to the door and stood with his arms folded. 'Do you want to go to school?'

'Yes, sir.'

'It won't be easy studying and doing house work at the same time.'

'I will do my best, sir. Madam has said she will help me with my homework.'

'Has she, now?' Captain turned to me, and I nodded. He shrugged and said, 'Well, I suppose it's better than sitting at home twiddling your thumbs and watching television.'

FOUR

'Arun is having an affair,' said Mrs Krishnamurthy. That day she wore a bright yellow sari with a red border, the kind that priests wore at rich temples. A heap of jasmine buds stuck to the back of her head, held together with a round golden brooch. She had polished her nails cherry red since her last visit, and the tips were beginning to wear off. The fragrance she wore enveloped the room, engulfing the cheap room freshener of my chamber.

Mrs Krishnamurthy never appeared to move even the smallest part of her body without first giving it due thought. She did not have to say anything; even her smallest gestures – a wave of the hand, or an amused glance – carried immense poise. She would have been a fit queen to any kingdom. When she sat on my couch, I sometimes saw it morph into a throne, and the bunch of flowers would become a crown. Attendants would mill about, watching her every move, attending to her every whim.

With the tip of her forefinger, she pushed away a floating strand of hair.

'I did not confront him about it,' she said. 'That would amount to me questioning his fidelity, and men are touchy about these things. But I began to notice things.' She spoke without pause, never at a loss for the right word. 'I am a headmistress. All my life I have had to be able to tell when children are lying.'

Men who get married to such women generally end up having an affair. I had one or two clients who would answer to the call of 'Arun', whose descriptions of their wives matched Mrs Krishnamurthy's. That kind of luminous power and grace attracts men, and they realize only after getting too close that they ought to have just admired it from a distance.

'It doesn't bother me that he's sleeping with someone else,' she said. 'Whoever she is, he will realize that she cannot match me.' She held her head erect and twisted it just so that the sunlight from the window caught her jaw and cast half her face in shadow. 'This is not the first time he has gone chasing tail.'

On my pad I wrote to myself a note that it was typical. The Aruns of the world come back to the light because of the warmth it gives, and they're forever stuck in that spiral, like moths, slapping themselves repeatedly against a mercury bulb until they drop dead.

'Have you ever had an affair?' asked Mrs Krishnamurthy, and I sat up in my chair, suddenly alert. Her thin mouth twisted to one side. 'You have, then.'

'Would it matter to you if I have?'

'Ah, you're playing the psychologist's trick of turning it back on the questioner. No, I don't suppose it would matter to me at all if you did or did not have an affair. But I am curious. Will you tell me?'

'I am afraid I cannot.'

'Then I am going to assume you have. You're still at that age where men look at you twice.' Her tone of voice became whimsical, almost wistful. 'In a few years your beauty will desert you, dear, and no man will give you a second of his time. They make tall claims about love and about how looks don't matter, but all they want is a fresh young pair of legs and a wet burning hole between them.'

I tapped at the pad with the tip of my pencil. 'So you think Arun is with a younger woman?'

She smiled at me, as though at my naivety. 'Of course, dear. Men age well, don't they? At least in women's eyes they do. But what of us? Once we're past it, we're past it.' After a pause, she said, 'I look at the young women of today, complaining about the amount of attention they get from men. I think to my own young days, when we used to march by the college wall and turn our chins up at the young men from the boys' hostel perched upon it, who would throw whistles and badly hummed songs at us.' She smiled, and her white teeth showed. 'We were properly miffed too, of course, but what I wouldn't give now to have a man look at me with desire.'

'Would you?'

'Would you not?'

'I don't know,' I said. 'Perhaps I will know when I am your age. But I would like to have the benefit of your experience.'

'Ha, I know what you did there,' she said, reaching for her bag and pulling out a chapstick. She applied it on her lips and pressed them together once. 'When you've spent your whole life – almost thirty years – warding off male attention and being so sick of it, my dear, on the day you wake up and find that no one's looking at you and that your husband's looking elsewhere – well, let's say it comes as a bit of a surprise.'

I found myself wondering if Captain would one day begin looking elsewhere too. There were enough young women at the NGO who fawned over him, I knew. The world was not short on nineteen-year-old girls with aspirational crushes on ex-soldiers with a treasure trove of anecdotes and a ready line from Tennyson on hand. The tapping of my pen on the pad quickened. The idea of Captain holding someone else's hand, reciting love lines to someone else, made me slightly queasy.

'I would have thought you would be relieved,' I said.

'Relieved because I am finally not being scrutinized?'

'Something like that.'

'That's what I used to think, doctor,' she said. 'When I was young I could not wait to get old, because I thought it would nice to go out – for once! – in clothes that I am comfortable in rather than those that I look good in. How nice it must all be for these old women, I had thought, because no one heckled them on their way to the grocery store. No one tried to rub hands with them over the counter, no one grinded against them in crowded buses.'

'But it has not happened that way, for you?'

Mrs Krishnamurthy shook her head. 'No,' she said, 'now that I have become old, I wish there was some way to become young again. I would give anything – anything – to see that look of desire in a man's gaze directed at me again.'

The alarm set on my phone went off, and Mrs Krishnamurthy caught herself at the start of another sentence. She gathered herself with a neat shrug of her dainty shoulders, adjusted her sari to cover the loose folds of skin on her waist, and got up to her feet. She held out a hand for me and said, 'Until next time, then, doctor.'

Soon after Mrs Krishnamurthy left, Sridhar came into the room and locked the door. He said the next patient had called and cancelled. We had no more appointments for the day. He walked to the window and drew the curtains. Outside, I could hear the faint taps of Ankita's fingers on her keyboard. One of these days

I was going to have to give her a few days of paid leave, cancel all appointments, and lock myself up in the chamber with Sridhar. I was rather tired of biting on his finger to stifle my moans.

I shook my head at him. 'My thighs ache.'

'Did you sleep with him last night?'

'No, I think it's just that time of the month.'

For some reason that made him angry. 'You don't listen to me, Ramya. I've told you so many times not to put up with this.'

'Let's not talk of that again, Sridhar.'

'My parents are beginning to ask me to get married.'

'Then go ahead!' I teased him, but when he didn't see the funny side I became more serious. 'You're not going to propose to me, are you?'

He scratched his head for a few seconds, at different places. His hair tended to grow in a bush, and it had been a while since he had had a haircut. I had heard Ankita tell him he looked good after a haircut. I think he did too – long hair just made men look like they'd just come out of the caves – but just to see what he would do, I told him how handsome he looked with a large mop of hair on his head. People said women were prone to flattery, but if you say the right things, you could have men eating out of your hands.

'Well,' he said, looking away from me. 'What would you say if I *did* propose to you?'

'You're a PhD. I think you will see the futility in proposing to a married woman.'

'So you haven't thought of what I said? You promised.'

'Sridhar, I promised you nothing.'

'You promised to think about it.' He went down on his knees on the carpet and took my hands. He insisted on looking into my eyes when he took my hands, which always made me uncomfortable. 'Look at me,' he said.

I did, and to pass the awkward moment I gave him a kiss on the forehead.

'You and I will be very happy together, Ramya,' he said. 'I have told my parents about you.'

I pulled my hands away. 'You did what?'

'No, no,' he said, fumbling with his fingers. 'I did not tell them about you. I told them that I was seeing a girl, that if all went well, I will settle down with her.'

'Did you tell them how old this "girl" was?'

'What does age matter? It's just a number.'

'I thought so too, when I was twenty-five.'

'And now? Now you think I am too young for you or something?'

I smiled at him. 'I don't, Sridhar, but your parents will. In fact, I think Ankita likes you, and I think she's the right age for you too.'

'She's not the right one for me. You are.'

I sighed. Men were such children. If you wished to make them want something, deny it and they will forever beg you for it. Mrs Krishnamurthy's words came to my mind. How long after Sridhar has me before a young pretty graduate student at the university would give him a sidelong glance? And how long before he would have a chamber of his own one day, like this, in which he would entertain his employees?

'Neither of us is right for each other, Sridhar,' I told him, and palmed his cheek. 'Do not get entangled with me. I am gone in the head, and I will ruin you along with myself.'

'I will help you. We're psychologists! We will help each other.'

'I don't need help.'

'But you just said –'

'Yes, I know what I said. We will ruin each other if we get married. And you're twenty-five. Twenty-five! Go out there!

Meet new women, make love to them, make them love you. You have your whole life ahead of you, and you intend to spend it with a woman eight years older than you?'

'Yes.' He was cute in that moment, much like a hungry puppy. I couldn't resist leaning in and kissing him on the lips. For a moment, our mouths moved together. When we disengaged, my breath had grown heavier. 'My thighs still ache,' I whispered.

'Is it an ache that I can soothe?' he said.

'Probably. What do you propose to do?' I leaned back on the couch and began to unbutton my shirt. He had already moved closer to the edge of the couch, and was running his fingers up my skirt. Over the next hour or so, he first told me all the things he would do, then he did them. I bit into the cushion of the couch and listened, and felt, and smelled, and shook, and thrashed helplessly.

At the end of it all, the ache in my thighs had indeed dulled a little.

'How do you feel about marrying me now?' he asked, as my teeth loosened against the rubbery sponge of the sofa and my breathing slowed down a touch. 'I could attend to your aches and pains all day, every day.'

'Ooh,' I said, 'my own personal boy toy. You won't ever say no, will you?'

'Never.'

'Even if I called you to service more than once a day?'

'Any number of times a day.'

He was cute then, too. This time he was a puppy with an erection. If you wanted to ask a man for something, Vimla had said often over the years, do it when he has a throbbing member. Chances are he will say yes. I pulled Sridhar closer to me by his penis. I ran my fingernails along its length, and closed my palm over its tip. He closed his eyes, and the tendons of his neck tightened. I didn't have to do much else.

He collapsed onto the floor, and I went to the wash basin. The water ran over my hands, and the white stuff dissolved, ran a few circles around the drain, and disappeared. I could still heard Ankita's keyboard from the reception, overlaid on Sridhar's hoarse breathing. If I asked the questions now, the answers might be different, I thought, and it would embarrass him. So I walked back to the couch and sat at its foot, running my fingers through his hair, watching his lower back rise and fall. He lay on his stomach, his face hidden in the crook of his arm.

'Come,' I said softly. 'Wear your pants. We will go watch a movie.'

Evenings became homework times for Nari and me. We enrolled him in the English-medium government school down the road. Nari had studied till standard eight in Singavaram, so he did not have much trouble with the curriculum, though he did struggle with English. The school in Singavaram had been English medium, but the teachers would only speak Telugu, he told me. He had a natural way with Math; he had just to read a table for just five minutes and he would be able to narrate it upwards and downwards even in his sleep.

I did not know then – and I do not know now – why I cared for him so. First I thought it was because he reminded me of Albert, but now I have to admit that I was overcompensating for my guilt, trying my best to lure him into liking me so that he would preserve my secret. I did not anticipate that it could lead to other things.

I had a low study table fashioned for him out of teak, and got it painted a fresh bright orange. On that day he was sitting cross-legged on the floor by my chair with his head bent over a compound interest problem. I tried to lean over him so that I could see what he was doing. He often made a mistake in entering the right rate of return in the calculation, and I wanted to correct him. We were sitting in the upstairs lounge, and Captain was watching television downstairs. All was quiet except for the droning English accent of David Attenborough on *Discovery*, marvelling at the miracle of migratory birds.

Suddenly, all seemed to stand still between me and Nari as well when we both realized that my hair was hanging over the back of his neck. I had taken a bath just before sitting down with him that day, and little droplets of water dripped from the ends of my hair onto his neck. The pen in his hand stopped moving, and he looked up at me. This was perhaps the first time I noticed that his eyes were not black. They had a deep shade of misty green to them, which reminded me of a cat that used to come into our house on winter mornings in Goa when Vimla and I were kids.

We looked at each other. Once or twice our gaze wavered, but neither of us dared to break away. The pen dropped from his hand. He trailed his other arm over my lower back, and traced a line up my spine. I did not move, though every sinew in my body was screaming to me to run down the stairs, onto the balcony, into the bedroom – anywhere but here.

I closed my eyes. His fingers grew bolder and fiddled with the knot of my nightgown. He smelled of soaked almonds.

'Nari,' I said.

His hand left me, he moved away so that our bodies no longer touched. His hand picked up the pen and he turned to face the page. '5.5% compounded quarterly over three years,' he said. The hand that held the pen shivered, and the blue ink blotted upon the paper because his palm was sweaty.

'Yes,' I said, pulling back my hair and tying it up in two finger knots. 'How many periods do you have to calculate the interest over?'

'Quarterly over three years means...' he attempted to calculate, running his thumb up and down his forefinger.

'No finger counting, Nari.'

He dropped his hand and closed his eyes. 'Four quarters times three years.'

'Yes, good boy.'

'Twelve periods.'

'That's right. Do it on a fresh page.'

He turned the page with a sigh of relief, because the ink was beginning to stain his wrist. He stepped through the rest of the problem with no difficulty. When he finished it, he checked his answer with that given at the back of the textbook. Then he looked up at me, nervous at first, but I smiled at him and he smiled back.

'Good boy,' I said.

Downstairs, David Attenborough moved on to predatory spiders, and I thought some more of soaked almonds.

Dad ate five soaked almonds before breakfast every day. I have faint memories of Mummy and Dad in the kitchen, laughing about something in the morning light and feeding the pigeons that had nested in the window sill, under the leaves of the money plant. Vimla and I would make a game out of sliding open the door to watch the mother pigeon spread her wings out in a fan. As she frantically pecked at the air to get at our fingers, we would pull them back and chortle.

Mummy died when I was four, so I don't know if this really happened – the part about the mother pigeon could have, because throughout my nineteen years in the house, the window by the kitchen had been home to many generations of pigeons. The part I am not certain of is Mummy and Dad laughing together. The photograph I have of Mummy shows her standing over Dad as he sits with his legs crossed and fingers interlaced over his knee. They are both smiling, but they are not happy smiles. Albert used to say that all photographs were fake, that they only captured one perfect fake moment after another, and life would be much more interesting if we could capture those fleeting instants just before and after the click of the camera.

I have always wondered what Mummy and Dad would have looked like the second before their photographer asked them to smile. I asked Vimla if she had any more memories of Mummy than I did; after all, she had been six when Mummy passed away. What was her smile like, I asked her. What did she do when she was exasperated with our naughtiness? Did she hold her hips and sigh, or did she come after us with a raised rolling pin? Did she soak almonds every morning and give them to Dad right after his yoga? Did she cut off the edges of the bread when she made toast for us before packing us off to school?

I asked Vimla all this and so much more, but all she told me was that she remembered nothing. She keeps a copy of our parents' photograph on her person at all times, and when I asked her if she sometimes wondered about the sadness in Mummy's eyes or the iron in Dad's smile, she just shrugged and changed the subject.

That night I took a second shower before bed, but I still couldn't shake off the stench of Nari's touch on my back. Captain had looked up from his book – *Man's Search for Meaning* – to ask why I bathed twice. I lied that I spilled some egg yolk in my hair. He thankfully did not wish to know how it happened.

I took out the photograph and smoothed it on my knee. Four fold lines – two horizontal, two vertical – divided it into thirds, like a photographer's viewfinder would. On the top right corner a brown mark stood. It could have been coffee or mud or fire. Vimla's copy of the photograph, I knew, was pristine, laminated in thick plastic, clear of lines and spots.

They did not appear very old. Dad still had a full head of black hair. The skin under Mummy's eyes was smooth, and the veins had not yet begun to show on her hands. The picture could not have been taken long after their wedding, and yet the shadows had already descended. I knew they had an arranged marriage, and somewhere deep in my mind, I heard someone – some relative, some aunt, some grandmother – say that Mummy married Dad without even looking at him. But Dad had, and though he had hesitated at first because she was too short, he had said yes.

Would Mummy have changed it all if she had been alive? Somehow it seemed that she was the reason for all of this; for my eloping with Captain, for Dad's slow death, for his nightly visits to our rooms, for Vimla's clamping up and refusing to remember things from her childhood, for Captain raping and hitting me, for Vimla abusing her students and bribing them with grades in return for their silence, for everything, for nothing.

I don't remember being scared by an unwanted touch, perhaps because I knew them before I knew fear. I grew up thinking that fathers of all children did to them what ours did to us. Only after we became twelve or so and began to have friends who spoke about sex did we come to think of our situation as strange. Vimla woke up to it before I did, of course, and I remember the awful fight she had with Dad when he came to know that a boy had dropped her home on his Royal Enfield. That night in bed I asked her why she was bolting the door. She said, 'Because Dad is fucked up.'

And with Captain too, there was no fear when he touched me. My body would stiffen and go limp, something it had learnt to do over fourteen years of practice, but he did not scare me. There are many unpleasant situations in life that we grin and bear and get through; for me, this was just one of those. On days when I got touched I would just have an extra-long shower, and a little pall would settle over me for a day or two, but it always passed – until the next time.

But when Nari first touched me, when I felt his tendril-like hands snake up my back, I felt fear. It was a strange fear too, not the kind that would give you chills and drive you to scream and flee; no, this crept up on you and stayed there, and it seemed to tell you that there is nowhere to run. It was like waking up in the middle of the night and *knowing* that you would see a white face staring at you from the window only if you drew open the curtains, and the only thing you could do is go back to sleep and hope that the monster does too.

It was that fear that sat at the bottom of my stomach and knotted itself tight enough so I wouldn't miss it. As I folded my parents' photograph and put it back in the drawer, I found myself looking every second at the open door, expecting Nari to march into the room and take me right there, at the edge of the bed. They say predators can sense fright in their prey. I wondered if Nari had done so.

When a knock appeared on the door, I sat up, jolted. Captain entered, kicked the door close behind him. There was a whiff of Old Monk on his breath. And on nights when he drank Old Monk, he always came up to my room for the night. His drunken eyes rolled up at me. He said, 'Shall we sleep?'

I nodded. Strangely enough, I felt protected in Captain's arms that night.

When I woke up, day had not yet broken. Beside me Captain rolled away and resumed snoring. I wore my slippers and went down the stairs, into the kitchen. I boiled some water, poured it into a cup, and dropped two teabags into it. I picked it up and turned my back to the stove so that I could lean against the countertop. Directly in front of me, at the door, stood Nari, leaning awkwardly against the frame.

My first impulse was to hurl the tea in his face and run upstairs. Instead, I took a sip and watched him. That would require a lot of needless explanation to Captain. And Nari would not take happily to a charred face. He might decide that enough was enough, that it was time Captain knew about her wife's doings at the clinic. Another sip. I was alert to any small movements, and by the looks of it, he was too.

He was just a boy, I thought, and I was trained in dealing with people like him. Could I not speak with him and make him realize that the path he had started on would lead to no place other than ruin? Nothing had yet happened. If I could succeed in making him see his folly, I could pull him away from a life of hell. It would take no more than a few words.

I placed the cup by my side and nodded to him to enter the kitchen. He did, staying along the edge of the wall, as though I were a ghoul.

'How old are you, Nari?' I asked, keeping my voice low.

'Seventeen.'

'I am sure you feel old enough to have sex, do you not?' Experience had taught me that being direct was the best weapon of all. I saw doubt flash across his eyes, and he considered me suspiciously. 'We both know what happened last night when you were doing your homework.'

'I – I am sorry, madam. I did not know what I was doing.'

'No, you need not apologize.' I gestured to him to come closer. I took a step toward him and ruffled the hair on his head. 'You're a good boy. I know you had no bad intentions.'

He did not shrink away from my hand, but he shook his head. 'No, madam.'

'I know. I am certain that you feel that you're quite a man already, Nari.' I looked into his eyes. His growth spurt had been all vertical, and he stood at about three inches taller than me. In a year or two, I supposed, he would grow a few inches taller still. 'But you're not quite there yet. One day you will find a woman who loves you and whom you love, and with her, you can do all that you want to do.'

He nodded and shifted on his feet.

'But Nari,' I said, making sure that he looked at me, 'you should never, ever, take a woman to bed without asking her first. Okay?'

'Yes, madam.'

'It is love when she lets you do it, but rape when she doesn't let you do it. And if you rape someone, the police will come and put you in jail – for a very long time. Do you want that?'

'No, madam.'

'You want to go to school, don't you? And you want to go to college and get a job and earn a lot of money.'

'Yes, madam.'

'Then you will not think of me that way again. You will think of me as your sister, or your mother. I looked after you when you were sick, didn't I?'

He nodded, looking down at the floor.

'That makes me your mother, doesn't it?'

'Yes, madam.'

I took his chin and lifted it up so that our eyes met again. 'You scared me last night. I thought you may come into the bedroom and do scary things to me. You wouldn't do that to me, would you? If you do, the Captain will come to know, and the police will make your life a living hell, Nari. They will never let you come out, and they will make every inch of your body bleed. Is it worth it?'

His eyes had become wider and wider as I spoke, and now he shook his head.

'Good boy,' I said. 'Now I have one of your secrets, and you have one of mine. Shall we call each other quits?' I smiled. 'Cross my heart, I won't tell if you won't.'

He put his right hand over his head and said, 'Mother promise, I won't, madam.'

'Good boy. Now make some tea for Captain, will you, just the way he likes it, nice and strong.'

'Yes, madam'

'And then we can finish the last few compound interest problems that were left over from last night.' I went into the living room, picked up the newspaper, and sat on the couch studying the headlines but not reading them. My heart was leaping in joy for having escaped the clutches of my blackmailer. I wouldn't have any use for *The Psychology of Blackmail* anymore.

FIVE

On the day Nari first raped me, the sun had not come out until late evening. I had come home by around four o'clock, and had asked him to make some ginger tea for my headache. This could not have been much longer after our early morning conversation, perhaps a few days at most. He brought out the cup in both his hands and placed it on the edge of the table away from me, and took a step back to lean against the wall. I took the cup, held it to my lips, took a nice slow breath, feeling it already clear the mist in my head. 'Thank you, Nari,' I said.

He said, 'I want to fuck you.'

I resisted the urge to look up at him. Keeping my eyes fastened on the tea, I made a mental note of the time. It would be at least a couple of hours before Captain returned home. Could I buy time for that long? My voice threatened to break, so I steeled it with a half-cough and then said, 'We spoke about this, Nari. You said I was just like your mother or sister.'

'I didn't. You did.'

'You agreed with me.'

'I don't anymore.'

'Nari,' I said, looking up, 'I am a married woman. It is not right on your part to propose sex to a married woman.'

'You fuck that man in your clinic.'

I closed my eyes and cursed that morning. The one day Sridhar and I neglected to draw the curtains and shut the windows, Nari had to peep in and see us. 'There is also the fact that I do not wish to sleep with you.'

'Why not?' He looked about himself, and his voice went low. 'You ruffle my hair, you smile at me, you hug me –'

'As a sister, Nari! As a mother! We talked about it!'

'I never thought of you as my sister.'

'Then you should have told me. I would have done none of those things if you had told me that you cannot think of me as your mother or sister.'

'I am telling you now. I want to fuck you.'

'Nari, but I don't.'

'I want to fuck you anyway.'

I looked out of the open main door, at the gate. A vegetable vendor passed, pushing his cart and yelling at the top of his voice. He saw me and waved. I turned away. A part of me wanted to close the door lest people heard our conversation, but then a worm-like feeling had begun to creep down my spine. It told me to keep the door wide open.

I lowered my voice. 'I told you the other day. You should never take a woman against her wishes.'

'You will want it,' he said.

'I don't want it.'

'You don't want it *now*. But you will, once we begin.'

'I won't.'

'I still want to fuck you.'

'What if I say no?' I knew the answer but decided to ask anyway.

'You said that we both have secrets. You said you will keep my secret if I keep yours. But your secret is bigger than mine, isn't it, madam?'

'I don't know what you're trying to say. If I tell Captain that you made a move on me, and you asked me this obscene question, do you think he will let you live?'

'If I tell Captain about you and the man in the clinic, do you think he will let *you* live?'

'Then both of us die.'

'I won't, madam. I will run away to my village and till my farm, tend to my cows, live my life. Where will you run away?'

I could go to Goa, I thought to myself, see what had happened to the old house, if they still had the 'Bosanquets' nameplate at the gate. I could run up to Sammy's Shack to see if old Sam still mixed his drinks the same way, in little silver thimbles. I could look up Albert. He would certainly take me in. (Wouldn't he?) I could go to Chandigarh, to Vimla, though we had not spoken to each other in a year. Or I could tell Sridhar that I was ready to move in with him. He would jump at it.

But even as I thought them, a strange chill took hold of me, and my fingers twisted nervously together. Nari was right. My need was bigger than his. And Captain would far more easily forgive a seventeen-year-old's infatuation than his grown wife's deliberate adultery.

Nari smiled at me, as though my thoughts were written on my face. 'Captain will not be home for at least two hours more.'

I nodded.

'Plenty of time for us.' He came to my chair, and clumsily held out his hands. I placed mine in his and got to my feet. The cup of tea stood there, still full. He was yet nervous, struggling visibly to look me in the eye. But his grip was tight, and I thought of the coconut husk that he had ripped with his fingers. My hand seemed to disappear into his, and my fingers dangled, limp. He walked to the stairs and I went with him, leaving the front door ajar. We ascended the steps, one by one. Nari no longer looked like a boy to me.

We entered the visitor's bedroom, which held a single wooden cot and a mattress. 'Sit,' he commanded, and began to open the buttons of his blue shirt. I sat on the edge and watched him. He smiled at me. I did not smile back. He covered my cheek with his palm, looked into my eyes, pushed me back on the bed.

A sudden gust of wind blew and slammed the door of the room shut.

By the time Captain returned, I had showered and was dressed in my satin nightgown. Nari had changed into a fresh pair of blue shirt and shorts. As Captain sat on the couch and pulled at his shoelaces, Nari came with a cup of black coffee and stood by his side. I pretended to read Chapter Two of my book, which compared the relationship between the blackmailer and the victim to one of lovers, forever at war with each other but equally unable to wrench themselves apart.

Captain had an uncanny ability to sniff at the air and call out that something was not quite right. He did so now, and my armpits became moist. I'd never felt like I had cheated on Captain with Sridhar, but now I felt dirty and sweaty all over, as if ants were crawling over my skin and building little muddy hills, behind my knees, between my breasts, under my toes. Captain would know, I thought; it was only a matter of time. I looked at Nari and saw that his eyes were fastened on me.

'How was school today, Nari?' Captain was asking.

'It was good, sir,' said Nari. 'We learnt about circles.'

'Ah. Geometry.' He set his shoes aside and took the cup. Nari picked up the shoes and carried them to the rack outside the front door. 'There is no shampoo in the bathroom, Nari,' said Captain. 'Will you go and get some?'

'Yes, sir.'

After Nari had left, Captain leaned forward so that his elbows pressed against his thighs. 'What's wrong?

'Nothing,' I replied, not looking away from the book.

'There is something,' he said. 'It is best if you tell me right now. You know I will find out sooner or later.'

It was not a threat. Captain liked to be in the know. I think it is one of the characteristic traits of army people. They're so used to knowing things that other people don't know that they cannot handle not knowing things that they think everyone else knows. The only way to kill an army man's thirst for knowing is to deny that there is anything to know. That was what I managed with Sridhar. Captain had met him once or twice but had suspected nothing. No one who met Sridhar could ever suspect anything.

But now Captain had got the whiff. I did not know what tipped him off; maybe he caught something in the way Nari and I looked at each other. Tonight, if he wanted me in the bedroom, I would have to make sure that the lights were off. Otherwise he may see the bruises on my thighs and wonder some more.

'Nothing, Captain,' I said at last. 'I just have a headache. Can we have an early dinner today and retire for the night?'

'Sure,' he said, but he looked doubtfully at me.

The tingling sensation between my breasts intensified. I managed a smile in his direction, then went back to the book.

★

I went to the clinic early next morning, and on entering the office, I told Ankita to take a day off and cancel all my appointments. She asked if she should call Sridhar and ask him not to come in. I paused and looked at her, but her face showed no malice. So I shook my head. 'We have some papers to work on,' I told her.

'Yes, madam.'

I took the keys from her and bid her goodbye. At the door she stopped and half-turned to me. 'Madam,' she said, 'will I be paid for today?' I recalled from our hiring interview that Ankita had an ailing father in Ludhiana and that she sent home money every month. She earned some extra rupees by teaching Bharatanatyam to school kids.

I smiled at her. 'Yes, of course.'

She beamed and said, 'Thank you.'

As she turned and stepped out into the porch, I called out to her. She looked at me.

'Come here, Ankita.'

She came in and sat on one of the white plastic visitors' chairs. I held out a five-hundred-rupee note. 'Here.'

'I – what is this for, madam?'

'Just a bonus for your diligence and work ethic. I don't think I pay you enough for the amount of work you do for me.'

The girl smiled uncertainly. She could not be much older than twenty-two. Like most women of her age, she had all the looks to snare a man but none of the nous to keep him. I thought of Mrs Krishnamurthy, for no apparent reason.

Ankita took the money and put it into her purse. She wanted to say thank you, but her throat kept catching.

'How is your father now?'

'He – he is not okay. The doctor has said four months.'

'I am sorry to hear that.' I thought of Dad and Mummy and

the dead eyes and smooth fingers and sad smiles. 'Will you get your mother here after that?'

'I don't know. I haven't thought of it yet.'

'Well, if you need any help with anything, let me know, okay?'

She nodded and got up to leave. I felt compelled to give her advice. If I had had a younger sister, she would look remarkably like Ankita, I thought. 'Do you have a man in your life, Ankita?'

She shook her head.

'Can I tell you something, if you don't mind?'

'Yes, madam.'

'Remember this when a man does come into your life. They come chasing your body, every one of them. There are *no* exceptions.'

She gulped, and lowered her head. She had pretty hair, jet black, wavy, smooth and tough.

'They come for your body – that you cannot help. But they stay for your mind. If you wish to keep a man, remember to make him see your mind, and make him like what he sees.'

'Yes, madam.'

I laughed. 'Go now. I won't waste your holiday giving you sermons on picking up men!'

Ankita smiled and tottered off with a quick, girly wave at me from the doorway. As she motored off on her baby pink scooty, I twirled the bunch of keys around my index finger and laughed at what I had said.

Sridhar came in. I threw the keys in his direction and motioned him into the chamber. He locked the outer room and followed me. The first thing he did on entering was bolt the windows and draw the curtains. I switched on the tube lights, and we met in the middle of the room. His hand went to my breast, but I pushed it away. 'Today you're going to be mine,' I said. He smiled. I didn't. I knew what I had planned for him. He didn't.

I sat on the couch, leaned back, spread my arms and commanded: 'Kneel.' He did. 'Remove the first two buttons of your shirt and give me your belt.' It was a leather belt with a silver buckle. I rolled it around my hands and tested its strength. 'Give me your hands.' I wrapped the belt around his wrists and bound it so that the pin of the buckle stabbed his skin. He grimaced.

'Are you going to be a sissy and cry?' I asked.

Sridhar shook his head, and bit his lip.

I slapped him, with my palm across his left cheek, then with my knuckles across his right. My diamond ring scraped him on his chin and drew a scratch that first went white, then pink. I removed his glasses and tossed them on the chair. 'Can you see anything without them? Or are you blind?'

He nodded, said he could make out only shapes.

'So you're a little blind fuck, aren't you?' I reached for the cane from the umbrella stand. 'Have you ever been punished in school?' He shook his head. 'Ah, you must have been the smart kid in class, huh, always sitting in the front row, always the first to put up his hand, always being talked about in staff rooms.' I held the cane at both ends and bent it with my thumbs. 'Show me your hands.' He held them out in front of him, bound together by the belt. The pin had made a little red ridge on his left wrist, just under the line of his palm.

'Soft hands,' I murmured, pushing his fingertips down with the tip of the cane. 'Never been punished, never had a scar on them.' I lifted the cane and brought it down with force, stopping right at the moment before it landed. He had shut his eyes. 'Don't close your eyes, boy!' He opened them, and I saw bewilderment in his glance. 'Don't look me in the eye either,' I said. 'Look down at my feet.'

With the cane I smoothed his hands and tapped on them. His eyes were red, teary, angry. I raised the cane and brought it down with a whoosh on his right palm. It made no great sound, but he drew a sharp breath, and a red line appeared across his hand. Then I landed a blow on his other hand, this time harder. 'Ah,' he said, and looked up. 'You're not allowed to speak,' I told him. 'Every time you speak, you get whipped.' He hung his head, like a repentant sinner at a church. I eased myself onto the edge of the couch and hit him on his upper arm, then his shoulder. Each time the cane seared into his skin, he moaned with his lips stitched together.

I placed my right foot on his chest and pushed him onto the floor. Getting to my feet, I clasped my hands behind me and circled him. 'Such a pretty boy, and such a pussy! Remove your shirt.' He began to undo the rest of his shirt's buttons. 'Hurry up!' I said, and raised the cane over my shoulder. He quickly popped the last two buttons and his shirt dropped around his waist. 'Good boy.' I traced a line along the side of his shoulder, down his arm, and back up toward his chest and nipples. I ran a circle around his nipple. Then I brought it down to his stomach and drilled into his belly button. 'Does that hurt?' He squirmed but shook his head. 'Oh, you lying to me?' He shook his head harder.

I rasped his arms twice, and while he squirmed, I loosened the belt off his wrists, held it hanging off the cane, and threw it against the wall. 'Remove your pants.' He looked up at me, alarmed. I reassured him that I wouldn't pluck out his cock. I pushed him with my foot onto his back, and pulled at his lips with my toes. I slipped my big toe into his mouth. 'Suck on it,' I said, with the tip of my cane playing with his hair. I watched his mouth cover my toe and draw it in, I watched his hands fumble with the buckle of his pants. He removed his underwear too, which I picked up, crumpled into a ball and flung it against the wall. I brought my foot down from his mouth toward his erection, and waited for it to harden against my ankle.

I hiked my skirt, pushed my panties to one side, and sat on him such that his penis slid into me. I squeezed my clitoral muscles. He shut his eyes and groaned. 'Does that hurt?' I asked. He nodded. I squeezed some more. I picked up the belt, wrapped it around his neck, and pulled myself onto my knees so that he could push deeper into me. His hands clamped around my waist, and his thumbs opened me and plucked at my clitoris. I swayed on top of him, my eyes dilated, I dropped the belt. My hands fell on his chest, and my fingers closed around the hair on his chest. A hyena-like grunt escaped me. My thighs squeezed together, and my legs began to shake. I fell to the side. He ripped open my shirt. His mouth closed around my nipple.

I passed out.

Later, I applied butter to all the red lines on Sridhar's body. I kissed the bruises on his hands, the spots on his thighs. I slipped under his arm, ran my lips along his jaw. We cried, and for a long time we lay in each other's arms on the cold floor, between the couch and the chair, naked, staring at the ceiling. Then we fell asleep.

Since the events have become public, sections of the media have hinted that at some level, I was at fault for what Nari and Captain have done. How can three different men – they include my father in this – treat the same woman in almost exactly the same way without it being the woman's fault at some level? With Captain I am sometimes accused as being weak – as Sridhar did. With Dad I am too pliant, too blinded by love to take a stand, and with Nari I was unconsciously playing the role of the prowling cougar that I had become accustomed to.

I pity the women in these men's lives. They must have the picture of a woman as little more than a sex doll that comes to bed whenever the urge is upon them. They must all subscribe to the great wisdom in our scriptures which denounce independent, sexually open women. They must think that every woman that ever gets violated brings it upon herself in some way.

I did not wish it upon myself when I was a child, and I know Vimla didn't either. As soon as we were old enough to understand what was happening, we locked our bedroom from the inside and lay awake into the night, waiting for Dad's heavy step, the rattle of the bolt as he tried to push it open, and the odour of his aftershave mixed with vodka. He always shaved just before he visited us; perhaps he was concerned that his beard would prick our skin.

I did not wish it upon myself when I married Captain. Vimla had the courage to pack her bags and leave on her own. I didn't. When I first met Captain, I knew that he was going to be my ticket to freedom; where to, I did not know, and I still do not know, but anywhere out of Goa, anywhere out of this hell, I remember telling myself. So perhaps I played the role of the woman he wanted, by curtsying when I met him, by blushing when he knelt before me and recited Chaucer, by appearing charmed by the many tales he told me of trenches and tanks. But nowhere did I suggest to him that I would willingly bear abuse in his hands, though that is what I have done.

With Nari, too, the picture of me as a seductress is untrue. I never wore in his sight clothes unfit for a housewife, and I never spoke to him but as a mother or an elder sister. When I tended to his sickness, too, I was careful, because I knew what a monstrous age seventeen can be. I never touched him when I didn't need to, and in fact, until that evening when I leaned over his compound interest problem, there never has been, to my knowledge, even a whiff of sexual tension between us.

And what of Sridhar? It is he who pursued me, and it is he who began those little games that come so naturally to men. Some observers have noted that I abused my position at the clinic and seduced a poor, innocent PhD student. But when it comes to matters of sex, men lose their innocence at the age of twelve. Women, on the other hand, stay naive throughout their lives, I think. As I look back to the first few days of my meeting Sridhar, I do not remember any interest on my part to have an affair with him, but he would find reasons to be present in my chamber when he didn't need to, and he would smile and he would flirt. Men can smell vulnerability in a woman from a mile, like Captain, like Nari, like Sridhar.

Albert was probably the only man who never took advantage of me, but then he had his hands full of Vimla. Vimla's men never had time or eyes for anyone else; she wrapped them around her index finger so tightly and yet with so much apparent love that they would descend into some sort of trance, their eyes glazed, their mouths muttering some unintelligible nonsense as they held her skirt and followed her. After Vimla left Goa, Albert and I met a few times – platonically – on the beach, a few hundred meters down from Sammy's Shack. But the stars in Albert's eyes had long gone by then. He said they were still chasing Vimla, that they were still holding her skirt wherever she went.

Albert wore his curly hair long enough to completely cover the back of his neck. On some nights, Vimla would describe to me in great detail how she had pulled his hair while they cavorted behind the bushes on the beach under the full moon. 'If you haven't had sex on the beach, Ramya,' she would say, 'you have not lived at all.' I would listen to her words, close my eyes in the darkness, picture my own fingers wading through

Albert's hair as his eyes dilated with the pleasure that *I* was giving him. My knees would sink into the sand each time the waves went out, and his hands would caress my waist, and sometimes they would pull me down to his mouth so that we could kiss.

I would think of all that and touch myself. Deep into the night, after Vimla had slipped into sleep, I would watch the phosphorescent stars stuck to the ceiling of our bedroom and imagine them to be real. I would find constellations – of the crab, of the balance, of the divine twins – and I would let sleep take me only after I had had my fill of Albert.

Nari did not come to me every night. He did not come to me twice or thrice a week like Captain did, or every morning before the clients arrived, like Sridhar. He came to me without warning, each time. Sometimes a whole week would pass during which he would only watch, making no attempt to touch or smile. Sometimes he would pull me by the arm into the kitchen after having had me in the master bedroom that very morning. The one thing I learned to rely on with Nari was the unreliability of his timing. Whenever I found myself alone, with Captain in another room or out of the house, I expected him to pounce on me, and I became a wreck of frayed nerves.

I took to painting, therefore. Every day, after returning from work, I would set up my canvas in the upstairs area and paint whatever came to mind. The first few days I found myself unable to concentrate, and every few minutes I looked over my shoulder at the staircase, listening to the sounds of the television or of the vessels in the kitchen. I celebrated every moment that I spent in solitude, only to stumble with fear into the next, waiting, watching.

But things became better with time. I painted the sand, the waves, the sun. I painted the worn out board of Sammy's Shack with the two interlocking 'S' signs. I painted Albert's curly hair and Nari's face onto a head. I dressed Albert in Nari's blue shirt and shorts. I painted our old house, the kitchen window and the nesting pigeons. I painted Mummy and Dad as they appeared in the picture, only with their smiles a little happier. I painted the view of our bedroom's ceiling in the dark.

Nari always asked me if I liked what he was doing to me. I always said no. He would laugh and say he didn't believe me. On the day I painted Albert's hair on Nari's face, he saw the painting and asked if I was in love with him. I shook my head in shock, but he only smirked and walked away, nodding as if he understood. Whenever he called me into the room he began by going down on me, and whenever a moan escaped my clenched lips, he chuckled softly. He always brought a condom, always made sure that my nipples were erect before he inserted himself into me. That way I should perhaps say he was quite the gentleman.

The first time he saw me reach orgasm he looked at me in wonder. I hid my face from him and told him about the tickling analogy that I had told Mrs Krishnamurthy, but oh, how wrong it felt! How easy it was to tell someone about it and wonder at their naivety for not accepting it, and how much harder it was to accept it yourself. Every time we finished, I would beg Nari to stop doing this, but he would only stare at me with confusion and say that my body loved what he was doing to it. Only I was standing in the way, either because I did not know it or because I wasn't willing to accept it.

Every time his hands fell on my body I recoiled with revulsion. His mouth stank of almonds and cigarettes, and each time after he left, I would brush my teeth at least twice and spray it with mouth freshener to get rid of the smell. He was not good looking, he was not educated, he was not intelligent or articulate; he had none of the attributes of a man to whom I would be attracted. I told him that; that my body was responding merely to his touch. I told myself that. But the doubt remained. Why did my body not listen, then, to my mind? Why did I cream myself when he pressed his tongue to my clitoris and ran his middle finger down the length of my vulva? And when he entered me with his member and drilled into me with his thumb placed under the clitoral hood at just the right angle, why could I not persuade my body not to climax?

I remembered Mrs Krishnamurthy's words. I hated him for abusing me, but I hated him much more for making me suspect whether there was truth to his words; whether, after all, my body knew better than I did, whether, like all those sick men said, somewhere deep within me, a part of me governed by the primitive reptilian brain actually *liked* being raped.

I had my chance to hurt him when he asked me, a few days after I had my first orgasm with him, whether I would take him into my mouth. A man is at his most vulnerable in the hands of a woman when she has his member. I wanted more than anything in the world to make it so that he would do this to no other woman in his life. Consequences be damned. Yes, he would tell Captain about my affair with Sridhar, and he would make sure that I was ruined completely, but was I not ruined already?

I said yes, that I would, but when the moment came, when he slipped his condom off and stood on the bed over me, his legs spread, that old friend, fear, came back to me and held me in her grip. If I were to carry out my plan and hurt him, before he would tell Captain about me, he would have the chance, I knew, of having his way with me. And when it came to a physical fight, I was no match for Nari. He had the hands of a wrestler. If he wanted to, I was sure that he could take me by the legs and tear me apart, like he did with that coconut. At the end, then, like always, fear won, and I meekly guided him into my mouth, nodding at his whispered instructions. I kept my teeth away from the stem of his penis, and ran my tongue over its tip. His hands covered my head and his knees bent. His hips arched toward me. I almost choked.

But I did not bite.

SIX

Mrs Krishnamurthy wore a bright red sari that day. Golden rings hung off her ears. At the tip of her white nose ring sat a diamond the size of my thumbnail. As she spoke, it shifted once this way, once that, reflecting the morning light in various patterns. She sat in her usual pose, one leg crossed over the other, one hand laid flat over her thigh, the other stretched along the backrest of the couch.

'I am convinced he's having an affair,' she said.

'What makes you so certain?'

'It's his eyes. It's always the eyes, isn't it? He never looks at me directly when he speaks any more. He's always looking away, at his fingernails, out the window, at the television, anywhere but at me.'

'No hard evidence yet, then?'

Mrs Krishnamurthy shook her head. 'None. But I've seen enough. I think I am going to put a detective on him, try and follow him and see where he goes and whom he sees.'

'Have you tried talking to him about your suspicions?'

‘It’s not a suspicion,’ she said calmly. ‘I know he is sleeping with someone else.’

‘Do you know who he is sleeping with?’

‘Oh, I am sure it’s one of the teachers he works with. He has always had a thing for these intellectual teacher-type women, you know. He’s always saying this or that about the English teacher at his school, for example.’

‘Have you ever met her?’

‘No.’ She appeared shocked. ‘Why would I want to meet his colleagues?’

‘Maybe meeting her would give you more insights into whether they are in fact sleeping together or not.’

‘I don’t need any insights. I am convinced that they are sleeping together.’

I closed my mouth with a hand and sighed into it, so that she wouldn’t see. Suddenly I felt a wave of fatigue wash over me, and my eyes grew heavy. I wanted to hear no more of Mrs Krishnamurthy’s tale of woe. I cast a quick glance at the wall clock. Only fifteen minutes had passed.

Mrs Krishnamurthy leaned forward, looking intently at my hand. ‘What happened to you, dear? Somebody has been mistreating you, haven’t they?’

‘Oh, this, no, it’s nothing really.’

‘Well, it doesn’t look like nothing,’ she said, taking my hand in hers and looking at the bruised skin on my knuckles and wrist. I had received them the other day when Sridhar’s belt buckle had chafed against my hands. I had wrapped it around my palms as I straddled him, and I had pulled so hard that it cut my fingers.

‘No,’ I said again. Mrs Krishnamurthy had begun to run her fingers over the bruises. ‘It’s nothing.’

‘Poor child,’ she murmured. ‘You poor, poor child.’

I wheeled my chair close enough to her for our knees to touch. Mrs Krishnamurthy looked nothing like my mother – her angular face had a distinct unkindness to it that my mother's did not – but at that moment when she soothed my palms with her touch, I saw in her smile the same confused sadness that I had seen on my mother's face. I allowed her to caress my wrists and clasp my hand in both of hers.

I told her that her time was being wasted.

She shook her head with a thin smile. 'As long as we're talking, there is no question of time being wasted, doctor.'

'But we're not talking about you.'

'Which is great! I get so tired talking about myself all the time. Why don't you tell me about yourself?'

I tried to pull back my hands, but she held on, firm and gentle. She tilted her head at me and said, 'You're my daughter's age, dear, and if this were not your office, if this were just a room in which you and I met, would you not have told me what you're so worried about?'

I looked at the closed door to the reception. Beyond the wall, out of my sight, Ankita's keyboard went clack, clack, clack.

'You have dark circles around your eyes, you have bruises on your wrists and god knows where else,' said Mrs Krishnamurthy. 'You are probably going through a lot more than I am, and yet it is I who gets to speak with you every time I visit.' With her free hand she pushed a strand of hair on my forehead back behind my ear. 'Why don't we meet as two people, instead of as doctor and client?'

She guided me to the couch, sat me down next to her, and placed an arm around me. I began to talk. I told her about Captain, about Albert, about Sridhar, about Vimla, about Sammy's Shack, about Dad and Mummy. I told her about Nari, and how just the night before I had had yet another orgasm by his touch, and how much I hated myself for it. My eyes did not water, and my voice did not change. It all came out as though I was a talking doll whose switch had been turned on. I clicked my pen open and close throughout my monologue, and toward the end a knock appeared on the door. I looked up at the clock. It was ten past the hour.

'I am sorry,' I said, standing up and clearing my nose. 'I won't charge you for this, Mrs Krishnamurthy.'

'Don't be silly,' she said lightly. 'Charge me all you want.'

I called out to Sridhar at the door to wait a moment. While Mrs Krishnamurthy was gathering her things, I set my notepad and pen aside on the table and pushed the chair back to its usual place, a good seven feet away from the couch. My eyes refused to look at Mrs Krishnamurthy directly; I realized that I was at once quite afraid of her. She looked nothing like Mummy, not any more.

'Why don't you come down to our place for dinner tonight?' she asked. 'Arun will be at home, he said, so you can meet him and tell me if my suspicions are true or not.'

'I don't know how appropriate that will be,' I said.

'And we can also have a cup of coffee together,' she said, 'you and me, as friends.'

As friends. I gave her a tight smile. 'I will give you a call around four.'

When I got home, Nari assembled his writing desk and brought his schoolbag over. He had become bolder these last few days. Earlier, when Captain was home, he would not so much as raise his head and look at me. But now he had begun to rub my back when we passed each other in the kitchen, allowed our hands to touch for that one second longer every time we handed each other something, and then of course, he would lustfully look at me with those grey-green eyes, with Captain sitting in the same room between us.

He enjoyed homework. I made it a point to sit two feet away from him, but he had ways of pulling me closer to him. The easiest was to pretend that he was struggling with a problem or a sentence. I would drag my chair over and look at his page, and he would touch my breasts with the blunt tip of his pencil. My breathing would get heavier, and he would smile and go back to the book. For better or worse, he looked forward to homework because of the ways in which he could touch me without getting caught.

I entered the house and dropped my bag onto the sofa. Captain would return no earlier than six, and it was just four. Nari did not seem to be in the mood to take me to the bedroom, but he seemed eager to begin homework.

'Not today,' I told him, and his face fell. 'I have to visit a friend.'

'Why don't you go after homework, madam?'

'Our homework will take at least two hours, and Captain will be back by then.'

'So? You can go after he comes back.'

'He wouldn't like that.' Noticing the explanatory tone in my answers, I said firmly, 'And I do not need to take your advice on when to go visiting my friends.'

He smiled, in the way kids did when they saw through your bluff. He shrugged and lowered his hand toward his groin. That was how he indicated to me that he was ready. 'Not now, Nari,' I said.

'I will make it quick,' he said, and pointed to the kitchen.

'No.' He went into the kitchen and held the door open for me. I closed the main door and walked toward him. 'No,' I said, but he just grinned. When I entered the kitchen, he closed the door, picked me up in his arms, and mounted me on the countertop. I leaned back against the wall. He hiked my skirt, slid his brown hands up my thighs and slipped off my panties. He held them up to his nose and took a deep breath, his gaze locked with mine. 'You're already wet,' he said. I closed my eyes and backed further up, knowing he was right, trying to go somehow to that place where I had trained myself to go during those nights when Dad visited us when we were children.

But I did not succeed. Every time I willed myself to lift into the radium constellations of my ceiling, the flick of his tongue brought me back to the kitchen. Every time I visualized Sammy's Shack and the white noise of the waves, I heard my own answering groans to his. When I thought of sand trickling through my fingers, of water running over my arms, of Albert's curly hair waving in the wet breeze, his sloppy kisses yanked me back to the present, demanding that I enjoy it. He held my legs and pushed them back over my head, and with one knee hoisted over the counter, he ordered me to dress him with a condom.

He did not bother with my pleasure this time. 'I am going to fuck you,' he said with such malice that I nodded in fear. 'You're my bitch, and I will fuck your brains out, till you come so hard over my cock that you won't be able to walk for a week.' I kept nodding, and he closed his fingers around my throat and leaned over me so that he could look into my eyes. His teeth gritted, and as his hips worked, sending his penis in and out of me, a deep frown came over his brow, and he began to whine. 'Fuck. Fuck. Your. Brains. Yeah.' I kept nodding, blinking back tears, unable to hold back moans each time he thrust into me, snapping at his mouth with my teeth, my hands clutching onto his shoulders so that my nails dug into his skin.

I do not know what happened then, but when I woke up, I was curled into myself, turned over my side, facing the wall. I raised my head and looked over my shoulder and saw him standing by the sink with his erection pointing at me. His arms were folded across his chest, and he had a dull grin on his face. I turned back toward the wall and slept.

Mrs Krishnamurthy's house was at the other end of town, but on the bus route, and about a five-minute stroll from the main road. She lived in a duplex villa set in the middle of a gated property with security cameras and uniformed guards who pushed a register at every visitor and took their signature. I had not asked Mrs Krishnamurthy where her husband taught, but as I reached the house and looked at the car parked in the garage, I guessed that it was not a community school or a government college.

The sun had almost set by that time, and the lights that stood on either side of the walkway went on at once, without flickering. Well-tended hibiscus and sunflower bushes lay sprinkled upon the lawn. Grey pigeons with purple bands around their necks hopped on granite benches, now pecking, now preening, now gurgling. One of the guards came at them with his hands waving, and they dispersed at once, only to settle as a group on the adjoining bench, with one careful eye on their invader.

I rang the bell, and Mrs Krishnamurthy welcomed me in a satin nightgown much like my own. 'Come in, come in,' she said brightly, 'hope you had no difficulty in finding the house?'

'None,' I said.

She waved me onto a sofa, from which I faced a book shelf that took up half the opposite wall. I passed a quick eye through the contents, but the names *Hamlet*, Dickens and Frost jumped out at me. The living room was L-shaped, as it was in most of these newer duplex homes, with the long arm containing two sofas and with the dining table and chairs occupying the short one. The light was orange and dim, curiously the kind of light that was the worst to read in.

'We don't read here,' said Mrs Krishnamurthy, holding out a glass of water. 'This is the TV room, Arun calls it. We do all our reading upstairs.' I looked around. There was no television in sight.

'Where is he?' I said. 'I thought you said he was going to be home tonight.'

'Oh, that's what he said. But he got a call from the college, some papers to correct or something of that sort.' She waved at the air in her neat manner. 'I think he went to meet his little English teacher. Never mind, he will be back for dinner.'

On the side table, I saw a picture of a much younger looking Mrs Krishnamurthy with a bald, bespectacled man in a kurta and pyjama. If he had a satchel he would complete the typical look of a communist. His glasses resembled those of Harry Potter, and the moustache reminded me of Charlie Chaplin. He had frayed leather sandals on his feet, and around his shoulder Mrs Krishnamurthy had her arms thrown in a circle, bending toward him with her lips puckered, one leg raised behind her, eyes thrown in the direction of the camera.

I nodded at it with a smile. 'Cute.'

'Yes,' she said. 'It was.'

'He seems a bit older than you are.'

'Oh, no, he is only seven years older, but he lost most of his hair before he turned thirty. When my father first met him he asked for his birth certificate to prove his age.' She laughed and shook her head. 'How did your father react when you told him about your husband?'

'Oh, he had no reaction. My father had by then given up on most things in the living world.' She gave me a frown, as if wanting me to go on, but I didn't. Instead I said, 'I see quite a collection.'

'Arun is a big reader of classic literature. Agatha Christie does just fine for me, though.'

'Agatha Christie is good.'

'You like her too? I have at least one copy of all her books. You can borrow them if you want.'

'I think I will.'

Our old house in Goa was a single-storied structure built flat on a large piece of land. For large parts of my life, only Vimla, Dad and I lived in it. When three people live in a large house, and if none of them are great speakers, the house seems to take on a life of its own. It seems to breathe, heave, sigh and mourn. The sounds of the house become part of your life, and when you move to another in due course, you feel as though a dear friend has departed.

Now, as we sat together, Mrs Krishnamurthy and me, making small talk, the house awakened. A breeze blew in from the west, pushing aside the yellow curtains, and made the cover of the refrigerator fall. It had on it the picture of a cat and a dog sleeping together. Mrs Krishnamurthy hurried over to return it to its place, but I would have asked her not to bother. Let the house speak, I would have said.

'Would you like to come and sit here, by the dining table?' she asked me. 'The lights in the living room are a little depressing.'

I did not ask her why they had them then. I was beginning to think that the couple did not entertain much, if at all. I realized that I still did not know much about this woman. On the wall separating the dining room from the kitchen, a black thin lad with a flute was playing to a girl with a painted pot. She sat on a rock, rested her chin upon her long fingers, and gazed upon the boy, though she could be looking at the flute too. In the background were trees, grass and cows.

'This was Arun's pick at a handicrafts exhibition,' she said, her hand lingering over but not touching the flute. 'He says this is one of the rare paintings where the artist did not bother with niceties and made Krishna dark – as he was supposed to be.'

I pulled out one of the chairs – made of heavy teak – and sat on it. I placed my handbag on the glass top. From the window I saw that it had become dark already. Captain would have come home, and would have asked Nari where I was. Now he would be fidgeting over this 'friend' of mine. I didn't have any friends in Hyderabad. A tiny hole appeared in the pit of my stomach, as it did whenever I thought of Nari and Captain together, talking among themselves. I played with the strap of my handbag. The smell of cooked-just-right basmati rice floated into the room, at which Mrs Krishnamurthy stood up and said, 'We can eat if you're hungry. I don't think Arun will come just yet.'

Dinner passed in silence. We ate with our hands, so the only sounds came from the steel spoons and vessels when we served ourselves. The curd was thick and creamy, the mango pickle nice and sour. Despite the lack of conversation – or maybe because of it – I enjoyed the meal. After I had finished eating, I got up to wash my plate, but Mrs Krishnamurthy would not allow it, and she gathered up all the dishes and loaded the dishwasher with them.

We went up the stairs. On the way up I saw more photos of Mrs Krishnamurthy and Arun, at the Taj Mahal, at the Leaning Tower, at the Niagara, at the Golden Temple. In all of them they appeared happy and young and without a care. Mrs Krishnamurthy's hair in these photographs was thick and lustrous, and she looked at least ten years younger. She led me onto the balcony. We sat on the plastic swing. In the house to our left, a couple stood on the edge of their porch, the man with his hands folded, the woman with her arm around his waist. They both appeared to be looking up at the stars.

'Mrs Krishnamurthy,' I said, 'I should be going. This has been fun.'

'Call me Haritha,' she said. 'Nobody calls me that any more. Did you ever feel that getting married was a lot like giving up who you are?'

I nodded. The couple on the porch drew closer to one another. The sky turned a deeper shade of purple. The stars became brighter. Captain would be getting angrier by the second. I checked my phone. The screen was blank.

'Before I married Arun, I had a life. I had a career. I was somebody. But now the world sees me as his wife and nothing more. Hell, even I see myself primarily as his wife, as his caregiver. It makes me very – afraid.'

'That he will leave you?'

'That he has found someone else who will care for him like I do. When something becomes your identity, you become very scared to give it up, no matter how much you hate it.'

I thought of the fear that I had lived with all my life. Maybe it had been me all along, searching and embracing fear throughout my life, frightened that it would leave me, afraid that I would be nothing without it. Dad, Captain, Sridhar, Nari – all of them frightened me in one way or the other, and today if I were to define myself, I could do so only by the ties of fear that bound me to them, in different ways. What would I do without them? What would I do without these ropes that had bruised my wrists?

'I know what you're thinking,' said Mrs Krishnamurthy. 'They say that once a man takes your body, he leaves a part of him with you, at all times, whether you like it or not.'

I looked up at her, and wondered if she spoke of Arun or of Captain or of Nari. Then I lowered my head, realizing that it didn't matter. I never slept with Albert. He never touched any part of my body except my hands, and yet he was the one whom I thought of the most. You could leave a part of you with someone else without ever taking her body, I wanted to tell Mrs Krishnamurthy. But the air had begun to fill with fog. Words did not travel far enough or fast enough at such times.

'This just sounds like one of our therapy sessions,' she said. 'Now I am going to shut up and get you to speak, my dear.'

'I really have to go, Mrs Krishnamurthy.'

'You're going nowhere before we've had our wine.' She eased herself off the swing. 'Let me get you some. In the meantime, you think of what you're going to tell me when I return!' On the way down the stairs, she hummed to herself an old Frank Sinatra tune.

One of those fatigue headaches came over me at that moment, as I sat and watched the shapes of the couple on the adjoining porch dissolve into mere smudges. I leaned my head back. The shade had green and white stripes on it, and toward its edge, a picture of Mickey Mouse had been printed with his trademark grin and wink. He held a yellow and blue umbrella over his head.

I closed my eyes, and for once did not think of anyone at all. Each time my mind veered toward something and threatened to run away with it, I pulled her back and pointed her to the building ball of fog. But in just a few seconds, something or someone would emerge in the shadows and beckon to me, and I would just run away from them and stare, instead, at the white cloud.

I heard steps, and the accompanying Sinatra song. The swing creaked when Mrs Krishnamurthy sat next to me, and the glasses in her hand clinked against the bottle. I checked my phone again. The screen was still blank. The clock said half past eight.

I let my thumb hover for a moment on the green call button. I stared at Captain's picture. I pursed my lips. Then I shut the flap cover and put the phone aside.

By her decree, we spoke of happier times. She told me of her trips with Arun, of long lazy Sunday afternoons which they spent in bed, him reading Joyce, her reading the latest Dean Koontz novel. I spoke of the perfect golden brown to which D'Souza, the chef at Sammy's Shack, cooked his crabs. I told her about the laughter in the kitchen, the mother pigeon who fanned her wings out and pecked at the air when we opened the window.

'Where have all those times gone?' she asked me.

'I never wonder anymore,' I said, though I did every night.

'Tell me about your first kiss.'

During training for therapy, they taught practitioners different ways to turn topics of conversation around. The theory goes that when people say 'Tell me about something', all they want subconsciously is to share their own experiences, but because they don't want to be thought of as monopolizing the exchange, they begin by asking someone else to share first. So by long years of training, the words tumbled out on their own.

'I am sure mine is not as exciting as yours. Was it with Arun?'

She shook her head, and covered her mouth with her hand as she smiled. I could see the layers of grace and poise peel away with each gulp of wine. 'I seduced one of our manservants when I was fifteen.'

'Get out!'

'I did! I never told anyone, not even Arun. But this boy was so – so – delicious! He had this smooth olive skin and the dreamiest pair of eyes you could find on a boy – or at least I thought so then. So this one night, there was a big party at the house for all the grown-ups, and I was the only "child", so I was left to myself.' She stopped to take a sip, and she looked at one of the orange spots of light that bore through the curtain of fog. 'I went into the kitchen and found him sitting in one corner, playing by himself with a deck of cards.'

We had heard rumours among our girlfriends that so-and-so was lusting after her babysitter or her tutor, that so-and-so was sleeping with her driver and so on. I was intrigued then, as a twelve-year-old, but after I became older I rubbished most of those stories as fascinated fantasies of pubescent girls. But here was a confession from prim and proper Mrs Krishnamurthy herself. I wasn't consumed by interest, but I would be lying if I said it did not pique me just a little.

I leaned my head toward her with my mouth thrown open.

'I know,' she said, gushing and winking. 'Anyway, I closed the kitchen door. By this time we had already indulged in some touching, mind you. Nothing serious, just brushing of the hands, little squeezes here and there – mostly on my part, which would make him blush and look away.' She cleared her throat. 'So I went to him and asked him if we could play cards. Of course he said yes.'

'Of course he did,' I said.

She laughed. 'He had these strawberry coloured lips, full and shapely. I told him that we will play a game that I knew, and I made up the rules as I went along. I told him that every time I lost, he would have to give me a kiss on the lips.' She looked at me out of the corner of her eye. 'And you could bet that I lost a lot of games that night.'

I took a sip of my wine, and for a moment silence fell. The air was beginning to get chilly. Every time a breeze blew, Mrs Krishnamurthy shivered, and the hair on the back of my neck stood up. I took a larger gulp, almost finishing my glass, to steady my voice. Then I said, 'You were a little slut, weren't you?'

'Totally.'

'So what happened to the servant?'

'Oh, he left us in a few months. I think my parents suspected something. At that age, you think you're being very smart and very careful when all the while your parents are seeing right through you.'

'Never looked him up again?'

'No,' she said, with a hint of longing in her voice. 'Now it all belongs in a different world, almost as if that fifteen-year-old is some previous life version of me.'

'I know,' I said. 'I feel the same about my teenage years.' I thought of the girl who looked upon the balding head of Captain as he went down on one knee and said yes to his proposal of marriage. She was not me, not at all, just a girl who wished to run away and latched on to her first carrier. I wondered if twenty years into the future, I would look back and scoff at the thirty-three-year-old me, too.

'Arun hasn't come yet,' I said, trying to get away from narrating the experience of my own first kiss.

'Yes.' Her tone at once became wooden, matter-of-fact. 'It's too late for you to go home now. You should stay the night here.'

'Oh,' I said. My phone still hadn't rung. It was past nine now, and if Captain had not missed me till now, maybe he was already drunk and had passed out.

The fog had become heavier too. We could no longer see the adjoining building's balcony. 'Only if you have a spare room,' I said, 'and only if Arun wouldn't mind.'

'Oh, come on! This is as much my house as Arun's. Of course he wouldn't mind.' She took my glass, and I followed her into the room. As soon as the door closed behind us, we both sighed in relief at the warmth. I rubbed my hands together, and my eyes fell on yet another picture of the couple. In their pictures there wasn't even a tiny note of discontent that had entered their marriage. Albert was right, perhaps. Photographs always lied.

Descending the steps, Mrs Krishnamurthy cackled loudly. 'How exciting!' she said. 'A sleepover!'

Sleep did not come to me. Mrs Krishnamurthy had set me up in the queen-sized bed in the upstairs bedroom. For almost an hour I lay on my back, listening for a car in the driveway and a knock on the door. Neither happened. I remembered that the car park was already full, and that it was big enough for just one car. I thought of the distant fondness in Mrs Krishnamurthy's voice when she spoke of Arun. I thought of the photographs once again, how young she looked in every one of them. I tried to remember at least one in which she bore a resemblance to how she looked now. There were none.

Outside the window, the fog became denser. In one of Mrs Krishnamurthy's favourite Dean Koontz novels, such a night would not pass without something eerie happening. A lock would turn on its own, a door would sneak open, a ticking pendulum in a clock would abruptly stop, a doll would twist her head around and smile. I had noticed it since I stepped into the house; something about it sowed desolation deep in me. Where it came from, I didn't know. Something was amiss, in Mrs Krishnamurthy's cackling voice, in her childlike eagerness to have me spend the night, in her story about kissing her servant, in her confusion about her rape, in her insistence that her husband was having an affair.

I turned to my side, facing the window. After two minutes, I felt that a white face would appear at the glass any moment, and decided to turn away. If the face did appear, I hoped it would be quiet so that I wouldn't have to look at it. For some reason, the face I pictured resembled Arun, with the clean-shaven scalp and the bushy black moustache and the round spectacles.

The knob of the door to my room turned. I sat up. A torch light flashed at me, and I covered my eyes with my hand. 'Are you still up, Ramya?' said Mrs Krishnamurthy.

'Yes,' I replied, the relief spilling into my voice. 'It's that kind of night.'

'Isn't it?' She closed the door behind her and came to sit on the edge of the bed. 'Can I sleep with you, here? I feel scared and lonely without Arun.'

I tried to look at her expression, but all I saw in the dark was a black oval. Without waiting for my answer, she slid herself into the covers beside me. I moved a little toward my edge of the bed.

'Shall we keep a pillow between us?' she said, and laughed. 'The wine was good, wasn't it?'

'Yes, it's keeping us both awake, I think.'

She shivered and said, 'It's a scary night.'

'And this is a scary house.' I reached out and drew the curtains. Lowering myself onto the pillow, I said, 'Good night.'

'Good night, dear.'

Sometime during the middle of the night, I was awakened by Mrs Krishnamurthy's arm wrapped around me. She hugged me from behind, and slid her legs next to mine so that my feet were on hers. Her breath ran over my neck, then I felt her teeth dig into my skin. Just as I was about to turn around and ask her what she was doing, I felt her body shake against mine, and she began to sob.

For about thirty minutes she cried, and I patted her hand throughout. Then we fell asleep.

I woke up on an empty bed, and when I went down the stairs, Mrs Krishnamurthy was sitting at the dining table, looking into the distance, applying cheese spread to a slice of toast. I pulled out the same chair on which I had sat the night before. The yellow curtains had been drawn, and morning light filled the room.

'When did he die?' I asked her softly.

'Six years now.'

'How?'

'Car accident.' She sniffed. Placing the toast on my plate, she nodded at it. 'He had always been afraid of driving. I used to chide him for his cowardice. I used to say that real men drove bikes and cars.' She picked up a fresh slice in her left hand, looked deeply at it. 'He gave in to my nagging at last and bought a Swift Dzire. I made him take us out on long drives, on highways. "One of these days you will get us killed," he used to say.'

I bit into the bread, licked my lips of cheese, and listened.

'I was by his side when it happened. He tried to dodge an autorickshaw, went off the road and hit a tree. We were only doing thirty or so at the time, but the collision was hard enough to bring the steering compartment crashing into his ribcage. I had little scratches on my forehead, my hands, my arms. When I called out to him, he said, "Hmm." I came out of the car and went over to his side to free him. I could not. Two of the people who had gathered helped me get him out. By the time we laid him on the ground, I realized he wasn't breathing.'

That pinprick-like feeling that I had been aware of since last night – I finally knew what it was. It was the pall of death that had cocooned this house and Mrs Krishnamurthy. Whether she lapsed into denial occasionally and invented stories of her husband, I did not know, but now I understood why she had no qualms about paying for a session in which I did most of the talking. Now I knew why she wanted me to visit her.

Now I saw the meaning behind that girl-like squeak, the sheer grief and relief that lay just a thin layer beneath her sobs of the night before.

After breakfast, I got up to leave. She came to the door. 'You will come again, won't you?' she said.

I said that I would.

SEVEN

When I got home that morning, I saw Ankita sitting on my living room couch with her legs held together with her hands. She got up as I approached the front door and lifted my leg to unclasp my sandal. 'I am sorry, madam,' she said. 'I am so sorry.'

I understood. Though my chest felt as though it was going to open up, I kept my face steady. 'You should have asked me,' I said. I went in. The granite tiles froze my feet. Captain came out of the kitchen with a tray on which two cups sat. When he saw me he broke into a crooked smile, just with the muscles of his face. His eyes looked like those of a mongoose circling a dying snake.

'You have come,' he said, with forced mirth.

'Maybe I should go,' said Ankita, making toward the door.

'Oh, no! Wait, my girl. Wait. Let Ramya also hear what you have to say. After all, it is about her that we have been talking all this while, isn't it?' He waved me to the empty single seater. 'Why don't you sit down, darling?' Not once in our fourteen years of marriage had he called me *darling*. 'You will certainly live to be a hundred.' He held the tray so tight that it rattled. Keeping it on the table, he gestured to Ankita, who shook her head. 'Oh,' he said, tilting her head toward her courteously, 'I insist.' She looked into his eyes for a moment, then decided to take a cup. 'You too,' he said to me. I obeyed.

'We were talking about you and your good friend Sridhar,' said Captain, interlacing his fingers over his belly and leaning back in his chair. 'I have been in touch with Ankita for a few days now, and she has been keeping a watch over you in your clinic, and has been reporting a few things back to me.'

My hands did not tremble. I took a careful sip of my tea. The tiles did not seem all that cold anymore.

'Ankita,' he said, 'why don't you tell me again what madam did with her friend and – what's the word? Research assistant? – at the clinic.'

She had her head bent, and her eyes fastened on the cup in her hand. 'I – I am sorry, madam.'

'Did I ask you to apologize to her?'

'I – I didn't mean to pry, I didn't mean to hear, madam.'

'But you couldn't help it, could you, my dear girl, because madam was so damn loud.' He chuckled.

'Er, yes. I would try and drown the sounds out with my keyboard, but I would know. And Sridhar, too, he would tell me everything you did. Everything.'

That didn't surprise me, though it perhaps ought to have. Only for the shortest flash of an instant I felt a tug, but that was it. I had never hoped to be anything more than a conquest for Sridhar, and for a man like him, conquests came rarely. For some reason, my eyes pinched. I had to shut them and push the tears back. If he had had the nerve to brag about us to Ankita, who worked in the same office, then he would not have left alone the graduate faculty at the university. I wouldn't be surprised to find some rumours leaking among the professors either. There had been previous cases of sexual misconduct, but in each one of them the person in position of power had been male. It worked differently when the coin flipped. Now Sridhar would be an object of envy of all young men on campus, a veritable stud, while I would be looked upon as a poor, sexually frustrated woman who satisfied her needs by preying on young men that worked under her.

Well, perhaps I was all that. Accurate descriptions hurt more than wild ones.

'A few days ago, Mr Tirthankar came to our office and began to talk to me, and when he asked if all was straight between you and Sridhar, and when he offered me some reward for coming clean, I – I decided to tell him everything, madam. I hope you understand. You know how sick my father is, how much money we need for his treatment.'

I nodded and smiled at the tea. I was still thinking of Sridhar, the high-fives he must have received from his buddies at the university cafe. A woman kept her sexual relationships private, but a man thrived on them. Did he go back to school each afternoon after making love to me – after declaring his intentions to care for me – and narrate tall tales of how he fucked that slut in her office?

Captain had not said much for a while now. He shook his legs and tapped his thumbs together. He narrowed his eyes at me, as if he wished to bore into my mind with them and find out what I was thinking. If I could find my voice, I would tell him I wasn't thinking anything, that my mind was at that moment a shapeless screen of grey fog. I knew what he was thinking, though. Captain came from a world where punishment followed crime with swiftness and certainty. He was devising the various ways in which he would punish me, and when it came to such things, he could get quite creative.

From the corner of my vision, by the kitchen door, a blue spot moved. I dared not look up and meet Nari's searching gaze now, for if I did, I was certain that Captain would know about us in an instant. Now Nari had lost his bargaining chip with me, so I could tell Captain all that Nari had done to me in the last few months, but I chose to be quiet. When a volcano erupts in front of you, you don't stand and argue. If you can, you run for your life. If you cannot, you burn.

Ankita chose to run. 'I think I will leave,' she said, and got up.

'Yes,' said Captain, 'I think you should. Tell all your patients that madam will not come to the office today.'

As soon as Ankita left, Captain closed the door and yanked me by the arm up the stairs. I did not resist or cry out. If you have been abused for years, you grow a little shell inside you into which you can creep and disappear whenever you wish. Outrage, surprise, a sense of justice, humanity – all of these dissolve into nothing when there is a man twice your size throwing you into a room against the wall and raining blows on your back. I crawled on all fours to the corner and sat covering my head, counting the lashes, praying that each one would be the last.

Eventually, he stopped and sat on the edge of the bed to catch his breath. His left foot stood up on tiptoe, and his thigh shook furiously. He tapped the cane on the polished floor. My spine burned throughout its length, and when I gingerly touched myself in my sides, a searing bolt of pain and heat made me mewl.

'Yeah,' he said. 'You deserve all that pain, bitch! Look how much of it you've caused me.'

I raised my head just enough to eye his smooth skin, without a visible scar. I lowered it back again. When I leaned against the corner, my upper arm rubbed against it at the same spot he had held me. I pulled up my sleeve. A blue blotch throbbed just above my elbow, threatening to spread all the way up to my shoulder.

'I paid for your university. I paid for your PhD. Do you know how many people's cocks I had to suck to get you your title? I set up the clinic for you, I paid for it all. And in return you give me this? After all these years, you give me this to remember you by.' He sprang to his feet and came closer to me. I hid my face and bent so that my back faced him. 'Say something, you slut!' he said, and hit me across my left side. I groaned and turned over on my back, looking up at him. 'Say something. Is this how you repay all these years of my love towards you?'

I joined my hands, retching at the pain. 'I am sorry, Captain.'

'Sorry!' He inhaled throatily and spat on my face. 'Do you think your fucking apology will make it all right? Have you forgotten the vows you took when you married me? Look at me.' He dropped his cane and fell on his knees. He picked me up by the arms and lifted me up so that our noses touched. 'Look at me. I can have any woman I want – any woman! – but I have chosen to be faithful to you. But you, you wanton harlot!' This time he spat right between my nose and mouth.

I licked it away. 'I will do whatever you want. Punish me however you want.'

'Yeah, damn straight you will do whatever I want. You have lost all credibility now, all your claims to independence, all your high-flying psychoanalysis of everything that comes your way, all your *self righteousness*!' He pushed me against the wall so that my head crashed against it and left me stunned for a moment. 'Yes, I will strip you of all that because you deserve none of it. Oh, lord, if only I had the sense to marry your sister instead.'

The words floated to me and hung in the air, prodding me one by one. Did he say he should have married Vimla instead?

But Vimla had been with Albert when I had met Captain. Then into my semi-conscious head images began to flow, of Vimla and Captain trading glances and smiling, speaking in hushed tones about this or that in the old house in Goa.

Good old Vimla. Dad, then Albert, now Captain. She had exercised her elder sister rights over me by staking a claim to all the men in my life. Perhaps she would be glad to hear of Sridhar too, and of Nari.

'You will go nowhere from now,' said Captain. 'You will stay in this room for as long as I order you to. All your food will be brought in here. All your clothes will be provided to you. If you so much as put a foot outside this room, I swear to you, Ramya, that I will skin you alive.' A faint smile covered his lips. 'Don't worry, I have the equipment.'

I was too tired, too overcome by pain, to respond. I may have given him a half-nod.

'Nari will look after you,' he said, getting up to his feet and folding the sleeves of his shirt back to cover his wrists. Picking up the cane, he caressed its length with a tender forefinger and thumb. 'If you try to do anything silly, of course,' he said, 'like trying to escape or alert the neighbours, I will kill you.'

He wasn't joking. Captain did not joke. 'I just need some first aid,' I said.

'You will be fine. Most of your injuries are superficial. None of them will leave a scar.'

'They burn.'

'They will for a day or two.' He looked away from the cane at me, and I thought I saw the look in his eyes change. I thought I saw the man who hugged me on the day I told him I had a headache. 'But soon they will go away. If you don't think of them, they won't bother you.'

'Okay.'

He turned to leave. He stopped at the door. I slunk back deeper into the corner, and rolled over to my side. In a second or two, I heard the lock click.

People have asked me why I did not tell Captain then about Nari's abuse of me. Some have suggested that this indeed is the big flaw in my story, that if I really hated Nari as much as I said I did, I should have told Captain all about him the moment he got to know about me and Sridhar. The fact that I didn't meant, perhaps, that I was not being completely honest in telling my tale, they said. Perhaps I was picking what to reveal and what to keep hidden. I am well aware that Nari has his own story to tell those who are willing to listen, and I do not wish to rob him of his right to speak. I am certain that after people have heard from both of us, the truth will emerge.

I did not tell Captain about Nari when he confronted me about Sridhar because he was already quite worked up, and adding any fuel to the fire was unnecessary, I thought, especially because I was in the direct line. But after he had locked me up in the bedroom and I had a few moments to think to myself, it occurred to me that Nari might just be the one way through which I can escape this prison. Telling Captain about him would achieve little, apart from a few bruises and cuts on Nari's body. But if I could convince Nari to help me run away, I could lure him with promises of keeping our secret forever from Captain.

Nari would be afraid now, I knew. He would know that his cards had fallen to the table, face open, and that if I chose to play mine, all his hopes of a life in the city would evaporate. But he would also know that my freedom was in his hands – he is not as stupid as his looks and words make him seem – so maybe he would come to my room ready with a fresh trade. I did not know if he or I would make the first move, but whoever did, it was best on my part to keep my secret so that I could barter it for something else.

Whether or not I hate Nari is not the question, though if I must take a stand on the matter, I will say that I do. Though the amount of hatred I feel for him is quite small compared to what I once felt for Captain, it is there, and it will be there, I think, till I die. You just cannot forgive a man who squeezes your juice out of you against your will. Mrs Krishnamurthy was right; a part of them always stays with you, laughing in your face, spitting into your eyes, telling you that you were just too dumb to know that you enjoyed it.

He came in with strawberry jam on toast and a bottle of water on a tray. He sat cross-legged and watched me eat. The pain of Captain's lashes had lessened, somewhat. I had examined myself in the mirror and seen grey lines strewn all over my waist. The spot on the arm appeared to have grown larger too. But Captain knew a lot about hitting people in ways which left no marks. I munched slowly on the toast, now and then meeting Nari's gaze and holding, just to see who would look away first. It was always him.

Just as I was about to finish my food, he said, 'I thought you would tell him about us.'

'I didn't, but you know what will happen if I do, right?'

He nodded sullenly, rubbing his arms with his hands.

'And now that he knows about Sridhar and me, what are you going to blackmail me with?'

'Nothing.'

I took a large gulp of water from the bottle, and sighed when it slid down my throat. 'So shall I tell Captain about what you did to me all winter?' Another shake of the head. He kept his eyes firmly on the ground. 'Maybe I should. What do you think he will do to you? Break your legs? Or maybe he will break something else.'

Nari squirmed. 'He wouldn't do that.'

'Wouldn't he? Maybe we should tell him and find out. If I were you, I would run away right now.'

He looked up, and I saw defiance build in his eyes. 'If you were going to tell him, you would have by now. You need something from me, don't you?'

'What will I need from a piece of shit like you?'

'Maybe a good fuck?'

I couldn't help chuckling in disbelief. The boy still thought, of course, that I enjoyed all his advances. Maybe he thought I was just playing hard to get. In his vocabulary, no meant a shy yes in disguise. A yes, of course, meant that the woman saying it was a slut.

'No,' I said. 'No. I do not want a fuck from you. I swear to you that if you so much as touch me again – do you hear me? – I will tell Captain everything, and he will come after you.'

A frown came over his eyebrows, and he appeared confused. 'What do you want from me then?'

'Nothing.'

He grinned at me, scratched his head. 'You're lying. You're just a lying whore.'

The first sentence was true. I did not quite take to the tone in which he spoke the second. For a moment I wondered if I should do business with this boy, but then what other choice did I have? I could try and reach Sridhar or Mrs Krishnamurthy or even Ankita if I could get to a phone, but Captain would have given Nari strict instructions. I looked to my sides if I could find something heavy to swing at his head, but that kind of thing hardly worked outside movies and novels. Even if I did get hold of something, and even if I did find myself in a situation where he offered his head to me, I would have no idea how hard to hit him. I would end up either just tickling him or smashing his head in and killing him.

Neither of those would do. So I gritted my teeth and resolved to meet him, yet again, as an equal.

'I want you to help me escape from here,' I said.

'What if I don't?'

'You know the answer to that already, don't you?'

'I will do it if you let me fuck you.'

'No.'

He stood up and came closer to me. He placed his hand over my knee. I jerked it back. 'I think your need is bigger than mine.'

'No.'

He sat on the bed, fingered the blue patch of skin on my arm, and grimaced. 'That must hurt.'

'No.'

He nodded. 'I think it does, yes. And the longer you stay here, the more he will torture you, madam. Every night he will have his vodka and he will hit you so that all the marks will disappear by the next morning.'

'He will do the same to you.'

'If he gets hold of me,' said Nari, lightly. 'Also, you know how it is. You are the woman who has seduced her student. If you tell Captain that I raped you, he will say that you brought it on, that you seduced me.' The first fingers of dread gripped around my heart. My breath quickened. He continued in the same smooth voice. 'And I will tell him that too, of course. Whom will he believe? The wife who has just cheated on him or the innocent boy whose father saved his life?'

I wanted to say Captain would believe me, and I wanted to believe that was what would happen. But would he? We live at a time when women are held at least partially responsible for sexual crimes in which they become victims. Here, if it were my word against Nari's, whom would Captain believe?

I have played that question in my mind so many times over the last few months. I have asked myself if things would have happened differently had I chosen otherwise. But even today, if you asked me for my honest answer, I would have said that Captain would have believed Nari. He would not have allowed him to go scot-free, of course, but he would have pushed at least half the blame onto me. And that would have made my plight worse.

So I stopped straining against Nari's touch. His grin broadened. He hiked up my skirt and felt my thighs. 'You will help me escape, then?' I said. He pushed me onto the bed, unbuttoned his shirt and licked his lips. 'Yes,' he said hungrily. 'Oh, yes.'

I closed my eyes, and tried to lose myself in the pain of my wounds.

Captain dropped the ash of his pipe on the floor. 'Your boyfriend called today,' he said.

I was sitting on the corner of the bed farthest from him, my thighs wrapped in my arms, my knees supporting my chin. I closed my eyes for a moment. Ever since he had locked me up, the house seemed to have withdrawn further into darkness than before. He didn't seem to mind the gloomy shapes, or the silvery beam of moonlight that pierced the glass window on its way in. He held his right leg crossed over his thigh, and held the pipe by the head, gingerly, with the very tips of his thumb and forefinger.

'I told him that you have left town,' he said, running a dry tongue over his lips. 'He asked me when you will come back and I said that you wouldn't for a month at least. Do you agree with that?'

'If that's what you want.'

'Yes,' he said. 'That's what I want. Then he said something strange. He seemed to give me some sort of a warning.' He lifted the corner of his mouth. 'He said that if something were to happen to you, he would see to it that I get my just desserts.'

Good old Sridhar, I thought, forever the knight without armour or sword. 'He doesn't know what he is talking about. You should just let him be.'

'Oh, I wanted to,' said Captain. 'But he said so many more things. He said that he cared for you, and that he loved you –'

'He's just a kid.'

'Ah, just a kid, yes, like you were when I married you, eh?' He held the pipe up against the moonlight, then tapped it on the side with a finger. 'When you're young you feel that life is so easy, don't you? You think you will grow up, fall in love with one person, get married to them, have children, and live happily ever after. But something always goes wrong, doesn't it?'

He seemed to speak to his pipe as he said these words, looking at it with deep, soulful eyes, as though it could nod and agree with him. 'And you're always so sure when you fall in love. Now if I were to go and meet Sridhar tomorrow –'

'No.'

'No? Do you think I shouldn't? Then maybe I should.' His scalp glowed white, and when he ran his palm over it, he seemed to spread the diamond dust all over his hair, so that the tips of the strands became little pinpricks of light. 'He wanted to meet me. He said he wants to talk to me about you.'

'No.'

'No? I think the conversation could be rather charming. I will of course make sure that he doesn't have any sort of career at the university.' He put the pipe back in his mouth, and a line of smoke wriggled upward and hit the ceiling. 'They don't look too kindly upon young men who seduce their innocent bosses and influence them for grades,' he said, and showed his teeth.

'You don't need to do that to him.'

'Oh, I don't *need* to,' he said. 'But I think I will anyway.'

'It was not his fault. It was mine. You can do whatever you want to me.'

'Oh, but darling,' he said, and leaned forward in his chair. I shrank back. 'I love you. I am angry with you, of course, but I cannot bring myself to do much to you. Your lover – well, I don't love him. I don't hate him – hate is such an extreme word – but I do dislike him, and he seems eager to bring it upon himself.'

'He doesn't know what is going to happen to him.'

'Well, of course he doesn't. Why else will he wish to meet me and "talk things over"? How old is this young man?'

'Twenty-four, I think, or maybe twenty-five.'

'Yes,' he said, and took a long puff. Over the next few seconds, streams of smoke left his nostrils and dissolved into the air. 'Twenty-four is a good age to learn a few important life lessons, don't you think? Like whom not to piss off, whose wife not to sleep with, what to say, what not to say.'

'Captain,' I said, pleading. 'Let the boy go.'

'Oh, I would have, darling. I would have if he had not called on your phone today and said all that rubbish to me.'

I let out a breath and kept quiet. The more I pleaded, the more I drove him to do it. If I could not make things better for Sridhar, the least I could do was not make them worse. And perhaps for all of Captain's clout and cunning, Sridhar might yet wriggle free of his grasp. Maybe they would give him a temporary suspension; nothing more. Aside from our relationship, his research work had always been top notch. The university would know that.

'Another person called,' said Captain, and immediately I thought of Mrs Krishnamurthy. 'Is that the friend you spent the night with?'

'I spent the night at her place, yes.'

'But not with her, you say?' He turned over the pipe, leaning over to look into it better in the dim light. 'But she seemed concerned when I told her that you left town.'

'Yes, I told her I would be at the clinic this morning.'

'And yet, plans change, don't they? Why should she be so worried for you if you decide to go away unannounced? It's almost as if you had told her that I was this controlling, obsessive man who never let you do anything on your own.' He looked up.

'I did not tell her,' I said.

'Now why would you go around telling people such terrible lies, Ramya?' He tapped the pipe against the armrest of the chair, and extracted some tobacco that had stuck to the bottom. 'Crap.' He turned it upside down and hit it against the floor now, but nothing came out. 'Fuck!' After two more taps he hurled it against the wall with an angry grunt, breaking it in two. 'Stupid pipes,' he said, as his hands shivered. I shrank back, and wished I could close my eyes and go to sleep.

'And who is this woman? Is she your lover too? Huh? Did you sleep with her too?'

'No,' I said, though it was technically a lie. I did sleep with her, in the literal sense of the phrase. 'She's just a friend.'

'So now you're a lesbian as well? How did you miss telling me that?'

'I am not a lesbian, Captain.'

He got off the chair, walked to the door and swung it shut. 'This lady, this Mrs Krishnamurthy, how did you meet her?'

'She's my client.'

'A client who has become a friend,' he said, grinning. 'You

seem to make a habit of inappropriate relationships, darling. First you sleep with a college student, then you "make friends" with your client. What will your Association say if they learned of it, I wonder.'

'I had no sexual relationship with this woman.'

He placed his hand on his chest and sighed dramatically. 'Oh, you didn't have sex with her. Such a big relief! Then what were you doing, may I ask, when you slept over at her house?'

'I meant to return,' I said. 'But we were talking and it was late. She was telling me about her husband.'

'And you were telling her about yours, I am sure.'

'I did when she asked, but she didn't let me speak much. Captain, you must believe me, I said nothing bad about you.'

'If it was late,' he said menacingly, 'you should have called me. I would have sent the car. You could have booked a cab. But you chose to stay back.'

'I – yes, she was feeling lonely, and she requested me to stay the night. I did.'

'Bitch,' he said, and I couldn't tell if he meant me or Mrs Krishnamurthy. He began to pace the room. His bathroom slippers squeaked as he walked up to the window, paused to look out into the night, turned and went back to the door. I placed my forehead on my arms. I tried closing my eyes, but every time my mind would wander I would shake myself awake, wary that he could come over to me any time with his leather belt in hand.

As it happened, he did something quite different. He pulled the chair over to the side of the bed where I sat, and leaned forward in it so that I could smell the tobacco on his pyjamas. I lifted my head and looked at him wearily. He smiled at me. I smiled back at him, though fear pricked the back of my neck.

'I will tell you a story now,' he said, 'a nice little story of how I fucked your sister.'

EIGHT

I don't know how much of what he told me was true. Captain was in a foul mood that night, and he was eager to reveal the tryst between him and Vimla to me as payment for all the hurt I had heaped upon him by sleeping with various people. So it is, perhaps, okay to presume that he made up certain details. For instance, he may not have had sex with her the night before he proposed to me. He may not have eaten her out in the kitchen while the rest of the family sat down to dinner in the adjoining room the evening after our engagement.

Maybe the story was embellished by his mad urge to rouse jealousy in me, but the only detail that mattered to me was that Captain and Vimla slept together. I would know every nook and cranny if only I asked Vimla about it, but even that night, as Captain told me in excruciating detail how she had seduced him from right under my nose, I knew that I would never bring it up with her. And I never have. For one, I was reasonably certain that Vimla would have forgotten about it all. For another, she would just have been matter-of-fact about it and said, 'Yes, we did it a few times long ago. But it's all in the past, Ramya.'

Vimla lived her present too as though it were in her past, as though she could do nothing to change it, as though the mere idea of choice was utterly silly. Maybe it was the only way she could forgive Dad. After his death, Vimla would only speak of Dad's great qualities. She would tell aunts and cousins great stories of Dad's chivalry when he was courting Mummy, of his stoicism, of his refusal to touch alcohol throughout his life – even though Mummy fancied a peg of vodka with lemon every now and then, of his canniness with money and investments, of his charity work with blind children and single working mothers, of the quiet dignity with which he fought against the cancer that eventually claimed him.

She never alluded to the nights on which he visited us. When we were alone, I would find a way to steer our conversations to it, but when we arrived there she would just sigh and smile at me. It was all in the past, she would say, and there was no good in raking it all up. Of all the secret affairs she had with her students and colleagues she would say the same thing, that it was all in the past, that one should never sit in judgement of the past and wonder if it had been right or wrong, or how things would have turned out if this or that thing in the past had been otherwise. The only thing that mattered, she said, was the way things were *now*. Everything else was just commentary.

So getting confirmation from Captain's lips of his dalliance with Vimla did not make me angry. Vimla did not do it to hurt me. She never did things to hurt or please people. If she saw something that she thought she ought to try her hand at, she did. I am sure that when she saw Captain pursuing me, a part of her perhaps felt jealous, wanted all of it for herself, and wondered whether she could have him. After having him, of course, like with everything else she would have gotten bored of him and carried on her merry way. How her actions would make someone else feel never figured in Vimla's radar. In fact, that her actions have consequences is something Vimla has always been blissfully unaware of.

Whether or not she is your sister, you cannot feel anger toward such a person. You cannot feel sorry for them either, because they go through life with such utter abandon, like an invisible fairy let loose in a garden. Whenever I think of Vimla I think of her like that – with wings, light as the summer breeze, blowing kisses to all around her, touching this flower, tasting the honey from that hive, laughing with the birds, smiling at the sun, playing with the curls in her hair.

Captain became furious when he saw me react to his story with a grin and a shake of the head. He said I had lost all touch with my morals, that my father had reared me to become a slut that would sleep with anyone – male or female. He said that Vimla had been so much better than me in bed that he thought of her while doing me. That made me smile even more, because he did not know that I would give all my life twice over if only we could all go back and arrange for Captain to wed Vimla.

'You're smiling?' he said. 'How can you smile after knowing that I was cheating on you with your sister?' He got up, and made to loosen his belt. He was angry, I saw, and the only way he could let it all out was to land a few blows on me. I rolled over, pulled up my shirt, and waited. 'You slut,' he said. His voice thickened and slurred a little. The first abuses always stumbled. As he fell into the groove and got into the rhythm of it, they flowed off his tongue. I closed my eyes and thought of Vimla in the garden. I was at my usual place, behind the grilled gate, holding it tight with my hands and shaking it so that she would hear, look at me, and beckon me over. But she never did.

A knock appeared on the door. Captain stopped mid-speech and said, 'Who is it?'

Nari's voice said from the other side, 'There is a call for you, sir. Somebody from the NGO called. They said it's urgent.'

Breathing heavily and hoarsely, Captain lowered the belt and went to the door to open it.

Later that night, the knob of my bedroom door turned, and Nari came in. I had been expecting him. I got to my feet in the dark, threw the black sports bag over my shoulders, and took the bag of jewels in my hand. I was to hand it to him after he had gotten me out. I still had no idea where I was going to go or what I was going to do, but I had my diamond necklace, my engagement ring, a few thousands in my purse, and a platinum bracelet around my wrist. I was confident I could figure something out.

When he saw me in the dark, he came closer and made to kiss me. I pushed him away with both hands. 'Not now,' I said. 'Not anymore.' He pleaded with me to let him kiss me one last time. I did not say no because if you did not respond to Nari's pleas, he immediately descended to threats. He kicked the door close, and what began as a kiss became a lot more. I shut my eyes, bit my lower lip and tolerated it.

After he finished, he rolled off me, dressed and gruffly said, 'Come.'

We got down the stairs on tiptoe. From the downstairs bedroom, we heard Captain's steady snore. When we passed his room, Nari pointed to the drawer. I stole in, keeping my back to the wall and my eyes on Captain at all times, and found the keys to the cupboard. In three large steps I was on the other side of the bed. I slid the key into the hole and twisted it. I turned the handle, and when it made a clanging sound, I thought I heard Captain's breath falter. I waited. From the passage, Nari gestured to me. Captain turned away from me, onto his side. I rummaged in the inner door and found the cloth bag containing my passport, my bank pass book and my phone.

I did not bother to close the door of the cupboard on the way out. A light breeze blew in through the open window and made the door swing and creak. Nari frowned, and I went back to shut the door. Captain did not stir, but his snoring had stopped. When he did not snore, it meant that he was hovering just beneath the layer of semi-consciousness. Even the smallest sounds sometimes awoke him. I hoped that whatever Nari had given him was strong.

I came out of the room, but all this while I had not seen that the cloth bag I held in my hand was not tied at its mouth. As I lowered my shoulder bag and bent to open its zip, the cloth bag tilted a little, and out rolled a small silver turmeric container that I had brought with me from Goa. It dropped to the granite floor in a straight line and clattered when it hit.

Nari scrambled after it, muttering swear word after swear word as it eluded each of his frantic grabs. I just stood there and watched, looking at the main door and wondering if I could not just make a dash for it. I had taken a faltering step in that direction when I saw Captain's shadow fill the door frame.

I screamed, and Nari backed up against the staircase. The container came to a stop after rattling against the floor for what seemed like forever. All three of us stood watching it, as if we wanted it to stop its noise before we could begin ours. I walked backward until I hit the edge of the reading chair and plopped into it. Captain stood with his arms folded across his chest, and though in the dark I couldn't quite see his eyes, I knew that they were blood red and cold. After the vessel had quietened, he said in a flat voice, 'Where do you think you're going, Ramya?'

I shrugged. 'I was going to run away.' There was no point in lying after being caught red-handed. That would only anger him further.

'And where were you going to run away to?'

'I don't know,' I said. 'I was going to figure out once I got out of the house.'

Captain turned to look at Nari, then back at me. 'Did Nari see you and wake me up? Nari?'

'Sir, yes, sir,' said Nari, scuttling to his feet.

I laughed. 'Yeah, right. He was helping me run away, Captain. He is the man you want, not me.'

'Nari? I don't believe it.'

'You better believe it.' Sometimes, when you know that all is lost, you want to go down fighting, you want to take everyone down with you. People say that you need to lose fear to be able to speak bravely, but sometimes fear makes your lips move like nothing else. 'How else did I get out of the room upstairs? How else did I get the key to the cupboard which you wear around your pyjamas?'

Captain checked his pyjamas. I jingled the bunch in my hand. He looked up, wide-eyed. 'Yep,' I said, nodding. 'You get it, don't you?'

Nari began to tremble, and his teeth chattered. Captain switched on the light. I saw a trail of wet spots on Nari's blue shorts. It was when things like this happened that I forced myself to recall that he was but a boy. Captain was a scary man, though, even to grown, hardened men. 'Why?' he was saying, already moving toward Nari. 'Why did you do this?'

'Madam – madam –'

'Madam did *nothing*!' I said, jumping to my feet. Queerly, it seemed now as though it was Captain and me against Nari, and I felt secure. Nari had already exhausted his options by then, and he was no more than a blubbering ass. I thought it was perhaps the best time to stoke Captain's anger further by telling him. So I cleared my throat over the sound of Captain's weighty intakes of breath. He stopped.

'Captain,' I told him, 'Nari has been sexually abusing me for two months now.'

Nari whimpered, and his knees began to knock against one another, threatening to topple him over. He held onto the railing of the staircase and kept shaking his head, his lips moving in prayer, his eyes shut tight, tears streaming down them. I timed my revelation perfectly, I thought, for it had the desired effect on him.

But with regards to Captain I did not anticipate what happened next. He stopped moving toward Nari and changed course to approach me. 'He has been raping you?' he said. 'In my own home? And you did not tell me all this time?'

'He blackmailed me, Captain,' I said, moving back one step with each step he advanced. 'He said that if I told you, he would reveal my affair with Sridhar.'

'He – he's just a boy.'

'But he raped me, Captain. He raped your wife in your own home. He ate your food, took shelter in your house and he had sex with your wife. Are you going to stand for that? Can you not even protect your own wife from predators like him, Captain?'

'Hmm,' said Captain, his teeth emerging from between pursed lips. 'Hmm.' He waved on his feet and raised his arms like a big gorilla. He turned around to where Nari was standing, and began to close in on him. Nari stood his ground for the first two seconds, rubbing his hands, bending his knees and watching Captain. 'Get him, Captain,' I said. 'Make him regret every time he laid his hands on me!'

'Hmm,' said Captain from the bottom of his throat, his fists opening and closing, his each lumbering step closing the distance between him and his prey. It felt like watching the alpha male and the youngest member of a monkey group going head to head for mating rights. After a jump to the left and a leap to the right, Nari got onto the stairs and ran up, his bare feet pattering against the marble.

I took the brass flower vase from the dining table, threw out the wilting chrysanthemums from it and followed Captain up the stairs. When we got to the lounge and looked around, we saw the main bedroom door shut and heard the knob click as it locked. Captain wrenched out the Nepali spear that stood taped against the back wall with a single hand, as if he were picking a broom from the corner. Then he turned and tapped the door with the blunt tip. 'Nari!' he said. 'Come out and I will not do anything to you.'

I did not know how anyone with even the smallest brain in the world could believe Captain when he sounded like a mammoth whose tusks had been severed, but his voice sounded perfectly quiet and cultured. If there was one thing you could rely on with Captain, it was to keep cool in times of stress. 'Come out and we will all sit together and talk,' he said.

Nari did not reply, but a series of firm thuds came from the other side of the door. 'He is jamming the door with the chair,' I said, and Captain charged at it and pounded at the knob with the edge of his spear. It did not give. He took a few steps back and ran into it with his shoulder. It whined but did not budge. From inside the scrambling became more hurried, more frenetic. Captain knelt by the door and looked through the keyhole. 'Can't see a damn thing.' He slapped his hand against the flat surface. 'Nari,' he said, 'Nari, Nari, come out and we will just have a chat, all three of us. Just come out, okay?'

He then looked at me and saw the vase in my hands. He beckoned to me, snatched it off my hands and thumped it once with his hands. After having convinced himself of its strength, he let the spear drop to the side and held the vase in front of his chest. Then he rushed into the door. This time it creaked, and made a low cracking sound in protest. With a grunt of excitement, Captain slammed the vase once again into the door. On the third try, the door fell open and he waded in.

From the side, I saw Nari's arm rise up and fall. When he made contact with Captain's skull, it sounded like a school bell. Captain yelled. Nari raised his arm and brought it down again, quietly. Again a bell-like peal, and another cry of anguish. I stood at the door's opening, peering into the darkness, afraid to take a further step. Out here, the orange light of the street lamp at least made things faintly visible. Inside the room, but for the moonbeam through the glass window, it was black.

Captain's heavy frame hit the ground, and almost by instinct, I picked up the spear that he had left behind and took cover behind the door. 'Madam,' said Nari, 'I think Captain needs to be taken to the hospital.'

'You have killed him already,' I said, though I did not know if he was bluffing or was telling the truth. 'And now you will kill me.'

'I will not kill you, madam,' he said. 'I love you.'

I did not reply. I just stood there, with my spear raised, the point ready to thrust out when he passed through. For as long as it took for him to come out, I would stand there, I thought; even if I had to wait till the sun comes up. 'I am dropping my stick, madam,' he said then, 'and I am coming out.'

'All right,' I said. 'I am dropping my spear too.' I tapped the tip against the floor a couple of times to make it sound as though I had dropped it. When he appeared, I drove it right through his shoulder and arm. Then I stepped into the room, brought out the flower vase, hit Nari on the head with it, drawing a little blood and knocking him out.

I went into the bedroom and turned on the light. Only when I saw the blood on the floor did the smell really hit my nose and travel up to the spot between my eyes. I knelt by Captain and checked his breath. There was none. I held his wrist and tried to find a pulse. Then I placed my hands on his chest, my lips on his, and blew and pressed as correctly as I could remember from high school first aid drills. When he didn't wake up, I located the phone in his pocket and called the police station.

I sat on the edge of the bed at such an angle that I could keep an eye on both of them. I held in my hand the stick that Nari had used to kill Captain, half-expecting that he would get up before the police could arrive, that he would charge at me with the spear and I would have to defend myself with this lump of wood. I wondered if I should go over to him and give him another knock on the head, a harder one this time, so that he would be out cold good and proper. But I did not want to accidentally kill him.

So I waited. I do not remember very well what went through my mind in those forty-five minutes. It is not every day that a woman finds herself locked inside a house with a dead body and an unconscious man. I think I spent the time recalling all the old songs that my father used to listen to: KL Saigal, Hemant Kumar, Kishore Kumar, Shamshad Begum and so on. I fancy that I may have even hummed a few tunes, to forget the pounding in my head. Once or twice I thought I saw Nari stir, and truth be told, I *wished* for him to stir, because if he were to die, I would be left with two dead bodies to account for, and I knew quite well what the on-duty police officer would then think.

Nari did not move, though. As it turned out, the blow I landed on his head had been just the right kind to render him unconscious for a good seven hours, so I needn't have worried. By the time I'd exhausted the songs I knew from the forties and was half-way through the fifties, I heard the police siren, and I practically flew down the stairs to open the door for them.

People have asked me if I miss Captain. The only correct answer I can give to that is that I miss parts of him. I miss parts of Nari, too, as I miss Sridhar and Albert and Vimla and Dad and Mummy. Once a person becomes an intimate part of your life, I don't think it is possible to ever let them go. They leave a part of themselves with you for safekeeping, I think, even those you think you hate – or *especially* the ones you hate. Vimla may flit about and say that 'it was all in the past, dear', but the people and things of your past make your present, and no matter how hard you try and shrug them off, I don't think you truly succeed.

Vimla did not come to Captain's funeral. She sent a card with one hasty line scribbled upon it that she was devastated to hear the news. Another card came from Captain's sister in the United States, with a handwritten note assuring me that his soul would rest in peace, and that all financial matters would be explained by their lawyer in due course of time.

A group of kids came from the NGO and sang 'We Shall Overcome' and 'Vande Maataram'. The local Citizen Club's president attended with a group of uniformed elderly gentlemen, and they gave Captain a guard of honour. Mrs Krishnamurthy and Sridhar stood to the side, hands clasped in front of them, heads bowed. I did not tell either of them what Captain had meant to do to them. It would serve no purpose.

That evening, as I paid off the last of the managers at the funeral home, somebody from the Pension Office called me.

The man's voice was squeaky thin and glassy. 'If you come to our office with your documents, madam,' he said, 'your husband's pension will be transferred to your name.'

Similar calls came over the next few days from the people at life insurance (who wanted me to buy a policy for myself), the bank and the stockbrokers. I re-opened my clinic after all affairs had been laid to rest, and Mrs Krishnamurthy was my first patient once again. Sridhar offered to assist me as before, and he also suggested we should move in together, but I declined both offers. I told him we should not be in touch anymore, and though I saw sadness in his eyes, he would get over it. The truth was that our relationship had never been an equal one. If I ever felt affectionate toward him, it was the affection of a schoolteacher, perhaps, for her dumbest student.

Then Mrs Krishnamurthy asked me over for dinner again, and I went carrying with me a saucer-sized plum cake, which we ate sitting on the swing on her balcony, sipping on red wine. This time the night was clear, and for the longest time we chatted – about our first kisses, our worst crushes, the ways in which we thought as teens we would lose our virginity, the wonder and ugliness of love, the need and value of friends.

I slept over at her place too, that night.

TESTIMONY II

ONE

The following is a translation into English of Narayana's statement in Telugu given to his lawyer, Mr Anant Murthy, who compiled the material over six weekly interviews with the accused, each lasting about an hour. For the benefit of those who wish to confirm the veracity of the views put forth in this statement, attached are the original audio tapes in Telugu, in the voice of the accused.

The firm of Chettinad, Roy and Kumar, with whom Mr Anant Murthy is employed at the time of this writing, does not endorse or condemn anything said in this statement. As a prestigious law firm which the country has come to respect, we believe in producing evidence from a neutral standpoint and allowing our robust judicial process to take its course.

The first time I saw Ramya madam, I was reminded of my mother. The way her cheeks rose when she smiled. The way her eyes twinkled. The curve of her mouth. The dimple on her chin. She has a habit of swabbing her forehead with the back of her hand when she speaks. My mother used to do that too, even when there was no sweat on her brow, even though her hair was all tied up neatly in a bun.

When Captain sir came to Singavaram and my father asked him to take me with him, he looked at me and said, 'Will you work for me, big boy?' I only nodded and mumbled something about school, but father was quick to silence me with an abuse. 'Work with Captain sir at whatever he gives you. Don't worry about school, living with him will be all the school you need.'

On the bus ride from Singavaram to Hyderabad, Captain sir told me that his wife would look after me well. 'I will not say that you should forget your parents, Nari,' he said, 'but Ramya and I will try our best to be your parents from now on.' I had in my bag three pairs of blue shirts and shorts. My father's wife got them stitched so that I could wear them to school in Singavaram. All my other clothes were torn, so she said that I should wear these until Diwali, when Raghuramayya the landlord, would give father a sweet packet, a hundred-rupee note, a sari for her, a skirt for Raji and a shirt piece for me.

It was morning when I reached Captain sir's house in Hyderabad, but it was raining, and all the curtains in the house had been drawn shut. The lights were off. I waited outside the front door after Captain sir went in. The colony was not that much bigger than our neighbourhood in the village. The only difference here was that no one seemed to have muddy toes from having worked in a field. They wore suits and shirts and pants instead of dhotis and white shirts with Reynolds pens tucked into their pockets. At the front door of the house next door, an elderly woman came to pick up the newspaper. As she straightened up, she trained her eyes on me and sniffed disapprovingly.

A cat walked along the compound wall and sat between the both of us, rubbing its front paw to its forehead and then licking it. It had a little golden bell around its neck that tinkled every time it moved. Unlike the stark thin, starving cats of Singavaram, it looked at peace with its bulging stomach, and I recalled Raghuramayya's words that people in Hyderabad were overfed.

I turned away when I heard anklets on the staircase. A light scent of fresh jasmines entered the air and stood for a second in front of my eyes, but then a breeze blew in and it was gone. Ramya madam stood before me with her hands on her hips, examining me as though I were a goat in a market.

'Can he do the dishes?' she asked.

'Yes, of course he can,' said Captain sir, inserting his thumbs into the rings of his breeches. 'He can clean the house, cook for us, make tea.' He looked at me. 'Can't you, Nari?'

I nodded. 'Yes, madam, I will do anything you want.'

Madam did not look convinced. Her eyes travelled slowly down to my feet and back up to my face again. 'He looks quite young.'

'Old enough to do our housework,' said Captain.

Her nails were long, oval and curved. They were not painted. She held a book in her left hand, her middle finger wedged in between the pages. Her long fingers wrapped around the spine as though clawing at it, wishing to rip it to shreds. She eyed my black asbestos case, the white steel lock hanging by its bolt, and shrugged. 'I suppose there is no harm,' she said. 'But let's make sure this one doesn't grow horns and start wagging its tail.'

She turned and went up the stairs. I lugged my case into the living room, after having first left my slippers out on the doorstep. I was not too concerned with how she spoke with me – my mother used to do that too, to me and to my father, before she would seat us down and feed us. Women like to do that, I think, because they like to show that they have authority over the men in their lives. It is not because they're wanting in love. My father's wife told me when I left that every woman has a mother in her, that every woman longs to care for and nurture, that I should find a mother in Captain sir's wife. 'It is all how you see it, Nari,' she said. 'The amount of love you get depends only on the amount of love you give. Captain madam will scold you sometimes, but don't use that as an excuse to dislike her. If you look upon her as a mother, she will be one to you.'

I felt rather like I was a girl about to go away to her marital home.

It was a big house. Captain showed me to a wooden closet under the staircase and told me to keep my box in it. He took me into the kitchen and got me to climb over a chair so that I could bring down the cotton mattress, mat and pillow that sat amid dust and cobwebs inside the top corner shelf. After I had taken them out and cleaned them, he gave me three bed sheets and a pillow cover.

'No, Captain sir,' I told him, 'We never used to cover our pillows in Singavaram.'

He smiled. 'Here you will cover them, and you will wash them too when they get dirty, all right? If you're going to live in my house, you're going to be clean and healthy.'

'Yes, sir.'

He beckoned me into the storage room, set between the kitchen and the bathroom. 'Here's where you will keep your sleeping stuff.' He pointed to the floor in the middle of the living room. 'And here's where you will sleep.'

'Yes, sir.'

'You will have a bath only in this bathroom,' he said, swinging the door open and shut. 'You will bolt it from the inside when you use it, and after you use it, you will clean it with phenyl and hot water.' He tapped the big switch with the thick red line on it. 'Pressing this will send hot water into that blue vessel there.'

'Yes, sir.'

'Now go and have a bath. We will talk later.'

I hunched in front of my box, unbuttoned the top right pocket of my shirt and produced the key. I took out a bundle of clothes – a fresh pair of blue shirt and shorts, a white vest and a black torn underwear – and made for the bathroom. I kept my head down at all times, as Raji had told me to. *Don't stare at everything in their house*, she had warned me. My eyes grew wide at everything I saw, the grey polished wash basin, the fluffy white towel that hung on the ring beside it, mats in front of every door, the white marble floor spotless and glistening.

In the bathroom I spread my arms and realized that my hands did not touch either wall. I filled the bucket with cold water – I did not trust the blue hot water vessel just yet – and ran my fingers on the steel taps and pipes. There was no sign of rust. The toes of my feet curled and uncurled over the ridges between the white tiles of the floor. I picked up the red soap in the box and held it to my nose. It smelled of roses, and when I applied it, it cooled my skin. I felt like I was eating peppermint, only through my skin. On the window ledge sat a shampoo bottle and a few other bottles with pink and yellow lids. I read the words written on them – I can read English, a little bit – but they made no sense.

The water softly glided off my arms and knees, dripped off my hair over my nose onto my lips and chin. I put my tongue out and tasted it. Unlike the water in the village wells, when it slid down my throat, it quenched my thirst though it was only a drop. After emptying each mug over my head, I waited till the sounds died, the patter of water hitting the tiles, the gurgle of it flowing toward and through the steel saucer in the corner riddled with black holes, the splash of my tapping feet. In the quiet that followed I paused a moment, pricked up my ears so that I could hear the drip-drip-drip from my fingertips to the floor.

Two roses, one red and one pink, one small and one big, one green leaf with a saw-like edge, one thorn that grew in a straight line and bent a little downward at the very end, and a green stem. This was printed on each tile of the wall, and I remember I looked at it and laughed out, burying my fingers inside my wet hair and throwing my neck back. I checked all corners for lizards. I did not find any. It did not feel right, having a bath without a lizard or two watching you, without a spider spinning webs in spaces, lying in wait, without the chirring of crickets interrupting your songs and laughs.

After soaping myself, I knelt in front of the transparent plastic bucket and stared at the clear water. No green moss floated in it. I wished the bucket was as large as a well so that I could leap into it. I could dive down to the smooth plastic bottom and crawl over it so that my chest scrapes against it. I could bruise my arms and knees, but I would not run out of breath, I thought. One could not think of running out of breath in such clear waters. I held the edges of the bucket in both hands and immersed my head in it, to see if it was true. I began to count up, and just as I was about to rejoice that it was indeed true, my eyes began to bulge, my fingers began to tighten, and I came up gasping for air.

More than anything that happened at Captain sir's house, and a lot happened after I went there, this first bath is the one thing that I remember most. Even today I dream of it.

After I came out of the bathroom, Captain sir called me into his room and briefed me about the timings of the house.

'I leave the house at seven,' he said, stretching his legs out on the bed. Sir did not look to me like an army man. I thought that soldiers always walked with their chest puffed out, shoulders erect, in polished black shoes and green socks. The soldier of my mind was always fit and strong, whether he rode horses or ran miles. Sir huffed and puffed whenever he had to go up the stairs or come down them. I think it was one of the reasons why he made his bedroom on the ground floor – so that he could escape negotiating the staircase. 'I like to have tea before I leave, strong and hot.'

'Yes, sir.'

'Madam leaves the house at nine. She has a cup of coffee, with two teaspoons of milk and a pinch of sugar, no more.' He paused and eyed me with a frown. 'You know how to make tea and coffee, don't you?'

'Yes, sir.'

'Good. Ramya returns home before I do, at around four o'clock. She would like a glass of milk and a few salt biscuits. The packet is on the fridge.'

'Yes, sir.'

'You will have to pack lunch for her in the morning, and cook dinner for both of us in the evening.'

'No lunch for you, sir?'

Sir smoothened his hair over his head. 'No,' he said, looking at his reflection in the glass door of the bookshelf on the opposite wall. 'I eat little, and I eat outside whenever I am hungry.' He smiled at me and patted his stomach. 'I have to lose a few kilos, you know.'

'Yes, sir.'

'Madam will tell you what to make and how to make it. She likes salt and masala in her food. Her favourites are potato, ladies finger and brinjal. If I were you, I would stay away from the 'c' words – cabbage and cauliflower.'

'Yes, sir.'

'You do know how to cook, don't you?'

'Yes, sir,' I said. 'A little bit.'

'Our maid, Yasmin, will come for a week from now, and she will tell you all that you need to know. We have told her we will no longer need her after next week.'

'Yes, sir.'

'But no gossip, eh?' He grinned at me. 'We don't keep more than one servant at a time in the house because all they do is chatter away.'

'Yes, sir.'

'On weekends we don't generally go out, so you will have to cook all three meals for all of us. On weekdays you can rest during the day and do whatever you want.' His tapping fingers stopped. 'Say, what do you want to do during the day?'

'Anything you want, sir.'

'Your father was telling me that you used to go to the school in Singavaram. Is that right?'

'Yes, sir.'

'How much have you studied?'

'Up until eighth standard, sir.'

Captain sir's eyebrows went up, and I felt happy. 'Good,' he said. 'Very good. Then we should join you in a school. Do you want to study further?'

'Yes, sir, very much.'

'Then it's settled. You will go to school in the mornings. Madam will help you with your homework.'

'Thank you, sir.'

Captain sir gave a brisk nod. 'Now run along and unpack your things, boy. And don't disturb me or madam until four in the evening.' He slid down the bed and turned over on his side. 'Sunday afternoons mean siesta.'

'Yes, sir,' I said, and closed the door of the bedroom.

I unrolled my mat and laid it out in the middle of the living room. On it, I spread my mattress and covered it with the white bed sheet that Captain sir had given me. It had tiny yellow and green flowers printed on it. I slipped the pillow into its cover and slapped it a couple of times. When I finally fell on my back, the mattress seemed to hug me and massage my aching muscles. I closed my eyes for a moment, placing my hands under my head, crushing the pillow with my elbows and forearms.

I turned my head to the left, and saw closed teak doors. It had holes cut out in various patterns, and through them I saw a dim orange light flicker within. There was no smell of burning incense in the air, but I joined my hands and murmured a prayer. I prayed that my father and sister would be happy forever with the money that I would earn from Captain sir and send them. Raji should go to a big school in Hyderabad and grow up and get a job in one of these big companies. Father's wife should own at least one sari for each festival of the year.

The mattress became a little warm now, and I went back to looking at the ceiling. I could not help grinning like an idiot because Captain sir said he would send me to school, and if I could stay here and learn the ways of the big people – how to make tea for them, how to cook for them, how to speak like them – then who knew where I could go? Maybe in a few years, I would earn enough to open a little betel nut shop outside an Udupi restaurant and make my own life. Or maybe if Captain sent me to college, I could get a real job.

I threw my arm back over my head and pulled my box closer. I rummaged within it and found my Ponds powder bottle. I held it over my hand and shook it. Mother always said I looked like a hero when I applied powder to my face. Placing the bottle back into the box and pushing it away with my foot, I rubbed my hands, smelled them and applied the powder to my cheeks first, then carefully spread it all over my face. Then I lay back down and went to sleep with a smile on my face.

★

Yasmin and I met that evening. She walked in with her hips waving like a dancer's, though she was dressed in a salwar kameez. She would leave her Hawai slippers out by the gate and walk toward the doorstep on tiptoe, avoiding the puddles of water left by the water tank, and on the window sill she would hang her black gown. She dressed in greens and reds most of the time, with an occasional bow to white, on which days she would grumble about the amount of dirt it would catch and the number of hours she would have to spend scrubbing it with soap after going home.

She looked to me a lady of maybe thirty, but on that first day she spoke of her pregnant daughter, which meant that either she had aged extremely well or that she had married as a child and gave birth as soon as she was physically able. I expressed surprise at the fact that she had a daughter, and she tittered and blushed. I never did find out when she got married, but I suppose it is not that important.

She gave me three lists: the first had all the food items that neither madam nor Captain sir liked to eat, the second of things that madam liked but sir didn't, the third of things that sir liked and madam didn't. I asked for a list of things that both of them liked, and she turned away with a snicker, as though I had asked the stupidest question.

Yasmin liked to talk while she worked. If she bore any animosity towards me for taking her job, she did not show it. She had brought a notebook along with her and wrote down all the things she told me – how much salt to put into the sambar, how to cut the cucumbers just right so that the juice doesn't spill (this one had a picture), what flavour goes with what and which two things should never, ever, be added together into any dish – that kind of thing. She asked me if I could read, and when I nodded, she smiled in approval, and gave me a piece of jaggery as reward.

'I don't know how you will manage,' she would say. 'I am writing everything down. If you have any doubts about doing any of this, you should call me, okay?' She waved her phone at me. 'I am writing down my number. Don't call me in the mornings because I will be busy in the apartment down the road. They keep their house so dirty and they pay such peanuts for all the work I do for them. These rich people –' she looked around her, and after having ascertained that neither madam nor sir were within earshot, continued in a lower voice, 'these rich people are *snarky*.'

I asked her what that word meant, but then I had not known her enough to realize that when Yasmin spoke, she did not listen. It was a bit like these old walkie-talkies where one speaker had to say 'over' before the other could reply. It was more difficult with Yasmin because she never said 'over'. You had to hear for clues that indicated she was done talking, and you could do that only after having spent some time with her.

'People like you are cutting my business, coming from the village and charging less than I do. But you don't have to live in the city, do you? You don't have a good-for-nothing husband and a daughter with a belly that you have to feed, do you?' She sniffed, and rubbed the skin under her eyes with the back of her hand which held the knife. I looked down at the board to see what she was cutting. They were not onions. 'Get a house here in Hyderabad, go to the grocer and see if you can get anything to eat for under hundred rupees.' A snort came out of her. 'Hmph, a "house" – is that what you call the *dump* we live in? A house? *Haan,* so what are you doing, boy? Don't just stand there and watch the oil burn. Why don't you do something useful and chop up some chillies? Go, go.' And as I scampered away to the fridge, she mumbled to herself about the malpractices of doctors.

When I returned with my hands full of green chillies, she waved me to the sink. 'Wash.' She stepped aside and resumed her work with the knife. 'He says we need a scan. Every time we go to him we need a scan. Every time we go to him we have to pay him a thousand. I told my little Afsana that having children is not a big thing. I had her, didn't I? I was speaking with experience, wasn't I? It's not like her husband is going to look after her. The very first month her belly began to show, both of them came to my house and gave us sweets. Sweets! I could have just chopped their noses off right then.' She carved at the air with the knife. I took a little step away from her.

'Oye, what are you doing? That's not how you wash chillies. Keep them in a sieve, here.' She threw at me one of the big filters hanging on the nail above the stove. 'And wash them properly, until they're nice and soft. I don't know how you will manage once I am gone. Make sure you don't get fired by madam.' Whenever she mentioned madam, her voice dropped, and her eyes bounded about nervously. 'She is a feisty woman, I tell you.'

And so on it went.

Every day for that week, she arrived at eight, after Captain sir left, and swayed out of the house at ten, an hour or so after madam. The one thing that never stopped working, no matter what she was doing – dishes, cleaning, cooking – was her mouth. Whether anyone was within earshot or not didn't seem to matter.

One of the things I noticed right in the first few days is that Captain sir and Ramya madam did not seem to have any friends. They both went their own way in the morning, of course, and they would come back in the evening and say some pleasant things to each other before retiring to their respective bedrooms. On Sundays they stayed in but hardly looked at one another.

Captain kept to his room downstairs, madam to hers upstairs. During meal times they would come together, but even that only occasionally. Sometimes madam would say she had a headache and ask me to bring her meal up to her room.

I became the heaviest watcher of television. I liked 'Tom and Jerry' on *Cartoon Network* the best. After lunch every day, I would spread my mattress in front of the god's chamber and lie down facing the television, giggling away and then slipping into sleep. Neither Captain sir nor madam seemed to watch much television, not even by themselves.

They had very few visitors. Once when the hand shower in the upstairs bathroom had to be fixed, a plumber came in blue overalls and a cap with a red 'R' printed on it, whistling a tune which I did not know but sounded pleasant to the ear. Another time a switch in sir's study was not working, so a boy with big eyes and a heavy grey backpack came to replace it. He had crummy fingers blackened by soot. Another time a plain-dressed man came when Captain sir was not at home and went away when I told him so.

But apart from these, no one seemed to come to meet them, and they never went out to meet anyone, at least not to my knowledge. On my first day at the house, I remembered thinking that it was as silent as a temple. As the days wore on, I began to think that it was more like a graveyard.

Captain sir was nice to me, though. Every evening he would ask me what I did, if I was liking it, if I had any problems, if my family back home were okay – sometimes, on Sunday afternoons, he would sit and watch Tom and Jerry with me. Madam, on the other hand, never seemed to even look at me as I moved about the house. For her, I was little more than a machine that made tea, I think. I noticed she treated Yasmin the same way – she only acknowledged her presence when Yasmin had either done something wrong or when she needed some work to be done.

It didn't bother me, no. Masters have to pay servants well and give them food, shelter and clothing. They don't have to be friends with them. I only mention it now because it was so different, the way Captain sir and madam treated me. And also because things would begin to change in the way madam treated me too, in due course.

If I should put my finger on one incident which triggered most of what has happened, it was probably the small argument that sir and madam had about my going to school. It was one of the weeknights – this I remember because this evening Captain sir wore those black belts around his shoulder to prop up his breeches, and he wore them only when he went to the NGO. They were both sitting on the sofa, each looking up at the ceiling, lost in thought. At last, Captain sir said, 'Maybe it's time that Nari should go to school.'

Madam immediately lowered her head and narrowed her eyes at Captain. I watched them from the kitchen door. 'To school?' she said. 'Why? So that I can begin serving him?'

'No,' said Captain sir patiently. Whenever they talked, it seemed to me that his voice was always lower than hers. She had a sharp tongue, and most of her words had razor-sharp edges. 'He will still do all the work in the house. But in the afternoons he only watches television and sleeps. That's no way for a seventeen-year-old to spend his time.'

'You didn't bring him here to educate him. You brought him here to be our servant.'

'That's true. But his father –'

'Oh, yes,' she said, waving her hand in front of her and looking away. 'He saved your life.'

'Yes, and Nari went to school till the eighth standard in Singavaram. If we could get him to somehow pass his tenth, then I can set him up in small jobs at the NGO.'

'I will tell Yasmin to start coming again, then.'

Captain sir looked at me, then back at madam. 'No, Ramya, we don't need Yasmin. Nari has said that he will manage both his studies and the work in the house.'

'Well, I am not going to do any of the house work, okay? I don't care if your little boy gets an education or not. I need someone to do the work in the house. This is what we agreed upon. Don't you remember, Captain?'

'Yes, yes, of course.'

'And you don't realize how these people think. You get them educated and tomorrow they will think they're too smart for you. They begin talking back to you, they begin disobeying, they begin stealing, and all these other things.'

'Come on, Ramya.'

Madam got to her feet and picked up her purse. She walked briskly to the staircase saying, 'Do whatever you want. When did you ever ask my opinion with the intention of actually respecting it?' She climbed two stairs, then looked at me. 'You,' she said, 'get me a cup of really strong coffee. No milk.'

'Yes, madam,' I said.

TWO

I don't think Ramya madam looked me straight in the eye and spoke directly to me even a dozen times until she fell sick and I tended for her. She could have still seen me the same way, as a machine that gave care in return for money, and she could have continued on after she had become well in the same vein as before, never meeting her gaze with mine, but she changed. Looking back, this was probably the very beginning of her affection towards me – and in spite of all that has happened, I still believe she was pushed into doing what she did out of fondness for me, at some level.

This happened towards the end of summer, two months ago, when the rains came to Hyderabad a little later than usual. The summer heat had receded, and the air hung heavy with moisture, but clouds never gathered. Many in the city fell to the virus. Even I had a bout of cough and cold for three days, but when it hit madam, it hit her hard. She had acute pains in her joints and muscles, she had running temperature, extreme fatigue, and for those few days, she looked like she had already died and was visiting us from the other world.

The doctor – one of those rare visitors to the house, a short bald man with a sly, untrustworthy smile – prescribed rest, painkillers and plenty of fluids. At about the same time, the NGO in which Captain sir volunteered began a few new projects which required him to be present, so the task of looking after madam fell upon me. The first day, when I pushed myself into the bedroom with my back, holding in my hands a tray with a cup of milk on it, she grimaced and croaked.

'Captain sir is not here,' I said, looking down. 'And the doctor said you have to have milk twice a day.' I dared not look at her, not only because I was scared to look into her eyes, but also because she had become such a faint shadow of herself, I felt that she would disappear if I were to sneeze at her. She just moaned in response and waved me in. The air in the room carried the smell of balm – probably Amrutanjan, though it could have been Zandu Balm – and when I went closer to her I saw the pale yellow shade into which her pink skin had deteriorated.

I put the milk on the table, helped her sit up against the bed rest, and held her hands as they closed around the glass. I stayed with her all the while she sipped it. Once her hands shivered so much that I had to take the glass away and massage them gently, and wait for them to become steady again. While she pressed her hands together, I held the glass to her lips, and she closed her eyes as she drank.

After the glass had been emptied, I sat by her and watched her eyelids droop. I hummed an old song of the village, one which farmers used to sing in summers when looking up at the skies. It had a lilting, slow tune to it, and I made sure that the sound came from the bottom of my throat, like mother used to do to put us to sleep. In a few minutes, madam's breathing became regular, and her fingers relaxed around the edge of the blanket she had wrapped around herself. Her lips had become pasty and glassy. I placed my hand on her forehead to check her temperature. The warmth did not alarm me. I smoothed her brow and watched her sleep.

She woke up every ten minutes or so with a start, and each time she would look at me with her eyes thrown open wide, as though questioning my presence in the room. But in a second she would remember, relax, rest her head to one side and nod off to sleep. Her front hair danced in the fan's breeze and tickled her nose, so I tucked it behind her ear and got up to turn off the switch.

Her eyes opened the very instant the fan stopped, and she raised her eyebrows. She pointed upwards and frowned. 'No, madam,' I said. 'You're sick and cold. The fan will make it worse.'

She looked at me with the petulance of a child, but she was too tired to fight me. I checked her temperature again and gave her a tablet with a glass of water. She swallowed it, her face contorting into an expression of pain when the water slid down her throat. She pointed to the glass cup and said in a croaking whisper: 'Milk.'

'Shall I get you some?'

She nodded. By the time I returned with the full glass, she was sleeping. I placed the milk on the table and sat on the floor by the wall. Her cheeks had gone inward, like someone had pushed them in, and the dimple on her chin was all but gone. I thought of mother's last days, and how she had suffered. I watched madam, and though she looked peaceful I felt like crying. I wanted to go back to mother and look after her.

In a few minutes she woke up, again with a start, but this time when she looked at me, her eyes softened, and the smallest hint of a smile crossed her lips. When she reached out for the milk, I hurried up to the table and removed the layer of cream that had gathered on top with my index finger. Yasmin had told me that madam hated cream in her milk – though she loved it in her yoghurt.

She held the glass with her hands, stronger this time, and drank it all in one go, without lowering it even once. Then she fell back asleep.

Until she got better, I looked after her. By the second or third day she had recovered enough to speak, so when I went up to give her milk or lemon juice or a plate of biscuits, she would ask me to stay for a while longer so that we could chat. She asked me about my parents, about my sister, about my school in Singavaram. She told me a little about herself too, about her father and sister and this boy she used to like called Albert.

'I keep wishing to go back to Goa and search for Albert, to see what he is doing, to see if he is happy,' she said. 'But then I remind myself that I am married, that it would help me in no way at all if I were to see him now. If he is unhappy, I cannot help him. If he is happy, I cannot join him.' She gazed at the yellowed nails of her right hand, laid out flat against her left palm. A corner of the little fingernail had chipped. 'What about you, Nari?' she asked. 'Did you not have any girls in your school that you liked?'

I giggled and scratched my head. 'No, madam.'

'Come on, you're lying! A man with your eyes – did I tell you? The colour of Albert's eyes is the same as yours. And when he spoke he used to look around himself the same way too, like he was afraid of someone catching him.'

'I am not afraid, madam.'

'But you have those eyes,' she said, and sat up to look at me more closely. I shrank away from her, more out of bashfulness than fright. 'You have those eyes that can make a woman weak in her knees. You will one day grow up to be a handsome man, you know?'

'Heh. My mother always said so.'

'But your mother is biased. I am not.' She swallowed and made a face. She took a gulp of water and cleared her throat. 'This damned throat. It scratches when I swallow. Will you come and apply some balm to it, Nari, while I lie down?'

'Yes, madam.'

She eased herself to the middle of the bed, and patted the mattress. 'You can sit here, by my side.'

'No, madam, I –'

'Come, now. You have looked after me when I was sick. Can I not let you sit on the bed while you tend to me? Bring the bottle from that shelf, will you?'

I do not know if her intentions were innocent on this day. Now as I recite the story, I am asking myself how I could have been so stupid as to not see the signs that she had begun to seduce me, but maybe now I am biased by the knowledge of what has happened since. Whatever may be the case, in my mind there was not even the beginning of an inkling of what was to come. I just thought she was being kind and grateful.

I sat on the bed with my legs thrown to the side, my feet touching the ground. In one hand I held the bottle, and with two fingers of the other I rolled off a bit of balm and applied it to her throat. She craned her neck and sighed. 'Go in circles,' she said. 'Start at my chin and go down to the base of my neck.'

I did as I was told, and after I had done her neck, she pointed me to her forehead, then her upper lip, just under her nose. The high cheekbones rose and fell with each stroke of my fingers, and each time my hand returned to the bottle, she half-opened her eyes and smiled at me, her chin curling inward right in the middle. She had two smaller dimples on her cheeks too, which I noticed for the first time.

'So tell me,' she said, her eyes closing, 'how many girls have become heartbroken because of you?'

'I – I don't know, madam.'

'Liar. You boys always know.'

I did not reply. I thought of the summer afternoons in Raghuramayya's mango orchard, and the moonlit nights in the shade of the old tamarind tree where his wife and I would meet. Raghuramayya had married a girl at least twenty-five years younger than he, and if he had known that she made eyes at me, he would have beheaded my father. I told Savitramma that, but she would smile and squeeze my cheeks. She was perhaps twenty-four or so when I was twelve, but she wore those heavy kanjivaram saris wherever she went, and she dressed her forehead with a big red dot and always chewed betel leaves. These made her look older than she was. When she came to meet me, though, she wore a blouse, a skirt and a pair of silver anklets.

'I guess you won't tell me,' said madam. 'You can stop now. Have you made anything for dinner?'

'No, madam.'

'Will you mash some potatoes for me? And make some dal too. I feel like having pickle today, now that I can feel things on my tongue.'

'Yes, madam.'

I returned the bottle of balm to the shelf. When I was at the door, madam called me. I turned around. 'You want to go to school, don't you?' she said. I nodded. 'Well, then, I will help you with your homework, if you don't mind.'

'Yes, madam,' I said, beaming, 'thank you, madam.' I ran down the stairs to the kitchen. She laughed at my enthusiasm, and called out to me to be careful, but I was already out of earshot and cutting up the potatoes.

That night I dreamed of Savitramma. The first time she called me home was the night before Janmashtami. Raghuramayya had left for town in his cart that evening, and Savitramma sent Narsayya the cowherd to my house and requested my mother to send a jar of tamarind pickle with me. I had begun working at Raghuramayya's house a month before, and throughout the time, Savitramma would watch me, chewing on something or the other and smile. She would sit on the big swinging plank with one leg stretched out, break peanut shells on the wooden surface, and toss the nuts into her mouth. Once or twice she called me over and looked deep into my eyes. 'Who gave you these, boy?' she would say. 'You look like a big strong tomcat.'

Throughout the month she found ways to be in the same room as me whenever she could. She rubbed my hands when we gave each other something, she sidled up to me when we cooked together in the kitchen. She squeezed my cheeks and pinched my nose. The night before Raghuramayya was to leave for town, she came into the bathroom when I was heating up water for his bath, and pushed me against the wall. Pinning both my hands on either side, she said, 'Tomorrow night, boy, you and me, in this house.' She licked her lips, and just as her tongue was about to disappear into her mouth, she looked at me as though something struck her. She leaned closer to me, ran her tongue in one long, slow, luscious stroke along the length of my bottom lip.

She was shorter than me even then, and her hands were but half the size of mine. So she did not pin me to the wall with the help of her physical might. But there was great strength in the gleam of her eyes, in the flash of her teeth. No man in the village dared to look her in the eye when she spoke, not even Raghuramayya.

'You won't tell anyone, will you, boy?' she said.

I shook my head in great fright.

'Good, because if you do, no one will believe you.' She tossed her head to one side to push aside a lock of hair that had strayed onto her forehead. 'I will say that you raped me, and what do you think will happen then?'

'They will kill me,' I said.

'Forget about "them", boy. Raghuramayya will see to it that you're burned alive in front of everyone in the village. You don't want to stoke his anger, believe me.' Her face softened, and broke into a smile. 'But why do we speak of such bad things now when I am inviting you to take me?' She bit the corner of her lower lip, and looked sidelong at me. 'I will show you the time of your life, my little prince.'

I went to her house that night, bearing a jar of freshly made tamarind pickle. As soon as I reached the main gate of the house, she came to the porch, holding a lantern. To Narsayya she said, 'Your wife came looking for you, Narsayya. Tomorrow is Janmashtami. Good husbands don't leave their wives alone on this night.' From me she took the jar, opened it with a twist, held it to her nose. 'Did your mother remember to add lemon to this?' she asked sternly.

'Yes,' I said, bowing down, as Narsayya set out on his bicycle and shut the main gate behind him.

She did not pounce on me. We went into the house together, hand in hand. She shut the doors and windows. She took me to the central courtyard of the house, where she had a *nawar* cot laid out in the middle, with jasmine petals sprinkled upon it. Above us was a clear, starlit sky. She set the lantern at the edge of the raised platform, and turned the knob, increasing the intensity of the flame, bathing the surroundings in a soft, orange light. She sent me away to put the pickle jar in the kitchen, and by the time I returned, she had let her sari drop. She sat with her back to me, and as I stood at the edge of the cot, clenching and unclenching my hands again and again, she looked at me over her shoulder and said, 'Come.'

I sat at the very edge, farthest from her, my forehead beaded with drops of sweat. For a long moment, neither of us moved. Then she extended her arm and gripped my wrist. She pulled me toward her, and turning around, looked again into my eyes. 'My little prince,' she said. 'You have eyes that a woman can get lost in forever.' She guided my hand to her waist. My fingers lay limp on her skin, neither moving nor squeezing. 'You're scared,' she whispered into my ear. She nibbled on the lobe. 'You've never been with a woman, have you?' Her hand travelled down my body, back up again. She ran a finger along my jaw, sinking her teeth into my neck, then my shoulder, then my lower lip. She tugged at it, and with two little movements of her fingers the first two buttons of my shirt popped open.

'Come,' she said.

In my dream I saw her in Captain sir's kitchen, in the living room, by the god's chamber, sitting on the stairs, in madam's bed, wrapped in her flower blanket, calling to me, teaching me things, abusing me with a grin on her face, commanding me, crawling on top of me, running her fingers over my tongue, straddling me with her thighs, under the light of the bed lamp near which I slept, the flowers printed on my bed sheet throwing out fragrance into the air.

I woke up with a start. It was almost morning. I was swathed in sweat, and I was panting, like I had run a great distance. But it felt nice, too.

Even after she left, Yasmin and I used to meet outside the vegetable market behind Captain sir's house. The first time I saw her, she was popping green berries into her mouth while sitting on the front step of the newspaper shop, looking around her with a brown vegetable bag slung on her shoulder. She had her black gown on, but her face was uncovered. When she saw me she smiled and motioned me over.

'Arey, Nari, you are still with the Captain sir?' she said.

'Yes,' I said happily. 'Captain sir is going to send me to school, he said!'

'Arey waah, very nice.' She opened her palm. I took two berries and pocketed them. 'And her highness? How is she doing?'

'Madam? Okay. She got sick this last week. She went back to her clinic today.'

'Oh, god, she got sick,' said Yasmin, tittering in her loud way, making the tea-drinkers around us look up. 'She is such a witch when she is well, she must have been a proper bitch when she was sick.'

'She's not too bad,' I said. 'She offered to help me with my homework.'

Yasmin had a long nose, and lips that bend down toward her chin when she smiled. Her teeth had an orange shade to them, and there was a big gap where her left canine should have been. 'Homework and everything, huh? Looks like you have managed to charm her with your eyes, boy.' She got up to her feet with a growl of effort, and rubbed her knees a few times. 'These legs are killing me. My husband cares for nothing but his club and his cards. One of these days I will kill him and run away.' She caught herself, as though suddenly realizing I was with her. 'Don't look at me like that,' she said. 'I will not really kill him.'

We walked to the end of the street together, where the Radha Krishna temple stood in the corner. She touched her heart and closed her eyes as we passed. 'Poor Captain sir,' she said. 'I don't know what he sees in her, huh?'

'I don't know.'

'Whatever someone asks, "I don't know". What *do* you know, boy? Have you not seen how he follows her and does everything she says? And have you not heard how she speaks to him? I may not be educated like you are –' she tapped me on the head with a knuckle '– but I can tell when a man is happy and when he's not. *That* man is *not* happy.'

I turned to the temple and began to pray. Why should I put my foot in all of this? What happened between sir and madam was their business. They did not pay me to talk to Yasmin about their marriage or happiness. Of course, Captain sir was always gentle, always kind, always speaking in soft tones, and madam was always on the edge of abuse. And madam looked so much younger than Captain sir too. So much younger and so pretty – if Yasmin asked what Captain sir saw in madam, one could also ask what madam saw in Captain sir.

'You're a damned rascal, that's what you are,' she muttered. 'Just make sure you don't get into trouble with the madam, all right?' She lowered her voice. 'The rumour is that she has a taste for younger men with beautiful eyes.'

I blushed at that quite by instinct, and she knocked me on the head again. 'Look at you, colouring like a tomato! Keep yourself away from those clawing fingers, my boy. Did you not see her fingernails? They belong to a tigress, they do!'

Savitramma had long fingernails too, but they did not have the same curve of madam's. Hers were flat, and pressed down, and not less beautiful. I had heard the same tales about Savitramma too, in the village – about her taste for young flesh, about her long clawing fingers, always spoken about in hushed tones whenever Raghuramayya's bullock cart passed clacking by.

'Where do these rumours come from?' I asked her.

'Oh, you don't want to know,' she said. 'I used to work for them, remember? I used to find – stains – on the bedsheet, and during the daytime too, after I had changed them in the morning. So they cannot belong to Captain sir because he's out all day.'

'So is madam,' I said stubbornly. For some reason my nose became hot at the thought of madam with another man in the bedroom. How hurt would Captain sir be if he found out. 'You're just making things up, old woman!'

'Believe me or not,' said Yasmin, looking at me from top to bottom. 'But I have seen her come back from her clinic before lunch on some days, and she would speak so sweetly to me, as though I was her mother. "Yasmin," she would say, in a voice dipped in honey, "you've been working so hard. Why don't you take the rest of the day off and come in the evening to make dinner?" And when I returned in the evening, I would look at the stained bedsheet put out to wash.'

'Rubbish!' I said. 'Shame on you for spreading stories about people that put food on your table, Yasmin.'

'Oh, lighten up, you goat!' she said, making to slap me but stopping to squeeze my cheeks instead. 'You should put some flesh in these cheeks of yours and you will be delicious, won't you? I am sure the madam has seen it, and that's why she has been sweet talking you.'

I shook myself free of her grasp and took a few steps back, out of her reach. 'Well, off you go now,' I said, 'or your new mistress will begin to think *you* have a taste for young flesh. And let me do my work too.'

She threw her head back and laughed heartily. 'What a way to talk to a lady who taught you to cook.' She lowered her burkha and started on her way. 'Keep seeing me, boy,' she said, looking over her shoulder. 'Don't be a stranger.'

I waved and ran back to the market. The empty sack dangled off my shoulder. My slippers slapped against the dusty road.

By the time I got home after picking up vegetables, it was already half-past seven. Captain sir had already left. The sounds from upstairs suggested that madam was up and was getting ready for work. She must have heard me come in, because as soon as I closed the front door, she called out to see if it was me.

'Yes, madam,' I replied, and hurried into the kitchen to make preparations for lunch. I had only twenty minutes to cook up something. I cursed Yasmin under my breath, one for wasting my time with mindless chatter, and two for having no quick recipes in her book. Even the quickest Yasmin dish took at least an hour to make. One of her rules was never to turn the stove's flame to 'high'. Only lazy people did that, she said.

I emptied the milk packets into a vessel and lit the stove. Just as I finished making coffee and pouring it into a cup, madam came down the stairs, adjusting her sari and checking her handbag. She sat on the couch and tapped her foot on the floor. I came rushing out and placed the cup on the table top. 'Lunch is not ready, is it?' she said.

'No, madam.'

'Don't worry. I will eat out today.' She picked up the cup and took a sip. 'No sugar in this.'

'Oh, no. I am so sorry, madam.' I ran back into the kitchen and came out armed with the sugar tin, mentally hurling another volley of choice abuses at Yasmin. Madam did not say anything. She tapped her foot faster. I added the sugar, stirred it and pushed it toward her. She sipped and nodded.

'Don't make this a habit,' she said.

'No, madam.'

'When you go to school, time will be harder to manage. I hope you do it properly without me having to tell you off.'

'I will, madam, promise.'

She finished her cup with a few quick gulps and got up to go. 'I may come home a little later than usual today. I have a lot of clients to catch up on.'

'Yes, madam.'

'Tell Captain that I will join him for dinner.'

'Yes, madam.'

'And you don't waste your time watching television. Make lunch for yourself, then make dinner, and start reading your textbooks. Especially Mathematics.'

'Yes, madam.'

If I had done what she asked me to do, I think things would have been different. If I had just made lunch for myself, dinner for Captain sir and madam, and settled down with my books, stayed out of trouble, maybe I would still be working for them. Maybe Captain sir would still be alive. But then maybe the same things would have happened in different ways. Maybe the seeds were sown much before this. Who really knows? What matters is what happened and how. Everything else is mere fantasy.

I felt bad about not having given madam lunch. I went straight into the kitchen after she left, and an hour later I emerged with a nice hot ladies finger curry, cooked with boiled potatoes and fried moong dal. I packed the lunch carrier with rice in one compartment, the curry in the second and curd in the third. I locked the house and set out in the direction of madam's office. It would take me half an hour to walk each way, and I could come back home with plenty of time, I thought, to make lunch.

I have asked myself a number of times why I did this in spite of madam's explicit instructions. The only reason that makes sense – to me or to anyone hearing this – is that I wanted to impress her. I wanted her to think well of me. It hurt me that she had just begun to warm to me during her sickness, and already I had done something to ruin it. I felt nice when she spoke to me in kind tones. As I said, she reminded me of my mother. And which son would not do all in his power to make his mother feel good?

I found the clinic with no difficulty – I had been to the area before, though not to the specific building – but as soon as I entered, I realized there were two gates to the premises. I had reached the building from the opposite end of the street, so I came upon the back gate first. I saw the cream-coloured door of the building shut in front of me, and I made my way through overgrown weeds and wildflowers along the side towards the front gate, beside the compound wall. It was after I had covered half the distance when I began to hear sounds – sounds of a rather untidy nature.

I came upon an open window, and through it I saw Ramya madam and a man, both naked, entwined with each other, on a couch. My first instinct was to run and pretend that I had seen nothing, and it would have worked, but at that very instant, a dry leaf must have crackled under my foot or something, because both of them turned to look at me straight in the eye.

I covered my forehead with my hand and turned away. I marched to the main gate and stood there, gulping, looking at the young girl who sat at the table, typing away on her computer. I waited for them to come out, as I knew they would.

THREE

The man stormed out of the room and gave me an earful. I didn't hear much of what he said, though I remember that he was quite severe with me. All the while he was speaking, I looked at madam, who stood behind his shoulder, her eyes cast down. After the man had finished, she lifted her gaze enough for me to see the gathering tears. 'You should not have come here, Nari,' she said, 'not without telling me.'

'I came to give you your lunch, madam,' I said, and held out the carrier.

She took it and said thank you. She said that I ought to go home now and that she would explain everything in the evening. All through this the girl at the table did not look up once from her computer screen.

On my walk back I thought of what I had seen, and what Yasmin had said about madam. The man I had seen in her office was certainly younger than her, and there seemed to be a certain easiness with which they moved, and I knew that this was not the first time they had come together. I remembered the awkwardness in my hands when I touched Savitramma the first time, and how things eased with time, as we met more and more often.

In our village, the old man who lived under the tree and saw to fevers – no one knew his name, he was just called 'grandfather' – warned us all that some women acquire the taste of nubile young male flesh, and once they do, it becomes an addiction, much like arrack or cards. He taught us to be wary of these women with long claws, because they snared you in their net and sucked the juice out of you. Once you went into their grip, you would not come out until they drop you and pursue another.

I reached home, left my slippers beside the shoe rack outside the door. I unlocked the door and went in. The air seemed still and dark. It was a cloudy, windless morning. I closed the door and made my way to the god's chamber. With my fingertips wedged in the holes, I tried to look in. The flame of the lamp stood steady, without shaking. A spot of vermillion had been applied to the forehead of the elephant-headed mud idol. I joined my hands and said a prayer.

The old man under the tree had said that when a woman pursued a youth, it stilled his breath, quickened the beat of his heart and heated his skin. Into his brain she sent worms that would breed and lay eggs. These worms would make him speak in foreign tongues and voices, and he would think of nothing and no one but his seducer. She would fill his mind, tire his body, sap him of his life force and leave him an empty shell. 'So keep away from them,' he had said, looking out of the side of his eye at Raghuramayya's house.

One night, when Savitramma and I met on the bank of the lake after the crescent moon had reached the top of the sky, I told her what grandfather had said. She laughed like the water, ran her fingers through my hair. 'Look at me, Nari,' she said. 'Do I look like a demon to you?' That night she had come in a white sari and black blouse. In the silver light of the moon, she looked like an angel. The lantern seemed to light her olive skin a deep brown from the inside, and the red round spot on her forehead made her look like Parvati. 'No,' I said. 'You do not.'

'It is only wrong if I do something to you that you do not like,' she said, taking my hand in hers and guiding it under her sari, to her breast. 'But you like what we do, don't you?' She squeezed her fingers, pressing my nails over the thin cotton fabric of her blouse so that they scratched her nipple. She bit the corner of her bottom lip and flashed her eye lashes. 'Hmm?'

I hesitated, wondering if I should tell her that I was confused, that though my body responded to her touches the way she wanted it to, my mind did not know what quite to make of it. She trailed her fingers down my body, and when she reached my manhood her eyes lit up. 'You seem to be ready,' she said, smiling. I looked down, gulped, and nodded, thinking that I must be if she said I was.

Savitramma never gave me fever or worms. She never sucked my youth. But grandfather was right in saying that she filled my mind. When I thrashed ripe corn and white juice flowed out of the seeds, I thought of her lips. When I milked the buffaloes in my backyard at dawn and heard the sound of the thin streams of milk hit the bucket, I thought of her laugh. When I watched over cut and dried mangoes in the afternoons with a stick in my hand to drive away crows, I thought of her scratches on my shoulders. When I sat at my seat and mixed rice with curry, I thought of the salty wet mound between her legs.

I thought of Yasmin's words – that madam had me in her sights – and prayed that it was not so. I asked the elephant-headed god for answers, for it was said in our village that he was so wise that there was no question in the whole universe that he had not heard before.

But then, they said, like all wise men, he preferred to be silent, only choosing to speak to those who truly needed him. I wished that I would be one of them.

In the evening, just as the clock struck four, madam came home. I had a cup of coffee ready for her. She walked in less belligerently than she usually did, and instead of throwing her bag onto the couch, she tucked it into her lap and covered it with both her hands. She took the cup in one hand. I stood at the kitchen door and watched.

'I know what you're thinking about this afternoon, Nari,' she said. 'You must think I am such a bad woman.'

I shook my head, though the thought had crossed my mind.

She smiled at me. 'Good old Nari, never can tell a lie, can you?'

I smiled back at her. My mother used to say the same thing, whenever I smuggled cream out of the pots and ate it on the sly. 'Do you love that man you were with?' I asked.

She thought about it for a while. 'Love,' she said. 'Love has got nothing to do with what I do with him.' She laughed shortly. 'I am a doctor of Psychology, so I should be able to tell you why I sleep with him, but I cannot. I cannot.'

'You don't love Captain sir?'

'No. Is it not plain to see that I don't?'

'Then why did you marry him?'

'I married him many, many years ago, Nari. I was a little girl then. I thought I loved him. Maybe I did too, in my own way. But now I no longer do.'

'Well,' I said, looking down because I had a feeling that I was stepping over the line. 'My mother always said that if it dies, it is not love.'

I thought she would rise and strike me, and her face hardened, as though she wanted to. But after holding the expression for two seconds, she broke into a smile. 'Maybe your mother is right. Maybe it never was love.'

'But you can fall in love with him now,' I said. 'Can't you? You make yourself fall in love with him, you can do it. He's a nice man, so kind and thoughtful and smart.'

'It doesn't work that way, Nari,' she said, smiling sadly.

'Then maybe you can leave him to be with that man I saw you with.'

'It doesn't work that way either.'

I began to shift on my legs. I told myself to shut up before I said something that would make her angry. I was afraid of displeasing her, but not because she would complain about me to Captain sir. I was afraid that she would no longer like me, that she would no longer wish to help me with my homework, that she would no longer smile at me.

'Do you know whom I love among all the men in my life right now?' she said.

I shook my head.

'I love *you*, Nari.'

I pretended for a second that she did not say that. I twisted my fingers, ran them through my hair, examined the hinges of the door, did everything I could to keep from looking at her. But she waited for me to finish, and in the end I did have to look at her. She was not smiling; her lips were set together, and her eyes hovered over me, not steady but not aimless either.

'You cared for me when I was sick,' she said. 'Do you know that nobody has done that for me in my life with the same love that you gave me?'

'I – I did not give you any love, madam.'

'You did. You gave me the love you would give to your mother, didn't you?'

I moved my head up and down, once.

'Then I should give you the love I would give to my son, shouldn't I?'

I remembered my father's wife's words that every woman had in her heart the capacity to give life, to care and to love. One only needed to know how to reach it. Without my knowledge my eyes filled with tears, and the tips of my eyelids burned.

'I will be like your mother,' she said. 'You need not worry about anything in this house from now on. If you have any problems with anything, I will take care of them for you. Will you take care of me too, like you did when I was sick?'

'Yes, madam,' I said.

'I will never have children, Nari, but you can be my child. Will you?'

'Yes, madam.'

'Then come and sit by me, will you, and I will tell you a few stories about Captain sir and about how nice a man he is.'

I went and sat on the floor at her feet, with my back pressed against the wall. In a clear, low tone, she began to recite the tale of their love, how as a young girl she had been smitten by Captain sir's grace and panache, how the affection between them has died over the years, with each time Captain sir slept with her without her permission, with each time Captain sir hit her and called her names, with each time Captain sir went out for days and came back with stains of lipstick on his collar and bite marks on his neck.

The more she talked, the more she looked like my mother. Sometimes in the middle of her narrative, she stopped to smile at me, and in these moments she wore the face of Savitramma when she told me of her travails with Raghuramayya. I sat with my hands placed flat on the floor on either side of me, staring down at my toenails.

'Tell me, Nari,' she said, 'do you think I should still be patient with Captain sir and learn to love him, even when there is no love that he can give me?'

I shook my head.

'Do you think I was wrong to find comfort and solace in the arms of another man who gave me all that I asked for?'

I thought of Savitramma, who had taken me into her arms for these very reasons. If that wasn't wrong, this wasn't too. So I shook my head again.

I saw Captain sir in a new light that night. He did the same things that he did every day, but I saw a steely glint in his eye, a vicious side to his smile, a deeper meaning in every word he spoke to madam. Underneath his soft and concerned questions, there was a patient, cold, sinister man. At least madam said so. I tried to see it, and I admit that I did for a few seconds, but as soon as he began to laugh and joke with me about the Tom and Jerry cartoon, I could not picture him as the overpowering tyrant with a loose tongue and a hot temper.

But I had heard of these men before, so kind and quiet at times and violent and unstoppable at others. Madam had seen more of him than me, so who was I to say that she was wrong? Why was I so eager to take his side? As I made my bed, with a murmur of greeting toward each other, madam and sir dispersed to their respective rooms. On most nights, they didn't sleep in the same room. On some nights, Captain sir stole up the stairs in the middle of the night, taking care not to wake me up.

On this day too, about an hour or so after the lights had gone out, sir emerged from the room. I lay still and kept my eyes closed. He stood over me for a few seconds with his head lowered down to his chest. Then he crossed me and made for the stairs. He ascended each step in a slow, thoughtful manner, like a bear testing a creaking bridge. The railing shook with each step he took, so hard did he grasp it as he pulled himself up. A strong whiff of alcohol followed him. I had to plug my nostrils with two fingers to stop myself from sneezing.

He disappeared from view at the top of the stairs. He did not knock on the door. He pushed it open. In the short moment for which he kept the door open, I heard madam's muffled voice. Then the door shut. The bolt clicked. After a few minutes of silence, I began to hear squeaks of the bed upstairs. I had heard these sounds before, of course, but they had never made me this angry. The sounds stopped for a while, then came again, this time louder. I heard Captain sir's grunts (of angry lust?) and madam's plaintive moans (of pain?). I burrowed under my pillow and held it over my head so that the sounds could not reach me. As I drifted into sleep, I vowed that if it ever came to it, I would do all that was in my power to protect madam from Captain sir.

'*Chup re*!' said Yasmin the next day, sitting on her usual step in front of the newspaper stand, tossing in green berries and chewing them with an open mouth. 'She told you one sad story and you fell for it? I thought village bumpkins like you are smarter than that!'

'She did not lie,' I said. 'I saw it in Captain sir's eyes.'

'*Arey waah*, now he can look at people's eyes and tell what they're thinking. Why don't you tell me what I am thinking? Haan?'

I looked into her eyes. She had dull black eyes, the kind that you would not remember the shape of even if you saw them a hundred times. 'You're thinking that you should go home and kill your husband.'

'*Hai-la*!' she said, closing her mouth with her hand. Then, recovering: 'You just guessed that, didn't you? Of course you did. But how stupid are you to be taken in by the tall tales of the witch?'

'I am not stupid,' I said.

'Hey boy,' she said, tapping the step next to her. 'Come sit here, will you?' I sat by her side, not close enough to be touching her. Yasmin got crazy when someone touched her by accident. I learnt that the hard way in the kitchen during the early days. After handing over some washed tomatoes to her, she took the knife, pointed at me, and said, 'Never again will you touch me without my permission, *samjhey*?'

Now, though, she ruffled my hair and said, 'You told me you saw her with her boyfriend?'

'Yes.'

'And now she has to find some way or the other to make it seem like she has not done a bad thing?'

'I suppose.'

'What better way of doing that than to say that her husband is really bad and drinks and beats her and has sex with her when she doesn't want to?'

'I suppose,' I said. 'But it's not like husbands like that don't exist, Yasmin. You have yours.'

'Haan, when did I say that it is impossible? But Captain sir? No. That man is the only reason I worked at the house for so long, I tell you. Every morning he would smile at me and wish me good morning. He would ask me about my husband, about my daughter, about my sugar and blood pressure, and he goes and teaches in all these schools for kids. If you say something about such a man, God will take your eyes, I tell you.'

'But –'

'And that lady? Not even on one day did she ever look at me in the face or talk to me directly. Not even once did she ask about my daughter, even when she was in labour! No, it's always "Did you make my tea, Yasmin?", "Why is there no salt in the curry, Yasmin?", or "No, Yasmin, we cannot give you two hundred rupees extra this month". The bitch!'

'Well –'

'Whereas Captain sir would always call me to the side and give me a few hundreds here and there. When I had my grandson, he gave me a full thousand rupees and asked me to buy new clothes and sweets. Do you know? And go to the NGO where he works. See what they think of him there. God will punish you badly when you talk ill of people like that. See, see if that woman doesn't get what she deserves.'

I did not try interrupting again. Yasmin was off on one of her monologues. The only thing one could do in such times is sit tight and wait for the torrent to end.

I first learnt of rape from the movies I saw in Singavaram, when I was about eight or nine. I used to steal coins from father's shirt or mother's maroon cloth bag whose mouth she tied with a bright blue ribbon. The potter's son, Venkatesh, and I ran away from school every Friday and walked up the cement road all the way to town to watch a movie, and would rush back in time so that people at home would not suspect anything. We sat in the first row, whistled when the hero arrived, threw coloured paper into the air when the camera panned to the bare thighs of the heroine, her painted fingernails, her bulging breasts.

We were too young to know why we did it, just as we were too young to understand what really was happening when the dark, bearded man carried the heroine into a room and locked it from inside. He would fall upon her and thrust his face into hers, and she would turn away, struggling, and offer him her cheeks on which he would bite. In most movies, of course, the hero would kick the door down and beat up the villain before he could undress the heroine. But in some, the man would subdue the woman, and later she would be seen clutching her sari to her mouth and weeping.

But as we grew, and as did our experiences of movie-watching, we understood that rape meant sexually taking a woman without her acceptance. The very first thing I thought of after gaining the knowledge was whether Savitramma was raping me. I was scared of asking the question of people, because I thought they would all think me to be a fool. There was no movie, as far as I could find, in which a woman raped a man. So it had to be impossible.

We also wondered, Venkatesh and I, though separately, whether the hero pursuing the heroine at the beginning of the movie – through songs and antics and such – was also a form of rape. After all, in every movie the same script plays itself out: the hero makes the first advance, the heroine doesn't like it, the hero persists, the heroine finally says yes, moved by the hero's commitment to love. We always felt that the villain was doing the same thing, taking the 'no' of the heroine as an invitation to keep going, because as everyone knows, when a woman says 'no', you only have to try harder.

I saw the same script of the movies play itself out, again and again, in life. A woman's first reaction to a man's proposal is always no, as it was when Venkatesh gave Lachi a datura plucked out of his backyard tree. She took it, but turned away with a snort and chided him angrily for pursuing her. She warned him of broken bones and scarred skin if she told her brother how Venkatesh was bothering her. He could have stopped then, and maybe he should have, but he didn't, and after two more months of flowers and gifts and stolen glances later, they met by the lakeside on a cold winter night.

Lachi kept him on tenterhooks, never fully giving in, always holding something back. She knew, like all women do, that once she gave herself completely, Venkatesh would not look at her with the same gaze, and perhaps his eyes would rove to some of the other young women in her class. She had learnt the rules: men had to actively pursue sex, women had to choose, to defer, to withhold, and if all goes well, to concede. It always began with a 'no' it seemed; and seen that way, every love story starts off being a story of coercion, of persuasion, of the man stalking the woman, offering her care and comfort, expecting sex in return, and of the woman warding off the man until she is sure that he is not *just* after the sex.

It becomes then a complex dance of men proposing and women – for the most part – rejecting, treading cautiously. Maybe for some men these signals are hard to understand, the script is too intricate. Maybe they do not see the need to follow the script every single time, maybe they see the woman's refusal as needless posturing in which she engages just to bide time, while in her heart she truly wants to say yes. Maybe all that separates a hero from a villain is this understanding of the finer nuances of how we are all meant to play this game. Maybe there is a thin line, after all, between love and rape.

And then there are women, too, who disregard the rules and take the men that they want without bothering to play the game of courtship. Savitramma pursued me against my will and had me, often, at different places, at different times. Hers was not a lust-driven, single bolt of passion. It was cold, planned and calculative. What did she want from me? What did she get? And what did she leave me with?

Was it possible at all for a woman to rape a man? If all rape meant was sex without consent, it could go both ways. Why, then, did the media and the news channels laugh at me when I said that Ramya madam had raped me?

The first time she touched me, which reminded me of Savitramma and sent chills down my knees, was on the first day I had been to school. I came back with a bag full of books and a diary full of homework. In the previous week, madam had arranged for a study table to be made for me. I went upstairs into the spare room and set my things. Then I went down to the kitchen and made tea for madam, who returned from work in half an hour or so.

She did not say much at first, but after her tea was done, she looked at me as though she remembered it just then. 'You went to school today, didn't you?' When I nodded, she smiled and said, 'Did you make any new friends?' I shook my head. 'Don't worry, you will make them soon enough. Did you get any homework?' I nodded. 'Let me go have a bath, and we'll begin immediately.'

While she had her bath I washed the teacups, dried them, placed them upside down in the blue basket. Then I went up and pulled out my books, one by one: first Mathematics, then English, then Social Studies, then Science. I held them up to my face, but like dead leaves they had no smell. When I turned the pages, they made crisp little noises.

She came out in a blue nightgown, drying her hair with a towel. She pulled a chair into the room and set it to my right. Just then we heard the sound of Captain sir's car, and by reflex I ran down the stairs and began making his tea. By the time he kicked off his shoes outside and walked into the room, I had already boiled the milk and was adding the tea leaves. He called out to me. 'How was school today, Nari?' he said. 'Did you get all your books and your uniform?'

I went to the door and said yes. He turned on the television and flipped the channel to Cartoon Network. The grinning faces of Tom and Jerry flashed on the screen. I returned to the kitchen, poured out the tea carefully, blowing at the cream so that it did not fall into the cup. Then I added a teaspoon of sugar and stirred.

By the time I got back to the study room, madam had dried her hair and was examining my diary. 'Fractions,' she said. I took my seat on the floor, cross-legged, at the study table. I sharpened my pencil, opened my book to Chapter Two and began to copy the questions that I was meant to work out. Madam's chair creaked against the floor as she pushed herself closer to my desk. She bent over me, and I was immediately aware of a pungent smell that I could not recognize. It did not belong to any flower that I knew, but it left a pleasant, smoky feeling in my mind. The tips of some strands of her wet hair brushed my shoulder. I could not gather the courage to push them away.

'Do you like the smell?' she asked in a soft whisper.

I did not look up from the book. But I nodded, bringing out my tongue to wet my lips once, because they had gone dry as paper. The tip of my pencil just stood there, dug into the page. We heard Captain sir's laughter from the room below, over the frenetic music of cat chasing mouse.

She pushed her hair away from my shoulder, and with the tips of her index and ring fingers, she rubbed the drops of water away. She leaned over, as though wishing to look more closely at what I was writing. Her foot slid beneath my thigh. With her toes bent forward, she scratched my heel. 'Why are you not writing anything?' she asked.

As if a spring had gone loose inside me I began to write, not knowing what or why. Her foot rubbed up and down my thigh. I fidgeted. 'Shh,' she said. 'Don't you like what I am doing?'

'I – I don't know.' I looked up from the page at her, but only for a flash of a second. My eyes dived down to the page, away from her searching gaze. I could see her smile, and her leg left me. She snaked an arm around me and pulled me close to her. My outer arm pressed against something spongy and soft, and I closed my eyes to think of something, anything outside of this room. Captain sir's laughter, yes, and images of Tom running round and round and round in pursuit of little brown Jerry.

She placed a dry kiss on my temple. 'Good old Nari,' she said, running her fingers through my hair. Then she kissed me on the cheek, this time for longer, and I felt her warm breath on my skin. A thin shooting pain arose in my head that mixed with the misty smell of her perfume and made me shake my head, more forcefully than I intended. She pulled back, surprised. She looked at me, first with a frown, then a little pink smile colouring her face.

I shut my book and stood up. 'I have to go,' I said. 'I have to make dinner.'

The smile on her face widened. I would be lying if I said I did not think she looked beautiful in that one moment. 'Go,' she said, 'but only for now.'

FOUR

I came down the stairs intending to tell Captain sir about madam, but by the time I reached the bottom, my step had slowed. Sir was lying on the couch with his hands on his stomach, clasping the remote under his entwined fingers. His eyes moved languidly from the television to me, and he raised his eyebrows. 'Finished your homework?' he said.

I nodded and went into the kitchen, flushed in the cheeks. I picked up vessels at random and began washing them. I filled one with rice. I soaked the grains, gathered them in my fingers and squeezed them dry. As I watched the water from the tap wash my hands clean, I heard the sound of her anklets on the stairs and my heart began to beat faster. I did not have to ask myself why I could not tell sir about what had happened upstairs; the answer was simple. I felt that if I were to speak to him about it, it would displease her and she would no longer smile at me, ruffle my hair, kiss me on my temple.

I turned and stood with my back pressing against the edge of the sink, my hands moving up and down the granite surface yellowed by the run of water. She threw a glance in my direction as she passed the kitchen, but she did not smile. Her expression had none of the warmth with which she had smiled at me upstairs. I felt a faint tickle behind my right knee, and at once I lifted my left leg and scratched the itch with my toenail. It did not carry the same touch, though.

One of the biggest questions that plague you when this happens – and I speak from my experiences with Savitramma as well – is that you wonder a lot whether or not you truly like what the woman is doing to your body. She told me that my body liked it, that she could tell by my hurried breath and the colour in my cheeks. But you always have this little thorn sticking out in your mind, and you wonder what it all means. Men are meant to be immune from thoughts such as these, if you believe what people generally tell you. We are not meant to question the nature and meaning of sex, and we're expected to pursue it purely for the pleasure it gives us. And yet here I was, standing in the kitchen and wondering – just like I had wondered about Savitramma – what Ramya madam was getting from me. What was I giving her that other men – Captain sir and that man in her clinic – could not give? And what was she taking from me – after saying that I was like her son – with such little regard for my feelings?

The channel changed to news, and over the sound of the water I heard the agitated tone of a woman reporter talking about something a politician had said. I was slicing potatoes at the time, so my focus kept shifting from the television to the cutting board. With potatoes, Yasmin had said, you had to make sure that all the pieces were roughly the same size and shape. It wasn't as easy as it sounded because they came in such different shapes – some round, some jagged, some small enough to slip between your fingers, some so big that they did not fit in your fist. It needed a certain technique that Yasmin had taught me, but I was not well versed enough yet that I could do it while listening to the television.

But a few minutes later, I was done, and then I heard Captain sir and madam talking. 'He doesn't have anything personal against women,' said sir. 'He is just quoting the facts.'

'The only fact that matters,' said madam, 'is that men are pigs.'

'That may be so, but when you dress like that, you're inviting trouble. Simple as that.'

'Why should it matter at all what I dress like?' said madam, and immediately I thought of her blue nightgown with the small white bubbles on it. 'Even if I walk down the street naked, I should be safe. And it's not like nuns and women in saris do not get raped.'

Captain's voice, as ever, was low and cool. 'He did not say any of that. He just said that if you wear clothes that invite attention, you will get all kinds of attention, both good and bad. You cannot choose the kind of people you will attract when you're choosing to dress in clothes that are meant to attract people. Isn't that easy to understand?'

'Maybe to a misogynist!' said madam. 'You know, I expected this from you. You've never, ever understood a woman in your life.'

'Maybe I haven't,' said Captain. I could not see their faces, but I could almost sense the tightening in his voice. 'But you don't exactly have a doctorate either when it comes to men.'

'What is there to understand in men? All they wish to do is control their women. It gives them their sense of pride, that they have their thumbs firmly planted on top of their wives, almost as if we were – circus mice.'

Their voices had gone up now, and the television was barely audible. The agitated reporter was saying something about patriarchy. I did not know then what the word meant. I made a mental note to look it up in the dictionary in English class the next day.

'Let me ask you a question,' said Captain sir, and the couch on which he sat creaked. 'A simple question. Will you answer it?' She did not respond, so after a second sir ploughed on. 'You wear attractive, revealing clothes all the time. Whom do you wear them for?'

'There's nothing wrong with wanting to look good.'

'Yes, but whom do you wish to look good for? Other women?'

'Yes.'

'No,' said captain, with a little tremor in his voice. 'You don't show off your body and dress well for other women. You do so to attract the eyes of men.'

'That's your theory. I don't agree with it.'

'Of course you don't, and it doesn't matter. It amazes me how out of touch women really are with their own behaviour.'

'And men with theirs. Just because a woman wears a sleeveless top doesn't mean she's asking you to fuck her like she's – she's – some *object*.'

'Can we have a discussion about anything – anything at all – without you crying at the end of it?'

There was a silence, one in which I heard the reporter interviewing a middle-aged couple who said that the politician ought to issue an apology for his words. They had a daughter whose life had been ruined, they said, and for one of the leaders of the country to suggest that it was somehow her fault was just unthinkable.

The television turned off. 'I am sorry,' said Captain sir. Only sobs and sniffles came from madam. I poured some oil into the pan and waited for two minutes for small bubbles to appear. I sprinkled some cumin seeds into it, then some mustard, and while they simmered I cut up some green chillies. Yasmin had taught me to cut the chillies along the length so that all the spiciness is preserved. It had been a while since we met, Yasmin and I. She had not been there at the newspaper stand these last few days, and the berry vendor had just shrugged and swatted away flies when I asked him about her.

After the chillies and the cut potatoes had gone in, I put a lid on the pan and turned down the flame of the stove. I folded my hands and turned around, listening to the quiet sounds of the living room – the tapping of sir's feet, the stretching of his fingers, the sighs, the occasional attempt at conversation and madam's taut, short replies.

Women grow up from a young age to be vain, of course. Whether that is learned or whether God created them that way, I don't know. They are taught from the time they are children that beauty is to be aspired for, cherished and valued. They revel in seeking male attention by their looks, and maybe they do it so subconsciously that they don't even pause to question why they do it. They know, deep in their bones, that beauty and youth are the two things that men look for in women, and forever run around those two things, madly clawing to clutch at them as they slip away.

There is vanity and insecurity in men too, but they concern status and wealth, not physical beauty. One could probably say that women are unlucky to be dealt these cards that they should forever clamour after the unattainable – lasting youth and beauty. For all the things that we hear about beauty being skin deep, one only has to look around to see the amount of beauty that looks down upon us every day, in movies, on television, on these big boards that the city erects at the end of every street. When the world is telling you that you're nothing if you're not beautiful, can you blame them for taking heed and moulding their lives that way?

These are not things that I thought of that day, as I waited for the potatoes to cook. Then I was but a simpleton and did not know the meaning of patriarchy, but I am fortunate that I thought of looking up the word in the dictionary, because that started me on a journey which gave me some of the answers that I was looking for. It also guided me to the one woman who perhaps truly loved me.

On that day, though, I merely waited for mist to cover the inside of the dome-shaped lid of the pan, pretending not to listen to the vile words that sir and madam hurled at each other – after her first bout of weeping had subsided. When the lid clouded over completely, I removed it and let the smoke rise to the chimney. I stirred the curry, watching for the sides of the potatoes to brown, at which I added the required amount of turmeric and salt. As the curry turned a delicious yellow, the smell tingled my nose and a smile came to my lips. No matter how many bad things happen in your life, I thought, as long as you have food to cook and eat, you are doing well enough. My mother used to say that food lovers are fortunate, because they will have fun at least three times a day.

Mother ate only when she was hungry; to her dying day she was thin as a beggar woman.

I sprinkled some chopped coriander on the curry and stirred it once again. When I covered the lid, all seemed to fall silent again, and I felt as though I was being reluctantly dragged back into the house from this wonderful world of spices and smells. But thankfully I could not hear any more voices. The television had come back on, and it was set to *National Geographic*, in which an old bearded white man was speaking about how ants went about collecting rice grains.

I figured they were hungry. After stirring the preparation one last time and sprinkling some shredded coconut and red chilli powder evenly on it, I turned the stove off and left it to cool down. With the wiping cloth thrown over my shoulder, I went to the door and said to them, 'We will eat in five minutes.'

Madam and sir sat at opposite ends of the dining table. The steel bowls were laid out between them. I sat in the far corner of the living room, beside the main door, one knee raised, with my plate on the floor in front of me. The first course passed in silence. When they ate my potato curry, I looked up at their faces to see if I could make out whether they liked it. But their faces were set tight, as though strings ran along the insides of their mouths, pulling the muscles wide apart.

This was not the peaceful, serene silence that you would find perhaps in a park early in the morning. This was the heavy, mournful silence, found at funerals; the kind of quiet that descends just before a bomb explodes. It made me sweat under the armpits, even though the fan was on.

At the beginning of the second course, after they served themselves sambar and took a mouthful each, madam spoke.

'My whole life –' she said, and I saw her teeth grit behind her pale, tightened lips. 'My whole life I have suffered for you. Never, not even once have you shown even the slightest interest in me, in my happiness, in my life –'

'Enough, Ramya,' said Captain sir. 'We will talk about this later.'

'Ah, later, later, later! God forbid that someone hears, someone in the neighbourhood, our servants, our friends, our colleagues – to all of these we're the model couple, aren't we, Abhilash? You with your suave manners and courteous habits and me the ideal army wife, always clucking like a hen whenever you signal. That is what you want out of a wife, don't you? You should have told me that when you were wooing me, I would never have come away with you. Never!'

Captain sir looked down at his plate, and seemed to be counting numbers in his head. The seconds passed. His hand worked in his plate, mixing the rice, turning the grains over, mixing, turning, mixing...

'Now don't you pretend that you cannot hear me,' said madam. 'Why do we keep up this charade, Abhilash? For whose sake? Remember the walks we had on the beaches of Goa? Remember?' At once her eyes began to water, but she blinked once forcefully, and again she was angry. 'You read poems to me. You made promises!'

'Poems are not what life is made of, Ramya.'

'Oh, but you told me that it was. You told me that you would recite Tennyson to me whenever I wished. You said our life would be one long walk on a Goan beach, where we can both dig our toes into the sand and count the waves.'

'I never said that. Don't put words into my mouth.'

'You didn't?' Her body shook with a sharp, sarcastic laugh. 'You're right. Maybe I'm recalling things from the dreams I had – from the dreams that *you showed me*. Where is that life, Abhilash? Where is the life in which you recited Tennyson to me?'

'Is that what this is all about?' said Captain sir, suddenly irritated. 'If so, I will read to you all the poems you want. All of them, as many times as you wish. Happy?'

'I came here trusting you.' Her words came out as whines now. 'I came here leaving my life, abandoning the people I loved, all for this – this pathetic excuse of a life you have given me. I was *happy* in Goa, damn it, I was happy and I was looking forward to life. I *wanted* to live.'

'I don't know what you wish me to do, Ramya,' said Captain sir. 'You said you wanted to be a psychologist. I paid for it. I got you a seat in the college. I paid for your PhD, I paid for the clinic that you now run. You have all that you want.'

Madam leaned back and cackled like an old crow, like a witch about to hatch a plan. 'Look at you, Abhilash. The biggest things that you've ever given me have the word "paid" in them. What do we have in common, Abhilash, apart from this house that we seem to share? Apart from the bed we share now and then, whenever it takes your fancy to *rape* me?'

'I don't –' said Captain sir, looking in my direction for a moment. I looked down at my plate and resumed eating. 'We better talk about this elsewhere.'

'Why? Because you're scared that Nari will hear us? Because you think that in the eyes of your servant your image will fall? Because you think it *fucking matters what Nari thinks of us?*'

'You – you knew how old I was when you got married to me,' he said. 'You always knew that we would have little in common. I – I told you to expect that.'

'Hah! Yes, you did, but so did you tell me that our love will never die. Now I wonder whether you ever loved me. Did you ever love me, Abhilash? Or was I just one of those butterflies that you caught in your net so that you can show me off to your club buddies? I am sure they think you quite the stud, having landed a girl so young and so pretty.'

'If you question my love for you, then I can question yours for me too.' His voice was but a bare whisper.

She looked at him closely, with a frown. A disbelieving smile came to her face. 'You don't have any idea, do you?' She shook her head. 'You actually think that I still love you. You fool, you big oaf, I have stopped loving you for almost seven years now. Almost seven years, and now you say you will "question" my love for you? Uh, yes, it's about time!'

'Let's not talk here, Ramya –'

Madam got up, and with a shriek, lifted her plate high above her head and sent it crashing against the floor. The brownish orange rice splattered against the wall and stuck to it. A stream of sambar flowed toward the main door and settled in a puddle, right beside where I sat. I got up to run into the kitchen for a piece of cloth, but she held out her hand at me. 'Sit, Nari,' she said quietly. 'Sit and eat. You're the only sane person in this house. At least you should eat well.' She crouched by the upturned plate and began to pick up the grains, one by one.

Sir shook his hand clean and got up from the table. He washed his hands in his plate, went into his room and slammed the door behind him.

Later, I cried while washing the dishes. The lights in the living room had been dimmed by then, and madam had already gone up to her room. From the thin line of light under Captain sir's door I could tell that he was either reading or sketching. Just the other day he drew my portrait in pencil and gave me these two big fang-like canines. It did not look funny, though madam had chuckled when she saw it. But I had to laugh because Captain sir drew it.

Doing dishes relaxes me like no other chore. There is something about rubbing the soap-laden green scrubber on the steel vessels that stimulates the mind, I think. In my time with Captain sir, I thought about more things, I remembered and recalled more incidents from my past, and I planned more about my future while I was doing dishes than at any other time. Today when I rolled my sleeves up my arms – more as a gesture, because the sleeves of my shirts were quite short to begin with – and picked up the plate which madam had hurled against the floor, I looked into my reflection, and thought I saw my mother.

When I think of my mother, the first thing I see are the bangles she used to wear on her wrists. A glass bangle, three mud bangles, then another glass bangle. When she spoke she liked to wave and gesture with her hands, so from quite a young age, I have learnt to associate her voice with the jingle of her bangles. Even when she didn't speak and was going about her work, whether it was cleaning the courtyard, placing balls of dung on rice flour patterns on the doorstep, stirring lentils in the big pot in the stove in the kitchen, or rubbing my forehead as I rested my head on her lap, the wrists clinked and tinkled, always. They woke me up every morning and put me to sleep every night.

Father and mother seldom fought. Father drank and smoked, but he cared for us as well. He had a job as a clerk at the post office, and he stamped on envelopes for a living. He left home early in the morning and returned before sunset. He ran errands for Raghuramayya whenever he was asked to. He was sensible with his money, as far as I knew. He never took loans, always saved a part of his income and paid our school fees on time. One could say that they did not have anything to fight about.

But I cannot say they never did. One day, we went to the wedding of my aunt's daughter in the neighbouring village. My aunt – father's elder sister – got married into a family of landowners, and ever since then she has not dressed in anything other than silk. The wedding took place on a two-acre field with food and dancing and games. Mother went to it wearing a cotton sari and her glass and mud bangles.

On the cart ride back, I could sense the same heaviness in the air that I had sensed this evening between madam and Captain sir. The driver chewed on a roll of tobacco, and slashed with his whip on the hides of his bullocks. The bells around their necks chimed as they shook their heads in vain attempts to free themselves. Each time they did, the driver said, '*Hye!*' and kicked them in the sides.

'Do you know what your sister said?' mother asked in a toneless voice.

Father stayed silent for a moment. Then he said, 'What?'

'She said that this will be the most lavish wedding in the family. And then she looked at me with this smile. "Not that it is important, dear." Why do you let her speak to me like that?'

'Well,' said father, 'what she said was true. It will probably be the most lavish wedding in the family.'

'Why? Won't we get Raji married the same way?'

Father laughed a little. Seated toward the front, Raji and I looked at each other. 'If we do,' he said, 'I will have to pawn our house, our cattle, our jewels – everything.'

'You should be ashamed for saying things like this,' said mother. 'Look at your sister's husband, how much he is spending for all of this.'

'But Venki, he's a landowner. Maybe we can borrow some of his farm land to get Raji married.' When mother did not answer, he asked, a little exasperated: 'Why are we speaking of her marriage now, anyway? It is at least fifteen years away.'

After that, no more words were exchanged, and once again we heard the sounds of the driver chewing, of his whip, of the thuds of his heels against the animals' ribs. We passed on a narrow path with paddy fields stretching out on both sides, and though summer had already begun, the breeze that blew from the west carried cool moisture with it. Raji and I hanged our tongues out like dogs.

The air had not become lighter, though, and that night, after the lamp had been dimmed and Raji put to sleep, they began to talk again. This time I was in the other room, so I could not see them, but I heard mother's bangles rattle incessantly over father's protests. Once in a while, one of them would lose their cool and be reminded by the other that the children were sleeping. I tried to plug my ears, to bury my head under the pillow, to sing songs loudly to myself, but the sounds wouldn't go away. At the end, I heard the snap of a wrist, one last clatter of mother's bangles, then her low wail, then silence.

I discovered in the morning that mother's mud bangles had all broken.

I finished the dishes, wiped my hands dry, turned off the light in the kitchen and gathered up my bedding from the storage room. I laid it out, joined my hands in the idol's direction, and fell on my back so that my head sank into the pillow. I fumbled in my pocket for my purse, and I opened it to look at the photograph of my father. (It had never struck me to keep my mother's picture with me, somehow.) He had a full head of black hair and a wide forehead. He was the fairest member of his family, and quite the pride of all his uncles and aunts. His childhood nickname was 'mango'.

As it turned out, what father said that day in the cart was right: it was too early to speak of Raji's marriage, then. When she was ten and I was twelve, mother fell sick – some said it was malaria, others said it was cholera, still others said it was some type of cancer. The doctors kept giving her tablet strip after tablet strip which she swallowed dutifully, though she grimaced every time I went into her room with a glass of water. Father still paid our fees on time, still did not take a loan from Raghuramayya, but he began to drink, just a little bit, only a glass or two, he said, after work, before the darkness set in.

The money he had set aside for Raji's marriage and my college had to be used for mother's treatment. She did not know this; to the last day she lived, she believed that Raji would get married in great style. Father did not discourage her fantasies; I think he knew much before either I or Raji did that she was slipping away. He was too kind a man to shatter a dying woman's dreams. So every time she asked if Raji's marriage would be grand, he said that it would be the grandest the village had ever seen.

I bent the photograph to one side, so that I could see it better in the light of the bed lamp. The first two buttons of his shirt were unbuttoned, and the collar was thrown back. His hair fell over his ears, completely covering them. In his eyes I saw a rich hope, and it seemed that he was looking into his future, confident that it would all turn out well and happy. I remembered him on the day mother died, with a sprinkling of haggard white hair on his chin and cheeks, almost bald, thinner than he had ever been, looking around him like a child lost in a fair, responding to questions only after a second or two of blinking.

I don't know what saddened father more – the fact that mother left us or that all the money we spent on her had counted for nothing. It may seem cruel that I speak of money and mother's death as if they were equally important, but her death brought closure to all of us – perhaps not to Raji because she was still too young, but certainly to both father and me. Only after she died could we finally sit down and look ahead to what we should do with our lives now that mother was beyond it all. That was when it came to us for the first time how much we had spent in frantic efforts to keep her alive, and neither of us could shake off the feeling that we had dumped all that money down the drain, into the doctors' pockets.

If it is true that the dead become souls, mother would have cried that we thought such things, that no sooner than a day after we had burned her body, we were counting our losses and lamenting on how much of a waste it was. Sometimes I wonder if father or I or Raji were to have died before mother did, would she have thought of all those days of caring for us as a waste? Would she have regretted looking after us and loving us? Would she have thought back to those nights on the nawar cot – on which she told me tale after tale to put me to sleep – and chided herself for pouring her life into me only to see me die?

We never talked about this, father and I. Before the end of the year – mother died in June – he was married again, and though we did not ask him, he told us that he was doing it for *our* sake, so that we would be well looked after. Raji took to the idea with more enthusiasm than I did. The first thing I noticed with father's new wife was that she did not wear bangles. She did not tell us stories. She was the widowed daughter of Ramayya, the head-clerk at the post office. Father became quite a hero in the village that year because he was 'giving a woman a new life' by marrying her. During the school day celebrations, they invited him as chief guest and asked him to speak on the primacy of women.

But something had left father when mother died. He no longer looked to the future with hope, like he did in the picture. He acquired a furtive look about him, like he had stolen something and that everyone around him knew. The father I looked up to when I grew up held his head high, smiled a lot and spoke with compassion. Now he was in a state of constant fear. I always thought that it was the dread of dying and facing mother's soul in the afterlife.

Captain sir's door unlocked, and I quickly returned my purse to my pocket. He turned off the light in his room and crossed me on the way to the stairs. He ascended them quietly, light as a cat. He knocked twice on madam's door, then pushed himself in. The latch fell into place. I flipped over onto my stomach and covered my head with the pillow. I willed sleep to come and take me before the bed began squeaking.

FIVE

I woke up with a strange fear tugging at my chest. Until after I had rolled up my mattress and allowed the fog of sleep to dissipate a little, I did not know what was causing it. The time was half past six. In about half an hour, Captain sir would leave the house, leaving me alone with madam for two hours. I sidled up to the god's chamber and peeped through the holes at the elephant-god's unseeing eyes. He seemed to smile at me. I got up to make tea for Captain sir.

I heard sounds from his room, sounds that I heard every morning – slippers, belt buckles, straps, the occasional whistle, a mumble here, a mutter there. Upstairs there was absolute silence. This was also usual, because madam did not wake up until after sir had left. But today I felt as though madam was lying awake in her bed, waiting for that moment when the door would close behind Captain sir, so that she could come swooping down on me. If she could do all that she did yesterday at homework with sir right here in the house, what would she do with him gone?

My hand trembled while adding the sugar, so that the spoon hit the side of the cup and spilled some crystals on the granite slab. I scooped them up with my free hand and dropped them into the sink. I stirred the tea slowly, listening for any sign of movement in the upstairs room. But there was none. I felt like a fawn probably feels when it has to go to the lake alone for a drink of water and behind every bush it *knows* that there is a tiger lurking.

Captain sir came out of the room and dragged his shoes over to the couch. I placed his tea on the table and stood there awkwardly, folding my hands. When he looked up, I thought he looked dishevelled and bored. 'Yes?' he said.

'Nothing, sir,' I said, and went back to the refuge of my kitchen door. He drank the tea, with small, tentative sips at first while he tied the laces on his shoes, but in hurried gulps afterward. He got up, took his bag and without the customary wave in my direction or the call to madam, he left. I went to the door and waited for his car to reverse out onto the road, and after he had driven away, I locked the gate and closed the main door.

Everything was still silent, but only for a short moment. She would have heard the car drive away, and the locking of the gate and the door, because as soon as I returned to the house, I heard her anklets in the bedroom. For some reason, the clinking reminded me of my mother's bangles. The door to her bedroom opened with a yawn and she appeared at the top of the stairs, only her hair visible. I wondered for a split second if I should gather the vegetable bag and make a run for the market, but that would only make her laugh and wait. She came down, tying her hair up with a blue elastic ribbon. Her armpits, hugged by the sleeves of her nightgown, were shaved, and hair was just about to sprout on them. Her complexion was black, almost blue under her arms.

Without a word, she took my wrist and dragged me into the kitchen. She closed the door. I didn't know why. She pushed me back against the edge of the counter and thumbed my lips. She stared into my eyes. 'These eyes will one day be the death of me,' she whispered, and trapped my lower lip between her teeth. She bit with enough venom to draw a little drop of blood on the inside of my lip, which she licked away. With her hands she worked the buttons of my shirt, easing each one open, then tracing a line down my chest with both her index fingers until she reached the next. When the last button came off, she placed her hands on my ribs with a hungry sigh, and moved them up to my nipples, her thumbs covering them, running around them in circles.

'You think I am beautiful?' she asked, one hand diving down to the buckle of my shorts and flipping it open in one deft motion.

I nodded. She *was* beautiful. My body trembled to her touch. She slid down the shorts, then my underwear. She gripped my penis in her hand. I looked down, her dark fingers wrapped around my member. At first her palm was cold, but as it began to run up and down, from the stem to the tip and back, it became warmer. I whimpered and managed to murmur a faint 'no'. She just grinned and said, 'You just said I was beautiful. Do you not want me? Do you not want this body? Hmm?' With her free hand she undid the buttons of her nightgown and let it slip a little so that I could see her shoulder blade, the beginning of her upper arm.

She knelt in front of me now, curled the fingers of one hand around my thigh so that her fingernails dug into the flesh. My arms flailed and hit the vessels around me. One of them crashed into Captain sir's empty cup. When she closed her mouth around my penis and touched the tip of her tongue to the tip of my cock, I exploded.

My body bucked like I was on top of an angry bull, but she didn't let go of me. The orgasm could not have lasted longer than five seconds, but if so, it was the longest five seconds of my life. She freed both her hands and hugged my torso so that her mouth would not leave my manhood, and the harder my body convulsed, the louder I groaned, the tighter her lips clamped around me and the quicker her tongue worked.

Only after I had gone limp as a sock, her mouth left me and there was not a trace of white left anywhere, either on my penis or on her mouth. She looked up at me, but I turned my face away from her. She held my chin and wrenched it so that she could look into my eyes. 'Am I beautiful enough for you or not?' she asked, harshly.

I just nodded.

I saw Yasmin at her usual spot in front of the magazine stand. I had to clean up the kitchen floor after madam let me go, so I came to the market thirty minutes or so later than I usually did. The sun was out and Yasmin had her black gown folded over her shoulder. A cloth bag hung around her one arm, and with the free hand she was vigorously fanning herself. I sensed that she had finished her day's quota of berries.

I went to her and said hello.

She shaded her forehead with one hand and looked up, at first not recognizing me. Then she said, '*Hoye*!' She struggled to get to her feet. I gave her my arm. 'Hoye! I haven't seen you in such a long time!'

'Yes,' I said, 'where did you run away to?'

'Oh, don't ask. I had to go and set right my son-in-law, the bastard.'

'Finished picking out your vegetables?'

'Yes, yes,' she said, giving me a peek into her bag. 'The brinjals are good and so are the onions. Don't take the potatoes – full of insects.'

I nodded. 'What was wrong with your son-in-law?'

'The same thing that goes wrong with all men when their women become pregnant,' she said, spitting to the side. She was dressed in bright yellow and green. Her teeth appeared to have become whiter than I remembered them. 'The bastard began to sleep with another woman, just a girl of seventeen, too!' We began to walk up the road, towards the Radha Krishna temple. 'Forget about me,' she said. 'Tell me about *you*, my prince with the dreamy eyes. Has the lady pounced on you yet or are you still keeping her clawing fingers away?'

'Stop that,' I said, suddenly angry, looking straight at the road.

'Oh, what a temper you have,' she said. 'Necessary, too, if you're going to deal with a bitch like that, huh?'

'She is not that bad.'

'Arey waah, you seem to like her a lot. *Chalo*, at least finally she has found a servant that doesn't hate her guts.'

We walked for a while in silence. I debated with myself whether or not I should tell Yasmin about what happened the previous evening at homework and that morning in the kitchen. But we were on an open road, with people all around us, within earshot. Maybe if we had been in a closed room that day, I would have told her. But then something else stopped me too. I thought that if I told Yasmin, word would spread to other buildings and other servants. If there was one thing that you could *not* rely on Yasmin for, it was to keep a secret.

'I went to my daughter's house and lived there for a full month,' she said. 'I watched them closely. My daughter is also a dumb idiot, never speaks up, always bears whatever that dog does to her. I think God fits such people together, you know, like he fit my husband with me. Even if I talk the whole day, he will just sit there, work away at his sewing machine, listening, uttering a sound here and there. But not one word comes out of him. Not one!'

I was not surprised to hear that. Yasmin spoke more in one day than ten people would in two.

'After ten days, I understood what was going on. You can tell when the man is sleeping with another woman. He is *happier*, you know. He begins to sing when he is shaving. He smiles to himself for no reason. He uses perfume on his clothes. You look for such small signs, I told my daughter, but will she listen? Just a dumb girl with no tongue in her mouth. So I followed him when he went to "work" the next day and caught him cavorting with the girl.'

'No!' I said.

'Oh, yes,' she said proudly, adjusting her hair. 'I carried a knife with me too, and I jumped into the room and told him I will cut off his dick if he insists on sleeping with other women. He tried to act all strong and manly, but when I pulled out the knife, I think he saw that I meant what I said. I did too.'

We came to the end of the road, and both of us turned to the temple to touch our hearts. People worked inside the temple compound. A new concrete stage was being erected, maybe for storytellers and singers and such. A priest came out of the main temple and walked onto the courtyard, dipping leaves into a brass vessel of water and hoisting them up into the air.

Yasmin took a few steps away from me to cross the road. 'I will have to go now, boy. The ladies will scream if I come late on my first day back at work. But tomorrow, tell me all about your madam and what she's making you do.' She winked.

'Sure,' I said uncomfortably, and turned back towards the market.

My favourite part of the school into which Captain sir and madam had put me was the library. It reminded me of the book house in Singavaram, in which Javed bhai used to sit looking through his monocle and mending his clocks. It was a rather run down hut, away from the rest of the village, close enough to the river to hear the sound of the water heaving against the grassy banks. One had to jump over paved stones and cross a thick pile of bushes to get to the house, and for a bunch of us, it was a daily routine straight after school. Javed bhai would welcome us with a wide grin and a fresh packet of Poppins. He always kept the yellow and pink ones for me.

The smell of the air in the book house was that of freshly cut onion, because Javed bhai made for himself onion pakodas every day for lunch. No matter how hot it was outside, it seemed to be cool and comfortable inside the book house because it sat in a small clearing in the woods, between the interlaced branches of a banyan and a rosewood tree. When you walked in, you always had the light, airy feeling in your head, as though it was just about to rain. Javed bhai used to ask us to smell the first pages of each book we picked up, so that we could feel the touch of all those who had opened the book before us. Books are a way of travelling, he told us, to another place and time.

Each time we skipped through his watch table into the inner room we had to deposit a rupee coin, and if we wished to borrow a book, that would be three rupees for three nights. For all his jokes and laughs, Javed bhai never allowed anyone to touch his books without payment, and I tried too often in vain to get him to give away a book to me for free. A librarian had to live too, he used to say, and with the price of onions going up so rapidly, how was he to manage if he gave credit to everyone who asked?

Javed bhai left Singavaram with his books without telling anyone. One day he was there, jolly and talkative as ever, looking over his clocks, and the next, when we rushed there after school, we found the house empty, as though it hadn't been occupied in years. The smell of onion still stuck to the wooden boards and shelves, and it still felt on entering it that it may rain at any time. Around the same time, a girl called Sahitya was found dead in the river. Rumours began to spread that perhaps these two incidents were not unconnected. The old man at the bottom of the tree said that Javed bhai stole Sahitya's soul and trapped it inside a book and that Javed was not a librarian but a soul collector. Now that he had got her soul, he had gone on, to other villages, in search of other innocent children.

Mother had prayed to many gods in gratitude when she heard this story, and she beat me black and blue with a wooden ruler for having gone to the book house, forgetting all those days on which she beamed with pride at me reading all the English books that I borrowed from Javed bhai. She gave a whole hundred and sixteen rupees and ten kilos of Basmati rice to the old man of the tree, and in return he blessed me that he would protect me all my life from the black force of Javed bhai.

The library in my school in Hyderabad did not have the same smell, nor did it have the same feel of rain. But the books in its shelves had the same musty feel, stained brown along the edges, the print so old that you could not make out the 'h' from the 'b'. It was not even as big as the book house was, having been pushed into a corner behind the staff room. There were only five bookshelves, a big one along the main wall and two small ones on either side of the photocopier.

Right on the first day, after lunch, when all the other children played in the ground, I had wandered over to the library and seen that it had two different dictionaries. On that day, I wanted to look up the meaning of the word 'patriarchy'. I remembered the spelling from the news report of the night before, and I knew that Mrs Pradhan would be there, ready to help me.

In the break between the second and third periods, I ran along the corridor, wishing all the teachers that passed me by and entered the library. Mrs Pradhan looked up from her computer screen, and it seemed to me that she was hiding behind the big open register kept on the table. She pushed her round glasses up her nose with her middle finger and smiled at me. 'Did you come to continue reading *Romeo and Juliet*?' she asked. She was dressed, as was common for her, in a white sari with a blue border. She looked very much like one of those women in detergent commercials on television, only older.

'No, madam,' I said, making straight to the main book shelf where the big books sat on top of each other. 'I want to look up a word.'

In those two months, the school library became my second home and Mrs Pradhan the big sister I never had. I call her that but she was older than Ramya madam, her hair almost completely grey with sacks of loose skin beneath her eyes and around her chin. Her spectacles hung around her neck on a lace-like brown string. Now and then she would remove them and chew on the temple tips while reading a book. Sometimes she would let them hang over her chest while she went to the shelves, hunting for a title. Most times when she spoke to me, though, she kept them on, and when she wished to reprimand me, she lowered them down her nose, so that she could peer over the edge of the thin black frame.

By name and bearing she should have been the principal, I thought many times, instead of the short Hanumanta Rao who carried a cane that was as big as him. She often told me that it was one of her dreams, to run a school in which students could study without fear of punishment or homework. She would call it Tiny Tots, she said, where all the teachers would be called

'Aunty'. I asked her if she planned to be the principal of this school, and she nodded.

'What would the children call you?' I asked.

'Why? Big Aunty, of course,' she said, and laughed. I could picture Mrs Pallavi Pradhan as 'big aunty', striding up and down corridors, addressing school assemblies, terrorizing kids and teachers alike. In fact, she would even find herself at home in an army camp. For her imposing size and personality, it was not hard to imagine grown, hard men quivering in their knees.

She brought rice in her lunchbox every day. Only the kind of pickle changed with the day of the week. Dried mango pickle was her favourite. She would sit by herself at her desk and read while she ate, with a duster poised on the pages of the book while she fiddled with her spoon and mixed the pickle into the rice. On the fourth or fifth day after I had joined school, I happened to be in the library while she ate, seated on the table right in front of the counter with a copy of *Gulliver's Travels* in front of me.

'Would you like to have some?' she said, and when I looked up, she nodded and raised her box. 'My daughter made it. She makes the best pickles.'

I hesitated, but I had had only two chapattis for lunch that day, and my stomach had already begun to grumble. Besides, I was reading the part of the book where the Lilliputians organize a feast to welcome Gulliver, and the illustration showed all kinds of tiny delicacies that made my mouth water. Mango pickle was not the same as chocolate cake, but it was better than nothing. So I took my own empty box and went to her table. She had two pieces in her pickle, of which she gave me the smaller one. With her spoon she spaded about a third of the rice from her box into mine. 'Eat,' she said. 'You look so thin and malnourished. Doesn't your mother feed you well?'

I didn't tell her that my mother was dead and that I lived away from my parents. I thought it would be mean of me to sound ungrateful for all that madam and sir were doing to send me to school. What if they were not my real parents? They were in all ways that mattered.

But something in my expression must have given it away, because Mrs Pradhan's face changed, first to concern, then to pity. 'Oh, you poor child,' she said. 'Don't worry, you can find a mother in any woman you meet.'

'My mother used to say the same thing,' I said.

'She was right, of course,' said Mrs Pradhan, the belligerence in her tone returning. She adjusted her glasses. 'You can come here every day at lunch time. We will share our lunch together. Okay?'

'Okay.'

So it was that I found a friend in school. I have often wondered why she kept to the library at all times, why she only ventured out to the school grounds during the assembly and school functions, and even then only made polite conversation with one or two teachers. That is the fate that befalls librarians, I think, because they must be present in the library throughout the day, and while the rest of the teachers had the staff room to relax and socialize in, the librarian must stick to her books, for both work and for pleasure. Maybe it is no surprise then that they don't make friends with any of their colleagues.

If I had known this on that first day she shared her food with me, that she was perhaps as lonely as I was, I would have given her some of the pity in which I wallowed so selfishly.

Soon I began to visit her anytime I could – during recess, between periods, in sports class – and we became more than just lunch sharers. She began to look over my shoulder as I read; she told me how to pronounce the difficult words (rendezvous with the silent 'z' and 's', for example); she spoke about the different levels in which one could derive meaning from the various works of literature by the great masters – Shakespeare, Dickens, Dumas. She started me off with the illustrated children's versions, but then quickly took me to the biggest shelf where the originals were kept. For each page of the children's book, she read out to me the passages from the original. In most cases I found the illustrations inadequate and the words complete.

And of course, by and by we came to talk about rape, too.

It is possible to make friends with fear. During the first few days after the morning episode in the kitchen, I found myself on edge almost every second of the day. The closer Ramya madam moved to me, even in the presence of Captain sir, my heart thudded, my palms got sweaty, my ears went cold. But your body makes sense of all that after you spend a few days in that state. Once it convinces itself that that is the common state, it adjusts and the fear becomes a companion whose presence you take for granted. I would stop short of calling it serenity, but you achieve a sense of detachment, going about your tasks and yet ready for that moment in which she would pounce.

Patterns emerged with time. She liked to call for me in the mornings, after sir's car drove off. If they engaged in sex the night before, chances were higher that she would want me the morning after. Most evenings, she was too tired after her office, so she preferred a foot rub. Once or twice she commanded me to move up from the feet to her calves, then to her thighs, then further up. But mostly she was content with comfort in the evenings. That November we had a cold wave with temperatures dropping to single digits even during the day. On some of these evenings, she took me upstairs to the bedroom, held me close, rocked me and told me to rock her back. On one of these occasions, she pressed her face to my chest and wept.

She fussed over me like my mother would. She got angry when my test marks were not good. She made sure that I did my homework every day. She cleared my doubts. On Sundays, she made *kheer* and fed it to me while we sat upstairs under the pretext of homework. Sundays were hard for her because Captain sir stayed home all day, and she had to find ways to be alone with me. Some of the excuses she gave Captain sir were so far-fetched that I do not know how he bought them.

Even when she did want me, it was not always sex. Sometimes she wanted to be touched or hugged a certain way. She would push her hair away, point to a spot on the back of her neck, and ask me to kiss it. She would give me her hands and ask to squeeze my palms against hers. She would lie down, place her feet on my chest and slide one foot up to my mouth. When I closed my teeth around her big toe, she would shut her eyes and cover her breasts with her hands. 'Lick my belly button,' she would say, or, 'Give me a nice thigh stretch.'

People have said that all of these don't constitute rape because by this time I had stopped actively objecting to her demands. But I *did* object the first few times, and it took me nowhere. Every time I said no, she would smile and continue what she was doing, and hold my own body as witness against my wishes. If I hated it so much, she said, why did I ejaculate when she sucked me? Why did my breathing get heavy when she kissed me? Why did she only have to run her fingernails down my chest for my nipples to perk up? 'Are you not a man?' she asked me a few times when I hesitated. 'Here I am, a woman, asking you to take me, ravish me, taste me, make me moan with desire for you and you're saying you don't want to?'

I did not have answers for any of those, so I did what any man would have done in my place. I stopped saying no. But that didn't stop these questions from popping up in my head every time she beckoned me into the room. I noticed that occasionally she would act very loving toward Captain sir while I worked in the kitchen. She would kiss him and slide her hands under his shirt, looking at me and biting the corner of her lips as she did so. I didn't know what any of it meant, and every time I went into the bathroom after she had drained me, I would sit on the toilet seat with my eyes covered with my hands, and think.

The biggest weight in my heart in those times was that I could not talk to anyone about this. On one side there was this big mountain of gratitude that I owed them both, for putting me up in their house, for looking after me, for giving me an education. On the other, she was eating me from the inside, little by little every day, telling me all the while that I should like it. Savitramma had done the same, pretending to give while she took ravenously. Father would beat me to death if I were to go back and tell him what had happened. He would say that it was all my fault for having poisoned my heart towards a woman who I ought to worship as a mother.

At night, I would pray that Captain sir would not cross me and go upstairs, because that would mean that she would be hungry for me the next morning. I would sit up, peek through the holes at the smiling eyes of the elephant god, and besiege him to put Captain sir into a nice deep sleep. I heard that the elephant god had never married, that he was a lifelong bachelor. Some of my churlish friends in the village used to say that no woman would want to marry someone with the head of an elephant, but then he is a god. If he were to set his eyes on a woman and tell himself that he must have her, he would have her. So it must have been his choice, to pursue knowledge and food instead of women, staying forever young in the process, with the smile never leaving his eyes.

Rather wise.

SIX

I had no plans of telling Mrs Pradhan anything about Ramya madam that day. In fact, our conversation began the same way it usually did: she asked me what book I wanted to read, I told her (it was *Moby Dick*), she gave me a copy, I retreated to the corner table, and she returned to her desk with a refilled cup of hot water. Towards the end of the lunch break, I looked up from the book to see that she had a strange, vacant look in her eyes. She was staring into the distance, past the open door, at the empty playground. This disturbed me. It was not common to see Mrs Pradhan idle.

I sat watching her for a while. She scratched the smooth surface of the cup in her hand. She sighed. She pursed her lips. She shook her head. She removed her glasses and pinched her eyes. She looked at the computer screen, but only now and then, guiltily. Again she lapsed into her reverie, remembering to take careful sips of water every few seconds.

Gathering the book in my hands, I went to the table closest to her desk and pulled out a chair. She did not notice me. I covered my mouth with my hand as I bent over the book, but my eyes stayed on her, waiting. At last, as the bell rang, she looked at me, flustered, as though she had just realized that I was still there.

'What is the matter, madam?' I said, closing the book.

'Nothing,' she said. Her usually well done hair today looked frizzy and unkempt. The ring on her finger was tilted to one side. There was an orange stain on the edge of her sari, just where it disappeared over her shoulder. Her eyes looked weary and red, as though she had not slept well. And perhaps for the first time since we met, she had no perfume on her. None of these would have happened if there was nothing on her mind.

But I did not push. I took out my lunch box and opened it. 'Do you want some?' I said.

'Don't you have to go to class?' The second bell rang on the stage, and the sound of steps began to rain on the corridor, as teachers marched from the staff room toward their classes.

'No,' I said. 'We have a drawing class next. I took permission to stay in the library.'

She appeared pleased. 'Good. Are you going to spend it reading Moby Dick?'

'And eat my chapattis. I have mango pickle with it.' I held it up to her. 'Not as tasty as your daughter's, but not that bad either.'

'Don't talk to me about my daughter,' she said angrily. 'The things she said to me today – sometimes I wonder if it is all worth it.'

'All what?'

'All of this – getting married, having kids, bringing them up, spending so much time and money and effort on them, only for them to grow up and kick you in the behind so hard that you remember it all your life.'

I lowered my head and ate. I was neither married nor had kids, so I did not know how to respond.

'Leave it,' she said in a softer voice, sighing. 'Let her do what she wants with her life. Who am I to tell her what to do?'

I nodded. 'That is probably wise –'

'But I am something, am I not? I am her mother. When she was a child, did she tell me what I should feed her? Did she tell me what clothes I should buy for her, what sports she should play, what instruments to take up? Did I ask for her permission before I helped her with her homework?'

I shook my head.

Her handkerchief came out. She blew her nose into it. Then she stared at the playground for a minute or two. 'She wants to get into the movies,' she said at last, and blew her nose into her handkerchief again. 'She says she wants to go to Bombay.'

I thought of myself and Venkatesh in the first row in Sridevi Talkies, whistling and throwing coloured paper into the air when the heroine walked in. We wouldn't if we knew that she was Mrs Pradhan's daughter, of course, but no one else around us would stop. I thought of the songs on television, where twenty or so village boys danced around one scantily clad woman with their tongues hanging out of their mouths. Venkatesh and I used to wonder which village had dances and women of that kind; it certainly did not happen in ours. But we liked it that someone out there in the big city thought that we spent our evenings drinking and dancing around slutty women, and we whistled harder and threw more paper into the air.

'You wanted to know what patriarchy was,' she said. 'Did you find out?'

I nodded, and rattled off the dictionary meaning. 'A form of social organization in which the father is the supreme authority in the family, the clan, or tribe, and descent is reckoned in the male line, with the children belonging to the father's clan or tribe.'

'Do you know what patriarchal societies do?' she asked. When I shook my head, she took off her glasses and placed them on the table, resting on the upper edges of the frame. 'They place exceedingly high value on the physical beauty of women and they teach women to value themselves purely in terms of their beauty.'

I thought of the heroines again, holding their hips and swaying them this way and that.

'And the true sign of patriarchy is that women believe that. They think they have nothing to offer but their beauty and their bodies. I told Madhu that's not true. I told her that if she went into the movies, she will become an object, an item. But she would not listen.'

Mrs Pradhan would love her daughter to be a librarian, I thought. She would love it if her daughter would tell her that she wished to lose herself in the study of literature, to forego her vanity and forge for herself an image based on intelligence, maturity and empathy. But by being such a woman, she would become another Mrs Pradhan in another school, eating lunch by herself, saying hello with an awkward tick, forever adjusting her glasses. She would be known to perhaps five or ten people in all her life. If on the other side of the coin you see a world of fame and adulation, who could resist reaching for it? I wondered if some small part of Mrs Pradhan felt envious of her daughter.

I asked her if she did. She laughed.

'Let me show this to you,' she said, and clicked a couple of times on her machine and turned the screen around so that I could see it. On it was a black-and-white image of a young woman dressed in a t-shirt and baggy pants, sitting on a rock with her hand laid on her thigh and the wind in her hair, her neck craned, her eyes covered with shades. She seemed to be looking up at something. She had a wide smile, her small white teeth peeping out between dark brown lips.

'Who do you think that is?'

I began to shake my head, but something about the manner in which she smiled as she said those words made me stop. 'You,' I said in wonder, drawing myself closer to the picture. 'You!'

'What did I tell you about patriarchal societies?' she said, her smile turning hard at the edges. 'We believe what we're told. We're as much to blame as the ones we shout and yell at when someone gets raped.'

'You – were in the movies?'

'Oh, no, not in the movies. But I was beautiful once, you see. And I was vain, and I was proud, and I turned heads wherever I went. Did I like it? Did I know it? Of course! Did I want it any other way? Only when someone whistled at me or sang a lurid song as I passed. But I knew I couldn't have one without the other.' I now recognized the vacant gaze in her eyes. She was not looking at the playground. 'We all manipulate the rules to our benefit, Nari, and cry foul when they turn against us.'

'Why don't you explain it to your daughter the way you're doing to me?' I said. 'Maybe she will listen.'

'She won't.' Mrs Pradhan shook her head. 'I didn't when I was young. I only realized it all after I got older, after all that beauty left me, bit by bit. Now all that is left of me is my mind, and I am terribly, terribly ashamed of my body.' She looked at me with reddened eyes. 'I don't get through one day without looking at myself in the mirror and grimacing. Whom do I have to thank for all of that?'

'The society?'

'Myself?' she said, as if wondering. She slipped one temple of her glasses into her mouth. 'Too often when we rail against society we forget that it is made up of people like us. I am trying to save Madhu from all this – all the brainwashing, all the subtle suggestions of image and physical beauty – but I suppose she has to learn her own way, as I did.' She tapped a finger on the raised temple of her spectacles a few times, then she chuckled. 'You must think me such a bore.'

'Oh,' I said, 'no, not at all. I – you just made me think, that's all.'

'I promise you that I will make it up to you by listening to all of your problems,' she said, replacing her glasses on the bridge of her nose and pushing them up. 'If you have any. But now bring that chapatti over here and let me have a taste.'

For the rest of the afternoon we did not speak about her daughter or the movies or item numbers. She said that the pickle reminded her of her mother's pickle and the terrace of her childhood home on which they used to dry the cut mangoes and salt them. 'This is good,' she said, licking her lips and the tips of her fingers. 'You know, I was an only child to my parents, born after four miscarriages. So you can imagine how naughty I must have been growing up.'

'I know a bit of that,' I said with a smile. 'I was the king of the house until my sister Raji was born. After that I became little more than a servant. No matter what she did or didn't do, it was my fault. I sometimes prayed to God to take her away in the middle of the night.'

'But he never did, of course,' she said.

I shook my head. 'Never did.'

'I can't imagine my childhood with a sibling. But now, I sometimes think that it would have been nice to have an older brother.' She looked at her oily hand. 'My father died last year.'

'My mother died five years ago,' I told her. 'I know what you mean.'

She took the last piece of chapatti and swept the bottom of the bowl with it, gathering the last bits of scattered oil from the pickle. Folding and placing it into her mouth, she said, 'We seem to have a lot in common, young man. Some day you will tell me your big story of woe, won't you? I promise I will listen to it as patiently as you listened to mine.'

'Definitely,' I said, but felt a little pluck at my chest as I did.

I went back to the library that day after school finished. Mrs Pradhan was dusting the desks with a newspaper. Moby Dick still lay open on its spine, and the pages fluttered back and forth in the breeze. In the corridor I heard voices and laughter of teachers as they bid one another goodbye. A great sea of blue uniforms, schoolbags and water bottles covered the playground. The sports master, Mr Sadanandam, waltzed over the stage, whistle in mouth, cane in hand, watching it all like a hawk, eager to pick out and summon any misbehaving children and rap them on their buttocks.

Mrs Pradhan looked up at me, and seemed to understand straight away why I was there. She nodded me to enter and went to return the newspaper to its shelf. I pulled out the chair opposite the open book and sat on it. The seat felt warm to my thighs. I placed my palms flat on the table and left an impression in the thin film of dust that had already begun to accumulate behind Mrs Pradhan.

She came back and sat opposite me, closing the book with a thud and pushing it away to the edge. 'You wanted to talk to me about something, Nari?' she said.

I nodded, but the prickly feeling of cold sweat on my back intensified. I felt like someone had tied my intestines in a knot and was now pulling the ends. My mouth had gone dry. I kept thinking of the trust that I was betraying, the secret that was meant to be just mine and Ramya madam's. Even now nothing was lost, I told myself. I could just turn back and flee the room and no one would know anything. I could think of something to tell Mrs Pradhan the next day.

'You're afraid to tell me,' said Mrs Pradhan. She leaned a touch closer and tried to meet my shifting eyes with hers. 'You don't need to be. I will listen to whatever you say, and I will not judge.'

I looked up at her. The evening light reflected off her glasses and gave her eyes a strange, translucent quality. They seemed to brim with concern – for my welfare – and fervour – to somehow help me cast away the pain.

So I began to tell her about Ramya madam. I began the tale right at the beginning, from the very first day I had begun work at Captain sir's house to the day on which she first helped me with my homework. Mrs Pradhan did as she promised; she listened. But as the story went on, I noticed that she became a little restless. The voices and laughter in the corridor had died down. Even Mr Sadanandam had left. The playground was once again empty, mired by a cloud of dust left behind by pounding boots. The sun had snuck behind the line of guava trees that stood along the outer edge of the school compound. Mrs Pradhan's eyes no longer had the same glassy look.

I then told her about the first time Ramya madam raped me, and at places Mrs Pradhan let out little gasps, of shock, of disgust, of disbelief. She kept looking at the front door as the shadows lengthened and darkened all around us. I thought she would get up and turn the lights on, but she didn't. Only when I looked a little more closely at her darting eyes did I realize that she was afraid. She was afraid of me.

I stopped speaking. My lips parted. She did not ask me to continue. 'I think you should go home now,' she said, a little squeak of fear accompanying her firm tone. 'It's late, and I should lock up the library. We'll speak tomorrow, I promise.'

I got up and gathered my bag and water bottle. 'I will help you lock up,' I said.

'No, no, that is not necessary at all.' She forced a smile. 'You go on home. I – have a little work that I have to finish. Please don't wait for me.'

I came out of the room and looked to my left, then to my right, along the corridor. On the edge of the stage, a boy and a girl in uniform sat with their legs dangling, talking among themselves, and looking up now and than at the main gate. Nothing else stirred in the whole compound. Even William's typewriter was silent. The staff room, the principal's office and the attender's chamber were all locked.

I set out in the direction of the back gate. It had got rather dark by the time I reached home.

They say a woman can smell deceit from a mile away. That evening, when I returned home, I found Ramya madam sitting with her legs crossed, not on her usual side chair, but on the one facing the door. Her right arm hugged the armrest, and her fingers wrapped around the edge. As I unlocked the door and let myself in, she stopped shaking her foot. She was in a red sari and a sleeveless black blouse.

'Where were you?' she said.

'Madam, I –'

'You've been coming late from school these last few days. Found a friend, have you?'

'No, madam, I – just spent some time in the library, that's all.'

She raised her eyebrow. 'The library, huh? You fancy the librarian so much?'

I did not know to this day how she read it in my eyes. Maybe I was not as good a liar as I thought I was. But once she made her guess, I began to sweat. She got up and walked slowly to me. She looked up into my eyes, tilted her head first to the left, then to her right. 'A fresh young thing, is she? Hotter than me?'

'Madam, no!' I said, suddenly awake to what she thought. 'She's old, much older than you are.'

'Ah,' said madam, 'then I have whetted your appetite for old ladies.'

'No, madam, it's not as you think.' Sweat poured down me now, from my temples, down my neck, under my armpits. 'We just talk.'

'Just talk, eh?' She took my collar in both hands and yanked at it. The top two buttons of my shirt popped open and fell to the ground. 'Like you and I talk, huh? What do you talk about?'

I tried to push her away, to shake myself free, but her grip was strong. My hands fell on her waist. 'Uh, we talk about books, mainly.'

'Oh, books! Books! You stay back after school to meet your librarian, and you tell me you talk about books and I should believe you?'

'I am telling you the truth, madam.'

'You little piece of shit,' she said in a low, deliberate voice. I blinked and covered my head with my hands. She let go of my shirt. 'You little ungrateful piece of shit.' She went into the bedroom and came out in a minute, holding Captain sir's cane in her hand. 'I gave you everything I had, didn't I?' She pushed me back with the edge of the cane, and when I backed up against the wall, she drew a line from the base of my neck down my chest, to my belly button. 'I gave you all that I had. Tell me, was there anything lacking in what I did for you?'

I sat down on my haunches, still covering myself with my hands. The cane travelled to the back of my neck, tracing light circles on my skin. I shook my head as hard as I could. 'No,' I said, and my voice came out in a whimper.

'I thought we had something special, Nari, you and I. It was going to be our little secret, wasn't it?' I lowered my head further and waited for a rasping blow, but it never came. '*Wasn't it?*' I looked up and nodded furiously. 'Get up.' She moved the cane up and down in straight vertical lines. I stumbled to my feet, using the wall as support. 'Get in.' I went into Captain sir's bedroom.

'Then what happened, Nari?' she said, following me in and slamming the door shut. 'Captain is not going to come back for another two hours from now, so you better start answering me. Or I will whip you until your pretty skin goes blue.'

'I – I don't know what you want me to say, madam. What shall I say?' I climbed the bed, sat on my knees, and joined my hands. 'Anything you want me to say, I will say it.'

'Ah.' She bent the cane between her hands with her thumbs. 'Now you're the obedient Nari who will do my bidding. What happened when you went to your librarian and talked about books? Hmm?' She tapped the edge of the bed with the cane and watched me. 'What else did you talk about?' Tap. Tap. Tap. 'Did you talk about me?' Tap. Tap. Tap.

'No.'

'Don't lie to me, Nari.'

'I – I did not tell her the whole thing.'

Her face changed. All this while a thin, diabolical smile was playing at the corner of her lips. But now it vanished, and her eyes became small white holes of hate. 'The whole thing,' she hissed. 'Does that mean you told her a part of the story?'

'Only a little part, I promise.'

'I took care of you, Nari,' she said in a low voice. The tendons in her neck stood out. 'I took care of you like a mother would. I gave you so much. I educated you. I sucked your god-damned cock. Did I not?' I crawled over to the edge of the bed farthest from her. She covered the distance in two steps and landed a full-blooded blow on my calf, saying, 'Did I not?'

'You did,' I said. 'You did, you did, you did.'

'Then you go out and tell people about us? Do you think I should go out and tell people too? Huh? Do you know what will happen if I do? Do you think anyone with a smidgen of a brain would actually *believe* you?'

I shook my head. I rubbed my calf and shook my head.

'Good,' she said, her voice low again. 'You're smarter than you look. Even your librarian – did she believe you? Did she say that she will help you?'

I thought of Mrs Pradhan's eyes when I told her the story. I saw the hope with which she looked at the front door as I recited my tale, a hope that someone would walk in and protect her from me. Not once in those three months had I seen her look at the front door with such longing, or at me with such fear. I shook my head, and for some reason tears streamed down my cheeks.

'She didn't, did she?' said madam. 'That's because she doesn't *understand* you, Nari, the way I do.' She hurled the cane against the wall and came closer. She clutched me to her bosom, and when I resisted, she took both my hands and put them on her breasts. 'She doesn't understand you, Nari. She doesn't understand *us*.'

I looked up into her eyes, but in the gathering darkness I could only see a dark shadow over her face. She removed her sari. She pushed me over the bed and sat on me. She leaned over, reached out behind her and snapped her bra open. She shoved her breasts into my face. 'Suck them,' she said. I did. 'Yes,' she said. 'Good boy. You love me, don't you?' I nodded, even as my hands fumbled over her outer thighs. 'Yes, good boy.' Then she pinned my hands to the bed and ran the tip of her tongue down my neck.

I lay there like a corpse, aware of the steady drone of the ceiling fan but not hearing it. She undressed me. She went down on me. She had sex with me. All the while she asked me if I loved her. And I kept nodding yes.

It may have been a week or ten days after this that things began to unravel. Life for me went back to normal in that gap. Things in school got a little strange. Mrs Pradhan stopped sharing her lunch with me. She employed a young boy who stood at the door and kept me in his sights at all times. Once or twice I went after school to make notes on Hamlet, and I noticed him loitering around the corridor as I entered. He followed me to the shelf and back to the table, always at a respectable distance. He stood behind my shoulder all the while I scribbled on my pad. Mrs Pradhan did not once look at me.

I stopped going to the library all that often, therefore. I ate my lunch on the stage now, by myself, watching the kids stumble and jump about as Mr Sadanandam strode up and down, his chest puffed out, an angry frown set into his face. Every time he walked passed me, I felt that he stopped for a second longer than necessary, as though he wished to breathe down my neck and let me know that he had me.

At home, not much had changed. Captain sir and madam fought four or five times at dinner that week, and on each night sir went to madam's room after the lights went out. And on each of the following mornings, after sir's car drove away, madam summoned me – to the upstairs bedroom, to the kitchen, once on the living room floor, once on the stairs even. She had begun to get dark circles around her eyes and her lips had turned a strange bluish colour.

On the last day of the week, she came home and left immediately after, saying that she had to go to a friend's house. About an hour after she left, Captain sir came home. He took off his shoes and stretched his bare feet on the table. Sipping the coffee I gave him, he sank himself in thought for a while. Then, as though awakened by a splash of water on the face, he jerked up and asked where madam was.

'She went to a friend's place,' I replied.

'A friend's place, huh?' said Captain sir. 'She's been visiting a lot of friends lately. Just the other day I called in on her office and the receptionist told me that she had taken the day off and gone out.'

I carried the coffee cup into the kitchen and began to wash it. I dipped my hand in the bowl of hot water by the stove and touched the cut brinjal pieces soaking in it. Not soft enough yet. The sound of beeping keys came from the living room. 'Hello?' said Captain sir. 'Ankita, this is Captain Tirthankar speaking'

I didn't know who Ankita was, but something about sir's manner, the sure, confident way in which he spoke, warned me that it was all going to end soon. He would know, I thought, staring at the water drain in the middle of the sink. He would know, and then so would the whole world. I could go to him now and tell him everything. But then I remembered Mrs Pradhan; if I could not convince her that I was speaking the truth, what chance had I with Captain sir? My only refuge was Ramya madam and the hope that she would somehow guide me through this unscathed.

'Yes,' sir was saying. 'I will meet you for dinner in half an hour. Do you have all the things that you said you would collect for me? Thank you! Thank you very much. If you also give me your bank account details, I will do the needful at my end. Oh, and yes, I will make sure your father gets the best treatment out there. I will personally refer him to Yashomati. I have a lot of contacts there.' He paused to listen for a moment. I looked over my shoulder, at the wide, plastic grin pasted across his face. 'Why, I should thank you, my dear girl, for all the help you've given me. Yes ... Yes. Let's say half-past seven, just in case there's traffic.'

He returned the phone to his pocket and pulled his shoes to him again. 'Nari!' he called out. I went to the kitchen door. 'I am going out for dinner. Don't make anything for me. Just you and madam today, okay?'

'Yes, sir,' I said.

'If madam comes, give me a call and I will hurry back home. Just tell her I am out to meet a friend.' He was buttoning up the sleeves of his shirt. 'If she asks who, tell her it's an old army colleague.' The buckles of his breeches went click. He slipped his socks on, wore his shoes, laced them up and marched to the door. 'See you later tonight, Nari.'

'Yes, sir.'

I locked the door and pressed my back to it, staring at the empty couches. There was no one else in the house, and yet I seemed to hear sounds – of Captain sir's cane, of the water in madam's shower, of the whistle on the pressure cooker, of the dinner plate hitting the floor and clanging away. I stood listening to them, and from beneath them all I heard the soft, clear, ringing laugh of Savitramma in the shadow of the jasmine tree on a moonlit night.

I went to the kitchen and checked the brinjal. They had soaked enough now. I emptied the water into the sink and turned on the stove. I washed the pan before placing it on the flame. In a few seconds the water drops began to run and vanish noisily. I dropped a spoon of oil in the middle and spread it with a spatula. Silence returned to my mind, amid all this. The sounds died down.

SEVEN

Madam did not come home that night. Sir returned at around eleven, after I had gone to sleep. I turned on my bed towards the wall as he entered, and when he saw me moving he asked if madam had come. I said no. He shut the main door, took off his shoes and made his way into the bedroom. He softly shut the door behind him, and immediately after, the fan began to creak.

The next morning I woke up early and left for the market with my vegetable bag, hoping to run into Yasmin. I found her at her usual spot, spitting out berry seeds. When she saw me, her smile faded, as though she could read my thoughts. She asked me how I was and told me that I should eat more because my bones were beginning to show.

'I need to talk to you, Yasmin,' I said.

She took me behind the newspaper shop, past a dump yard, on top of a large covered sewer. The stench in the air was unbearable. Looking at my expression she tapped me on the head with a knuckle. 'I don't have an AC room for you, boy. Whatever you want to say, say it here and no one but you and I will know of it.'

'It is about Ramya madam.'

She peered into her paper cone and fished for more berries with her finger. She found one and popped it into her mouth. Nodding at me, she said, 'I figured. The bitch has started fucking you, hasn't she?'

'Yes.' I did not tell her for exactly how long. 'She says she loves me.'

Yasmin burst out laughing and almost choked. She slapped herself on the scalp a few times, coughing. Her eyes watered. 'What did you say?' she said. 'She said she loves you and you, lover boy, you believe her?'

'Should I not?'

'Arey yaar,' she said, bundling up the paper cone and tossing it on the heap of waste. 'Let me tell you something about women of that type. Trust me, I know of them because my son-in-law slept with one of them. She will tell you that she loves you, but do you know how many other men she is saying the same things to? *Hain*?'

I shook my head.

'What about the boy in her office? Does she love him too? What about her husband? I suppose she loves him the most, which is why she is not leaving him.' She ran her tongue against her teeth and laid a hand on my shoulder. Yasmin had big, strong hands, almost as big as mine. 'Listen, boy,' she said, 'if you think she has anything for you that even resembles love, then you're just stupid.'

I said, 'But she doesn't listen to me. No matter how many times I say no, she – she –'

'Haan, of course. They've given you shelter, haven't they? And they're paying for your school as well. Of course she will think that she owns you.' Yasmin wagged a finger at me. 'But remember, she doesn't own you. *Nobody* owns you. Samjhey?'

'I – I don't know what to do. I feel like my chest is caving in every morning. Today when I woke up and realized that she wasn't at home, I felt so good. Every morning, every single morning, Yasmin, after Captain sir leaves –'

She looked closely at me. 'Hey,' she said, 'tell me something honestly, will you?' I nodded. 'Do you, at *any* level, *like* what she does to you?'

'No,' I said. 'No, well, I don't know!'

'Ah!'

'No, you don't understand. I think of her as my mother. She – she tells me stories, she helps me with my homework, she feeds me when Captain sir isn't looking.' I felt my eyes smarting, and I clutched the back of my hand to them to push back the tears. 'But for what she does to me when Captain sir isn't at home, she – she's just like my mother.'

'You haven't answered my question. Do you like it?'

'I don't,' I said, my voice rising and immediately falling to a whisper. 'But my body does!'

'So you – uh –'

'Yes. Yes. Yes!'

'But you don't like it.'

'No, of course not.' I suddenly noticed the buzz of flies around us. I waved them away, but they kept returning. They were everywhere, on the empty juice bottles, the rotting banana peels, the berry seeds that Yasmin had just chucked. 'Tell me, Yasmin, what should I do? Now I think Captain sir has found something out about madam. She did not come home last night, and sir spoke with someone on the phone – I – I am scared, Yasmin.'

'Oye,' she said, slapping me on the shoulder. I bent my head to my chest. A low wail came out of me, and I turned away, ashamed. 'Oye!' She held me by the collar and wrenched me around. 'You haven't done anything wrong, so stop crying first. Man! You're such a girl!'

She stood with her arms folded, watching me cry. When I finally stopped, she said, 'That took a while. Now look. Have you told anyone else but me about this?'

'I told the librarian at the school.'

'Did she go all nuts on you?'

'Yes, she – we were good friends. As soon as I told her about it, she became frightened of me. I could see it in her eyes.'

'Well,' said Yasmin, 'what do you expect? You tell anyone in the world that a woman raped you and people will say, what? Get real! They would say that you should just cooperate and enjoy it. Thank your lucky stars that a woman is fucking you.'

'But you believe me, don't you?' Whether she did or not, I could not tell. But she did not disbelieve me. At least she was willing to consider the possibility that I was speaking the truth. She frowned and sniffed and waved the flies away, looking in the direction of the magazine stand.

'Go and tell everything to Captain,' she said.

'Are you crazy? He will skin me alive!'

'You should tell him first – before she does. If she goes to him, he will hear her version first, and I am telling you, then he won't even listen to you. This way you at least get to tell him what you're going through.'

'But –'

'Buy for yourself a recorder,' she said, turning to me. 'Yes, do that, and turn it on when she comes on to you next time. Record everything, her voice, her words, everything, and play it for Captain.'

'Will you – come with me?'

She looked aghast at the suggestion. 'Me? What do you need me for, hotshot? It is not me whom his wife is fucking. If you drag me into this, the entire block will come to know of it, and then how will I feed my family? Eh? You better leave me out of this, okay?'

'But Yasmin, you're the first person who believed me. I need you by my side.'

I must have begun to cry again, because she looked at me with a tired expression, both hands on hips. 'All right, all right, just stop crying, you big baby. You first do what I said. Record all that happens, okay? You know how to work one of those things?'

'I think I do,' I said.

'They're not hard to figure out. Once you have two or three incidents recorded, bring them over to me first, all right?' She narrowed her eyes. 'You have to convince me first. Right now I am just taking you on your word. If – and only if – I see that you're speaking the truth, then I will come with you and speak to the Captain. All right?' She spat at the rubbish heap. 'What things you make me do – now dry your eyes quickly! Before someone starts talking about you and me in this dump. My old man will leave me then.'

She started back towards the main road, and after taking a few moments to compose myself, I ran and caught up with her at the market. We walked together to the end of the road in absolute silence. The new stage in the Radha Krishna temple compound was almost ready. They were putting up plantain and mango leaves on the eaves. Both of us turned to the idol and touched our hearts. I said a silent prayer. Without turning to me or a word of goodbye, Yasmin crossed the road and walked away.

As I turned the bend in the road leading up to the main gate of the house, I saw a tiny helmeted young woman speed away on her pink scooter. After a few seconds of puzzled recollection, I realized that she was the girl I had seen in madam's office on the day I saw her with that man. Was this the girl that Captain sir spoke to last night on the phone? My heart began to sink for

Ramya madam already, as I hurried up to the gate. Outside the door I saw her sea blue shoes. So she had come back.

I left my slippers and bounded in, to see Captain sir holding madam by her hair. The look of his eyes reminded me of a bull whose nose had been rubbed in red chilli powder. He took no notice of me, but Ramya madam cried out to me for help. At least she *started* to cry out, only to be quieted by a massive slap right across her face. 'Shut up!' he said, and she zipped her mouth close, whimpering mournfully like a piglet. He dragged her across to the staircase and pulled her up one step at a time, muttering things that I could not quite catch. She kept shaking her head to what he said, but she did not struggle to free herself. Her cheeks had already turned red. The blow I had witnessed had not been the first one.

I stood in the middle of the room, looking up at them, my full vegetable bag hanging off my arm. They disappeared into the upstairs bedroom, and as soon as the door closed behind them, everything went quiet. The coffee table was clean, the couch covers had been dusted and re-laid. I went into the kitchen and began to put the vegetables into the fridge. My ears perked up for any sound at all that would come from upstairs, but nothing did. My hands shivered. Twice I dropped potatoes on the floor and sent them rolling across the room to the staircase. After all the vegetables had gone in, I slid back the case and squatted at the base of the fridge, feeling the cold fumes from the fridge tickle my hair.

How much did she tell him about us? How much would she tell him during the course of this night, under the incessant rain of his beatings? Would he come down and drag me too, into the other room? I rubbed my arms, under the sleeves of my shirt, against the cold. I removed a bottle of water from the stand and poured it into my mouth. No matter how much I drank, the thirst did not die. The water crept over the corners of my mouth and spilled onto the floor.

I didn't know how long I sat there, but when the cuckoo clock chimed nine times, I got up out of habit, pulled two eggs into my hand and went into the kitchen. I lit up the stove, placed the small pan on the flame, and broke the eggs on its edge. As the yolk spread on the surface, I tried to listen again for sounds. But even then all was quiet.

He did not come downstairs until an hour had passed, long after the toast and omelette had gone soggy. There was no song on his lips this morning, but when he saw me, he smiled brightly, too brightly. He sat down at the table, folded the omelette in half, wedged it between two slices of bread, and ate it in three giant bites. He removed the lid from the top of the milk glass, took one or two careful sips, and after ascertaining that it was no longer hot enough to scald his lips, finished it too in three gulps. He sighed loudly, in apparent contentment. 'Thank you, Nari,' he said. 'That was a very good breakfast.'

I hung my head and did not say anything. At least the good thing about it was that madam had not yet told sir about us. I had to heed Yasmin's words: I had to be the first to tell sir, but I was yet to buy a voice recorder. I had no idea how much one of those things cost; from memory, I had perhaps three hundred rupees in my bag after the money order I had sent to Singavaram at the beginning of the month. I fervently hoped that it would be enough.

Captain sir went and sat on the main couch, behind the coffee table and folded one leg over another. 'Nari,' he said. 'Come here, will you?'

I went and sat on the floor next to the entrance to sir's bedroom. The morning breeze that drifted in through the main door chilled my upper arm. I slid a hand under my sleeve and rubbed it. I kept my head cocked upward, listening to what sir had to say. A faint tug of fear was still present in my mind.

'There is no use pretending that everything is all right,' said sir sternly, the harshness directed more toward himself than at me. 'You have seen what has happened, haven't you? Your madam has been unfaithful to me for a few months now, with a man who works with her at the clinic.'

I nodded, and only just stopped myself from saying: 'I know.'

'She will spend most of her time in the room upstairs from now on,' he said. 'She's not to be allowed to go to the clinic anymore or meet that man. In fact, she's not to be allowed to leave the house at all.' He had been looking down at his hands all this while. Now he eyed me. 'Do you think you can manage that?'

'Me, sir? But – how can I – madam –'

'She won't try anything,' said Captain. 'Even if she does, you're strong enough to overpower her. I am going to rely on you to keep her in the house, Nari, until all of this blows over.' He did not say when or how this would 'blow over', but I nodded. 'You're not going to abuse her, you understand,' he said. 'But you can use gentle force – *if* she resists. But she won't. I have made sure that she understands the consequences if she does.' At that moment I saw the gleam in Captain sir's eyes. He was enjoying this, I thought. He was not unhappy that this had happened. He was glad, he was alive because now he could exert his power over her and have no one question him. Suddenly the breeze did not seem all that chilly.

'It will take time for her to get over him,' he said, his eyes once again moving away from me to his hands. He had small hands for a man of his size – stubby fingers and puffy, water-balloon-like palms. The knuckles were barely visible even when he closed his fists. 'But she will, and all will be okay again. We can all go back to our normal lives.'

I felt like laughing at him. Savitramma used to say that we all live life bound by lines. Once we step over a line and cross it, often there was no going back, no matter how much we wished it. I felt like the three of us – Captain sir, madam and me – had stepped over that line that morning, into a new world. Going back to the old, 'normal' world was not going to be as easy as Captain sir seemed to think.

'We just need to give her time,' he said. 'Time heals everything. Everything!' He twisted his fingers together. 'We just need to give her time. And make sure that she doesn't meet the man she fell in love with. With enough time, she will forget him and she will come around. She will come back, Nari. She will come back. I am confident that she will.'

I raised my knees, rested my chin on them, gazed at the spotless white marble floor.

'You will help me bring her back into our lives, won't you, Nari?' he said, and I thought I detected a thin shiver in his voice. 'I need your help. Without your help, she will be gone. She will leave me. You have to help me.'

'Yes, sir,' I said, though I had no idea what I was saying yes to.

'Thank you, Nari,' he said. 'I knew I could rely on you. You're a good boy, Nari, and one day you will grow up to be a fine young man.' He sniffed, and reached into his breast pocket. He produced two keys bunched together in a ring. 'I have locked the upstairs room. Here are the keys. I will keep one, and you keep one. Okay?'

The breeze picked up, and the hair on his scalp shifted. He did not notice. He just ran an absent hand through it, ruining it even further. At once he looked dazed and confused. He fiddled with the ring and freed one key. Pushing the other one at me, he said, 'Now, madam will be hungry. Take something up for her to eat, will you?'

'Yes, sir,' I said, pocketing the key. I got up to go into the kitchen for a tray. As I was about to enter, sir called me and I stopped.

'And Nari,' he said, 'don't tell anyone about this, okay?'

'Yes, sir, of course.'

The sales boy at the store looked me up and down. 'How much do you have?' he said.

Mother always said never to tell people exactly how much money you have in your pocket. So I said, 'A hundred?'

He was no more than seventeen, this boy, with a thin black line of moustache colouring his upper lip. A tuft of hair stood out at the very base of his chin, and he kept caressing it with pride every two seconds. He turned an unused matchstick in his left ear and examined it closely. 'A hundred?' he said at last, not bothering to look at me. 'Come back next month. The cheapest one we have costs two hundred. What do you get for a hundred rupees these days?'

'Does it work?'

'Does it matter? You don't have two hundred, do you?'

I thought for a moment. 'I may.'

'Oh,' said the boy. 'You "may". Then I "may" show it to you, and it "may" work.'

The older man at the cash counter chuckled away while counting his notes, and I realized they were making fun of me. I considered walking out, but this was the only electronics store in the block, and I had to get back home quick, to keep watch on madam. So I swallowed and said, 'Show it to me.'

The boy's phone rang, and he whipped it out and spoke into it, turning back at the same time to reach up to one of the upper shelves. He pulled out a blue and white pack and looked at it, leaving the matchstick half-buried in his ear. 'I *said* I am sorry,' he spoke into the phone. 'How many times should I apologize to you over the same thing?' A female voice chattered away from the other end. He turned, slid the pack over and nodded at me. 'Baby, no, you know I did not mean that.'

'Put the phone down, Chotu,' said the man at the counter, still counting his notes.

'Baby, I have to go. Boss says I can't talk.' And he cut the girl mid-sentence. He rolled his eyes at me and shook his head. 'Never, ever have a girlfriend, my friend.'

'I never will,' I said, glad to be on his side. 'Will you please show me how this works?'

He pulled out the device from inside the pack, inserted the battery, and turned it on. 'Say something,' he said. 'What's your name?'

'Nari.'

'What's your girlfriend's name?'

Another chuckle came from the man counting the notes. I had half a mind to strike him across the face. Instead, 'I don't have a girlfriend,' I said.

'Good enough.' He turned the machine off, then pressed the button next to it. All our words got played back with reasonable clarity. I could tell my voice from his, which was the important thing. Even the cash-counting man's chuckle was distinct.

'Will it work even if I put it in my pocket while recording?'

The boy's interest went back to the matchstick, but he nodded.

'I will take it,' I said, and paid out the two hundred bucks.

At lunch, Ramya madam looked better than she had in the morning. Her hair was now more presentable, the marks on her face were already beginning to fade and she even managed a smile when I entered with a tray full of food. I had in my pocket my new possession. Though I was doubtful if she would be in the mood to pull me into bed today, I thought there was no harm in being ready.

She ate one small morsel at a time, stopping for a drink every few minutes. I sat at the far corner behind the door, watching her. After a while she said, 'Don't look at me like that, Nari. I am not going to try and escape from here.'

'Uh, no, madam –'

'And don't deny it either. I know what Captain must have told you. He asked you keep an eye on me, didn't he? You're my watchdog, eh?'

I looked down at the floor. I rubbed my bare feet on the cold marble.

'Good old Nari,' she said. 'As gullible as ever.' She removed the lid on the bowl of yoghurt, and emptied it over the rice on her plate. With a spoon she began to prod at it. 'You have a mind too, Nari,' she said. 'Don't forget that. You can see how Captain is treating me. Would you have let your father treat your mother this way?'

I shook my head. I was not lying. I really wouldn't have.

With the same spoon she took a bit of pickle and mixed it with the rice. 'This yoghurt is nice. Thank you, Nari.' She raised the plate off the tray and began to eat. She looked pained when she chewed on her food, and I guessed her jaw was giving her trouble. I could not bear to look, so I turned away.

'There is a good man inside you,' she said. 'You're a fine young man. You're considerate, you're kind and you're loyal. You know what is right and what is wrong.' She scraped the last bits of rice off her plate. 'You can see, can't you, who is right and who is wrong here – me or Captain?'

I nodded, not because I knew who was right – I didn't – but because I did not want her to take back any of her compliments. I felt nice when she talked to me. She approved of me. Unlike Captain sir, who thought I would one day grow up into a fine young man, she thought I was *already* one.

'Good old Nari,' she said again. 'You will take these plates away, won't you? And if you come back in a couple of hours, we will do your homework. I take it that you're not going to go to school while you keep watch on me. We have to make sure that doesn't affect your exams.'

I got up and gathered the bowls, one by one, and left the room. I locked it on the outside and made my way down to the kitchen.

I went back up to her room two hours later, as she had said, my schoolbag slung over my left shoulder, the recorder nestled in my right pocket. Looking back now, it amazes me how I never thought I was in any physical danger. It never occurred to me that madam had it in her to injure a person. If I had known, I would have thought twice before entering that room unless I absolutely had to.

As it was, she woke up just as I opened the lock and swung the door open. She smiled and motioned me over to the bed. She went to the bathroom for a few minutes, and returned fresh and bright. I thought this would be my chance, that she would come on to me now, that I could record everything and play it for Captain sir's benefit at the end of the day. One part of me was jubilant, for this could be the day I broke free of her, but another darker part of me cowered in disgust, for thinking that way about a woman who had been a mother and had given me so much.

But she did not touch me that afternoon. She helped me with profit and loss and percentages in Mathematics, the passive voice in English grammar, a particularly convoluted Telugu poem, and in understanding the functioning of the human heart. She got me to draw it on a piece of paper, in outline, and label the ventricles, the auricles and the valves. When I got it right, on the second try, she ran her fingers in my hair and pinched me affectionately on the cheek.

Once or twice when she moved closer to me or when she reached to pat me on my back, I thought that it would become something more, but it didn't. Perhaps she had enough on her mind with being imprisoned in her own house. Perhaps the injuries on her body from Captain sir's beatings had not healed. Whatever the reason, she let me go, two hours later, my homework complete, without once kissing me on the cheek. That had never happened before. I could not decide whether I was happy or sad about that. I was certainly confused.

Captain sir came home at his usual time, just after I had played the two recordings from that day to myself, at low volume. There was nothing in it that would convince sir that madam was abusing me. He pulled the door shut behind him and came to sit on the couch. I noticed that his shoulders sagged, as though a great invisible weight was pulling them down. I gave him his coffee.

'Did madam eat?'

'Yes, sir.'

'Did she eat well?'

'She ate the normal amount, sir.'

I knew right from wrong, madam had said. I knew what was to be done. It was madam who was imprisoned, but Captain sir looked like he was stuck in a prison of his own. His eyes had taken on the vacant, roving look of a madman. His hair appeared to have thinned from that morning. His cheeks had become sallow and his lips pale. What was right, then? To stand by and watch him punish his wife, obey him or turn against him?

He walked to the steps after finishing his coffee, his gait unsteady. After climbing the first four stairs he unbuckled his belt and pulled it out. The lock of the door clicked. It opened, then shut, with a mild thud. Silence descended on the house, just like the night before. I knew it was futile trying to listen, so I went into the kitchen and busied myself with preparing dinner.

Captain sir came out after an hour and a half or so, just as I had turned on the lights downstairs. The cuckoo clock showed ten minutes to seven. He fell into the couch with a loud sigh, and his body was bathed in sweat. 'Shall I turn on the fan?' I asked, but he shook his head, breathing through parted, parched lips.

'The bitch,' he said. 'The bitch wants a divorce.' His eyes rolled over to look at me. 'I am not going to give her a divorce.'

'Dinner is ready,' I said, and brought out the bowls – one with cauliflower curry, one carrying dal and the third with yoghurt. 'Is madam going to come down?'

'The hell she's going to come down. As long as she doesn't return to her senses she's not going to come out of that room.' His tongue came out, lashed against his lips. 'A few months of sex with a younger man and now she wants a divorce. See how ungrateful women can be, Nari. Don't get sucked into the wiles of a woman, I warn you.'

Looking at him I was reminded of one of those water animals in my science textbook – what was its name? – yes, a sea lion, I thought, or a walrus. His arms and legs were just flipper-like appendages to his bloated torso. 'Please come and eat, sir,' I said.

'Leave it there and go. Leave me alone.' Out came the tongue again and slipped back in. 'Go and give some to your madam. She will be hungry.'

'Yes, sir,' I said, and went in to get the tray and madam's plate from the utensils basket. By the time I came out, Captain sir had come to the table and was examining the contents of the various bowls. I filled two smaller bowls with the curry and dal, placed a glass of water on the tray and went up the stairs.

I forgot to take the recorder with me.

EIGHT

She was sitting with her knees raised and her head buried in between them. As I entered, she looked up. Her red eyes had black marks around them. Her hair looked dishevelled, the skin on her face appeared patchy, but she still looked beautiful, I thought. I placed the tray at the very edge of the bed. She shook her head. 'One of you comes and feeds me with a belt and a cane. Then the other one comes with food. You want to keep me alive only for him to beat me up, don't you?'

I looked toward the door, wondering if I should run out. She must have read my thoughts like she had done so many times before, and said quietly, 'Sit down, Nari.' I buckled down where I was. 'You're not going anywhere until I tell you to.' I nodded. 'Good boy.'

'You see how he treats me, don't you?' She lifted up her nightgown and showed me her stomach, filled with blue-black stains. 'Look! Look at each of these marks and understand that you have let him do that to me.'

'Madam, I –'

'You're all the same. You come here and sit dutifully, giving me food and then you go away and give him food. You stand by and watch as he imprisons me here, as he beats me and you pretend that you cannot hear my cries of help. What kind of man are you that cannot protect a woman in need of help?

'He is eating downstairs, isn't he? He will eat, he will regain his strength and he will come back here with his belt. Whether he will throw me against the wall or fuck me against my will, do you even care? You will just lie down on your bed and pray to your god – for what, Nari? For what do you pray? For courage? If you cannot find it in your heart, nobody will give it to you.'

'Madam,' I said, drawing away from her, yet not daring to get up and run. 'You're scaring me.'

'Am I? Am I? You have not yet seen him come at you with a raised cane. Then you will know what fear is. You know why he beat me today?' She pulled back the sleeve of her gown. Across her upper arm were plastered three red, burning stripes. 'I asked him for a divorce. And you know what he said? He said he would rather kill me than give me a divorce. Is this the kind of man you serve, Nari? Does it not boil your blood to work for a man like him?'

'Madam,' I said, joining my hands at her, 'please eat your food. I am powerless. I am powerless to help you. I truly wish to, but I can't!'

She got off the bed and came to me. Pointing to the wall, she said, 'Go there.' I crawled over to the corner of the wall, just beside the door hinge. She knelt in front of me and held my face in her hands. As she came closer, I saw the bruise marks on her cheeks, the slightly swollen bottom lip. 'Nari,' she whispered. 'I need your help. Captain will kill me otherwise.' She kissed me on my forehead, the tip of my nose, the corners of my mouth. 'You won't let him kill me, will you?'

'No,' I heard myself say.

She took my hands in hers and kissed the callouses at the base of my fingers. She pressed my palms to her eyes and wept into them. 'I need you,' she said. 'I need you.' She guided them to her breasts, and closed her eyes. 'Be gentle. I have not had a gentle man's touch in a month.' I cradled her breasts with my fingers and lifted them up. My thumbs touched her awakening nipples, and she sighed. 'Don't let him take me.' Tears dropped down onto the marble floor. 'Don't let him ever take me again.'

'I won't,' I said.

She began to unbutton my shirt, hurriedly, scratching my chest with her fingernails while doing so. I pushed back against the wall, watching her, even as my hands slid under her gown to fondle her sweat-soaked breasts. 'Remove it!' she ordered, and I obeyed her. In one smooth motion, it came off the top of her body and fell against the door. Then she fell back against the edge of the bed, panting, and we sat there for a moment, staring at each other, our lips parted, our eyes hazy and flickering.

'Do you want me?' she asked innocently, squeezing her breast in my direction.

I did not reply. I went after her and wrestled her to the ground. I sank my teeth into her neck. She chuckled and dug her fingernails into my back. 'You want me, don't you?' she said. 'Hmm?' Using her thighs, she toppled me over and mounted me, one hand clapped over my mouth, the other playing with my chest hair. 'See, this is how I like my men, yummy and full of verve.'

Somehow in the middle of all that insanity, my mind broke through the fog. 'Captain sir,' I said, looking at the tray of food, then back at her. 'He will hear us.'

'So he will,' she said, smiling. Strands of hair fell over her face, and she threw her head back to send them flying away. 'So he will. Let us behave ourselves, then, shall we, big boy?' She dipped two of her fingers into my mouth and rubbed the tip of my tongue with them. 'I will wait for you tomorrow, at our usual time.' She bent down, touched her lips to my chest and slid down to my torso. When she got to my thighs, she gripped the edges of my shorts and made as if to pull it down, but she stopped and smiled up at me. 'Behave,' she said.

When she let me go, I scampered to the corner and sat on my haunches, my shirt thrown over my shoulder. She clambered onto the bed, still topless, and bent over the tray of food. I watched her eat, not certain whether I was more scared of her or of Captain sir.

The next day, when I went back to her room with breakfast, I expected her to pounce on me, because sir had already left for work. I did not carry the recorder with me. I guess I had decided in my mind to rescue her. Rape is about power, people say, and she wielded power over me – my body, my thought, my soul. I don't believe it is possible for anyone who has not been under such complete control of someone else to fully understand what it is like. When she looked at me with tears in her eyes, my heart ached. When she touched me even with the tips of her fingers, my body burned. Once she asked me to help her, I could not possibly say no.

And yet I resented it all. It is perhaps not dissimilar to the smoker who hates every cigarette he smokes and still pines for the next. Or a drug addict whose limbs shudder until they get their poison. Mind over body, we're told repeatedly, but how often does body rule the mind? And where does body end and mind begin?

For anyone who wants answers to my actions, this is all I have. I feared her. That morning, as I carried breakfast up to her room, I even hated her. But I could not get enough of her. I begrudged her the ease with which she seemed to control me.

But she was like a mother to me. If a mother doesn't have the right to control her child, who does? Did I love her? Perhaps I did, but so many of us declare love without knowing what it is. Maybe my love was like that too. I certainly cannot explain what my love is like – greater minds than mine have failed to.

One thing I can tell you, though, is that my love rode on the twin horses of fear and torment. In stories I read of a love that is free of these things, that shines with a light so pure that it soothes the eyes that look straight at it. There is no blackness to this love, I am told, and it doesn't need a reason to be. I am yet to find that love in my life. I am yet to believe that it exists for real.

She took the toast and strawberry jam, the glass of milk. She did not look at me once while she ate, and at the end she said, in a matter-of-fact tone, 'We will escape tonight.'

'Okay,' I said.

'We're never going to come back here, Nari,' she said. 'I will take you to Goa. We will live in my old house. It will take some repair, but we will manage.'

'Okay.'

'I will put you in a school there. I will help you with your homework every day. I will give you all that Captain can give you, and I won't treat you as a servant.'

'Yes, madam.'

'But you have to listen carefully to what I am saying.' She was sitting on the bed, cross-legged. She wagged a finger. 'You cannot come with me tonight, okay? You have to come back here, and you have to make Captain believe that I have run away on my own accord. You have to act surprised.'

'Yes, madam.'

'I would suggest that you give an extra glass of wine to Captain tonight, to put him to sleep. And you have the same thing after I leave. When you wake up in the morning, deny everything. We will make it look like I have escaped on my own.'

'Yes, madam.'

'Now here's what you will do,' she said, and outlined the plan. Her eyes grew wide as she talked, more alive than I ever remembered them to be. I listened to all that she said, and though a part of me felt miserable for plotting behind Captain sir's back like this, there was no alternative. If madam had to escape this prison and live her own life – and she did – there was no other way but this. I was the only person in the world that could help her; how could I pretend as though I could not hear her cries?

Now I know that this was all bullshit, of course. She had friends in Hyderabad. There was that man in her office. There was that girl on the pink scooter. There was that other friend with whom she spent that night. If she truly wanted to escape, all she needed to do was ask me to inform any of these people about the situation and – if required – call the police. Why, she could have told me to go directly to the police myself. But she didn't.

It was later – much later – that I realized this was not at all about her wishing to escape. This was her means to get her revenge against Captain sir – by killing him.

The first inkling that not all was going according to plan hit me at night, after Captain sir had gone to sleep and I went up to open madam's door. She had no bags on her shoulder, just a pair of hand gloves that she was in the processing of slipping on – and Captain sir's walking stick leaning against the corner by her side. Only the bed lamp was turned on; in its light I saw half her face illuminated and the other half in shadow. When she smiled, she looked like a ghost. Once her hands went into the gloves, she stretched her fingers. I could see the shape of her fingernails through the latex. She picked up the stick and walked past me to the landing. She had her hair tied in a ponytail. She was still in her nightgown.

I followed her down the stairs, uncertain of what I must do. She went into Captain sir's bedroom, with me standing at the door. She tiptoed to the side of the bed. Sir was sleeping on his stomach, his face turned away, his arms hugging the pillow. One of his legs was raised, the other was stretched out straight along the length of the bed. Madam looked up at me, and put her finger to her lips. I nodded.

She held the stick in both hands and raised it over her head. With precision, she brought the weight of the metal tip down on Captain's head. There was a clang, like a steel plate hitting the floor. Captain did not stir. A murmur of protest seemed to begin to leave his lips, but it got curtailed and he became silent. I closed my mouth with my hand and pushed back against the wall, clawing at it with my fingers. A deep whine started in my throat, but when she shot me a look I swallowed it. I frantically looked for the heave and drop of his body, and almost cried out in relief when I found it, erratic and slow as it was. But then madam turned back to Captain sir and touched the scalp with the tip of the stick. She then turned sir over on his back. Then she raised it and thumped his head with all her might once again, just above the left eye.

Now sir's body went limp, and it seemed to relax against the cushion of the bed. I would not dare to feel his legs, but I knew that if I did, they would be cold. Madam put her finger under his nose for a second, then looked up at me. 'He's dead,' she said, and just as another whimper was about to escape me, she waddled across the bed on her knees, got off it, held me by the collar and pulled me into the living room.

'What have you done?' I said. 'What have you done? You were going to run away, escape and never come back! Oh god!'

'Shh,' she said, walking up and down the room, from the coffee table to the foot of the staircase and back. 'Gather yourself, Nari! You're the man here, for god's sake!'

'But – but – b-b-but –'

'You know I had to kill him,' she said in a quiet whisper. 'No matter where I run away to, he will find me. The only way I could get freedom from him was by killing him.'

'But – but now the police will come.'

'They will, but they won't know what has happened here. You won't tell them, will you?' She paused to look into the room and it seemed crazy to me that she was looking in on a dead body. Captain, dead. That still did not register. I half-expected him to get up and walk into the room now, running his fingers along the edge of his breeches. 'We have a bit of time now,' she said. 'Neither of us need to get caught in this. We can both get off and we can both go away and live together in Goa.' She dropped her voice further and smiled ruefully at me. 'Just like we spoke in the afternoon.'

'But they will know!' I said. 'They will know, all of them!'

'Nobody will know!' she hissed. 'Come with me. Help me carry him upstairs, will you?' She still had her gloves on and from the window I saw the orange street lamps light up a secluded street. I followed her and took sir's head and arms. She took the feet. We stopped once at the bottom of the stairs to catch our breath, and then once again at the top. By the time we got him into the room, we had begun to pant. Sir's eyes caught the glint of moonlight from the window and seemed to stare at me. I stepped over to the other side and drew the curtain.

'Thank god there isn't much bleeding,' she said, turning on the light. Go down and see if there is blood anywhere.

I walked down the path we had taken, examining every inch of the floor for marks. On the bed there was a little smudge, but it was colourless. I ran my finger on it and touched it to my nose. It had no smell. On the very edge of the bedsheet there was a slight discolouring. I called out to madam. When she came down, she ordered me to wash that part of the sheet with soap and water. 'You do this and come upstairs,' she said. 'We need to talk.'

After washing away all the stains that I could see, I went upstairs to the room. Ramya madam sat on one of the couches, cradling a spear in her hand – I guessed she dismounted it from the wall – waiting. The flower vase that usually stood on the corner table downstairs now sat by her feet. She waved me to the opposite wall. I went and sat there, willing myself not to turn and look into the room.

'If you and I both tell the same story, Nari,' she said, 'then no one can touch us. But if our versions differ, then they will find out everything. Do you understand?'

I nodded.

'Good. Now we will go over this as many times as you wish. We will get it right down to the smallest detail. All these days, Captain has been raping me, abusing me and has put me under house arrest. I asked him for a divorce and he refused me one. All of this will stay in our story. The less we divert from the truth, the better.'

'They will know,' I murmured. 'They will know everything, and they will put us both in prison. For the rest of our lives.'

'Today you were going to help me run away. You drugged Captain so that he wouldn't wake up when we leave the house. You went into the room in which Captain slept, and you opened the cupboard to get my passport and other documents. But then Captain woke up and he asked you what you were doing in his room. He drove you out into the living room, where I was sitting, and he came to know that you were helping me. So he came after you, and you ran up the stairs to hide in this room. Captain came after you with a flower vase.'

'Which one?'

'This one,' she said, pointing at the one at her feet. 'You locked yourself up in this room, but Captain broke it down. When he came into the room, you hit him on the head with this stick, just to defend yourself. After that first blow, he took this spear out of its wall socket and drove it through your shoulder. Clearly afraid for your life, and overcome with instinct, you manage to hit him again, this time from the front, and he fell to the ground.' She frowned at me, still cradling the stem of the spear in her hands. 'Do you understand?'

'But I don't have an injury on my shoulder,' I said.

She got up to her feet and walked over to me with the spear. She placed the point on my left shoulder and said, 'Now you will.' Then, without warning, she pulled it back and pushed it into the flesh just under my breast plate, and I squirmed in pain. 'There,' she said. 'It won't kill you.' She went back to the couch as I fell on my side, twisting. Bringing the vase over, she leaned over me. 'I am going to have to hit you on the head with this, Nari. It will knock you out. But again, it won't kill you.'

I lifted my hand to ward her off, but she held my wrist and pushed it to the side so that she could take a clean swing at my forehead. I heard the beginning of a loud twang deep inside my head, but before it could die out, blackness covered me.

When I came to, it was morning. It took me a moment to blink, look up at the ceiling and figure out where I was. Something clinked on my wrists and suddenly I remembered what had happened last night. I sat up, and saw that I was on the living room couch. My wrists were handcuffed.

Somewhere from another room, madam's voice floated into my ears. I heard my name mentioned once or twice, but I could not hear much of what was being said. The twang from the bump on my head had not yet subsided. My ears felt as though they were being pierced by needles. Two constables sat on either side of me, on the smaller chairs. One of them appeared to be preparing himself to ask me a question, and I closed my eyes and craned my neck against the couch. Let madam answer all the questions, I thought. The plan was hers. She would know what to say. Soon the handcuffs would be taken off, and we could leave for Goa or wherever madam decides that we should go.

I dreamed of Savitramma then. I did not see her in her white sari under the moonlight. Nor did I see her the way she met me on our second night together: clad in a wet brown cloth wrapped around her chest, with her one arm and shoulder bare, her nipple almost visible. I saw her as a shadow, set against the white cloth of Raghuramayya's bullock cart when they left the village. Rumours had begun to flow in the village that she was seeing a younger man, and after a few months of denying them, Raghuramayya took her away to her mother's place. That day, when the cart passed our house, I came running out and watched it until it disappeared around the bend that led to the bus stand and the main road. A dirty white cloth had been hung to cover the back of the cart, and her shadow etched itself on it, her hair swirling, her nose sharp and erect, her lips pursed, her chin set, and her neck, slender and graceful.

Raghuramayya returned to the village that very evening, without her. Nobody asked him where she went – people in the village did not ask questions of Raghuramayya – but it was not hard to guess. No one had seen or heard of her after that.

In a few months, just a few days before I was to leave to come to Hyderabad, Raghuramayya got married again, to the second daughter of a landlord from Lakkavaram. Once or twice the old man at the rock would refer to Savitramma as a witch and a cougar, but soon she slipped from people's memories, and now, I dare say if you were to go to Singavaram and mention the name of Savitramma, people would most likely look up and say, 'Who?'

But from my mind she will never be cast away. It is not my place to question whether she did the right or wrong thing by Raghuramayya, but by me she never did anything wrong. She looked after me much like my mother did. She fed me well during festivals, she read out to me from the Ramayana, she sang for me, she pined for me. She also took me to her bed. On the day that Raghuramayya returned without her, I went to the jasmine creeper by the lakeside and sat looking up at the moon. I threw stones into the brook, smelling the night air, hearing the sound of the waves that the breeze whipped up. I thought of her ringing laugh, and the way her eyes lit up whenever she spotted me in a crowd.

Something stirred next to me, and I opened my eyes. The stench of death came to my nose, and I knew where I was. Footsteps came down the stairs. Ramya madam was with a bigger man dressed in a khaki jacket. Madam was waving her hands, moving her fingers, pointing here and there as she talked. The man frowned and nodded, making notes in his pad. Now and then they looked at me, but their glances did not linger.

Madam finished speaking, and then looked at me with a thin smile. The man walked toward the exit, gesturing to the constables on his way. They sprang to their feet. One of them held me by the arm and pushed me toward the door. I looked over my shoulder at Ramya madam. She closed her eyes and opened them again in reassurance. 'I will come for you,' she said. 'You may have to spend a day or two in prison. Just a formality.'

I wore my slippers and went with the constables, past Captain sir's car, toward the blue jeep parked in front of the gate.

After two days in the Observation Home, I realized that madam was not coming for me. I asked the supervisor at the Home if Ramya madam had called, but he said no, and he looked at me as though I were a beast from a strange land. The attendants said a few things to me when I was alone, things that no respectable man would repeat to another. I wondered at their dislike for me, but what more could I do?

The amount of media coverage that this case has attracted has nothing to do with Captain sir's death, but with the alleged relationship between Ramya madam and me. I saw on the television at the Home – a week or so after I had been brought there – that people had this ridiculous notion that I was raping madam. I asked the supervisor where that came from, and again they saw me as they would a chimpanzee at a zoo, with a mixture of repugnance and curiosity.

In the middle of my second week, an elderly man in a black coat and white pants came to meet me. I had become weak with fever by then and had begun to vomit three times a day. He came and sat by me, and laid a hand on my knee. 'I have to come to take you home,' he said.

'Whose home?' I asked.

'Mrs Pradhan signed for your bail. She said that I should act on your behalf.'

'What does that mean?'

'I am going to try and get you free.'

'But I did not do anything.'

'We're going to prove that to everybody.'

I shook my head weakly. 'You don't understand. Ramya madam already knows that I have not done anything. She will tell everyone. Did you speak to her?'

The man did not say anything. 'Perhaps we should first take you home, get you washed up and ready for court.'

'For court? Madam said I won't need to go to court.'

'Narayana, you have to go to court. You have been accused of killing Captain Abhilash Tirthankar.'

I sat up on my ledge, and despite the splitting headache, managed to shake it clear. 'You think I killed Captain sir?'

'Your madam has said that you have,' he said. 'And she has also levelled charges of numerous counts of rape against you.'

I still could not understand what he said. It felt like he was speaking in a foreign language. Now, looking back, of course, I fully understood; I just was not ready to accept it as the truth. Now I also understand why Ramya madam must have decided after knocking me out to blame everything on me; it is so much easier to get people to believe that than the story she had narrated to me before I passed out. If one man dies and two people live, it makes sense for one of the survivors to blame the other for everything. There is nothing personal in this; it's just survival instinct.

I know all this now, but on that day I broke down and cried on the lawyer's arm. He soothed me with kind words and took me away to Mrs Pradhan's house. We did not speak much to each other that day; she made a bed for me, gave me some lime juice, some tablets, and some blankets. She arranged for my bath, gave me a fresh pair of clothes, and read *Pride and Prejudice* to me while I slept.

To my father, I wrote letters of assurance that everything will be all right. They have seen my pictures, of course, on television, and he had come to Captain sir's house only to be turned away from the gate. I asked after Raji's education and health. I even wished my stepmother well. It is amazing how easily you forgive people for their little errors when in the middle of a crisis. I think the right word for it is perspective.

I am not sure if I will come out of this with my name unsullied. Mr Anant Murthy says that the evidence is overwhelmingly against us, and that it will be extremely unlikely for us to win, barring any acts of god. When he said that I thought of the elephant god in the lamp lit chamber at sir's house, and his smiling eyes and his pot-like tummy. I envied him his wisdom, once again, for having stayed away from women his whole life. I had a feeling that if he could look at me now (of course he could), he would throw up his trunk into the air and laugh.

I also hope that if he can look at me right now, he will be my witness. After all, he has seen all that has happened in the house.

OTHER TESTIMONIES

This section contains transcripts of the testimonies of the people connected to this case, followed by the interrogator's comments.

SRIDHAR MALLELA

Pursuing PhD in Psychology at the University and Intern at Dr Ramya Tirthankar's clinic

I : What was the nature of your relationship with Ramya Tirthankar?

SM : It was one of sexual exploitation. She misused her position of authority and brought in a clearly unwelcome sexual component into our relationship.

I : Did you ever encourage such behaviour from Mrs Tirthankar?

SM : No, not to my knowledge.

I : So if someone were to say that you were a willing participant in your relationship with Mrs Tirthankar, that your bond was a consensual one, how would you respond to that?

SM : I would deny it quite vociferously. I am willing to believe, though, that Mrs Tirthankar may have found ways to convince herself that I was a willing participant. A common delusion among sexual abusers is that they insist the victim derived pleasure from their acts.

I : You have spoken about this to your superiors at the university?

SM : I have lodged a formal complaint, yes. On the termination of my internship with Mrs Tirthankar, I consulted my mentor and guide, Dr Awasthi, in the Psychology department. He insisted that I should make a complaint and ensure that the facts come out.

I : Have you spoken about your relationship with Mrs Tirthankar with anyone else, besides Dr Awasthi?

SM : No.

I : Not even to Miss Ankita Khandelwal, with whom you worked at Mrs Tirthankar's clinic?

SM : No. I never told Ankita anything about this. But there was often just a wall separating us from her. I cannot blame her for making her own assumptions based on what she could hear.

I : Do you allege that you made your discomfort plain to Mrs Tirthankar every time she approached you for a sexual liaison?

SM : Not every time, but for the first few times, yes. I made it quite clear that what she had in mind was unprofessional and exploitative.

I : Why only the first few times?

SM : After that, I resigned myself to the fact that she was not going to take no for an answer. She had the power to grade my work and make recommendations to the university, so I was naturally anxious not to ruffle her feathers in any way.

I : In Mrs Tirthankar's account of what has happened, she says that you were the one who first pursued her romantically. What do you say to that?

SM : I most emphatically deny it.

I : Did you at any time call Mr Abhilash Tirthankar?

SM : No, I did not. But I called Ramya's phone and he answered the call. So I did speak to him, yes.

I : Why did you call Mrs Tirthankar?

SM : She had not come to the clinic. She had not called either me or Ankita. As her subordinate, I think it's natural for me to call her in such circumstances. We had to know what to tell the patients, whether we had to wait for her or if we could take a day off.

I : What happened when you spoke to Mr Abhilash Tirthankar?

SM : He spoke to me rather rudely. He seemed to have convinced himself that I was the one who had seduced his wife. I tried to deny it but he spoke as though he knew everything already. He also said that he had ways to make sure that I would never get my PhD.

I : And what did you say to that?

SM : I was naturally afraid of what he would do to jeopardize my work. I told him that I wanted to sit with him and explain everything that had occurred.

I : Did you make any reference to Mrs Tirthankar during this conversation?

SM : Yes, I asked him if she was all right.

I : Why did it occur to you that she may not be all right?

SM : The whole thing had a suspicious ring to it. I called on her phone, but he picked up. He appeared to be drunk when he was talking to me. And his general tone was that of deep malice. I somehow got the inkling that he had done something to Mrs Tirthankar.

I : Did you threaten Mr Tirthankar that you would go to the police?

SM : No, not at all. I was in no position to threaten him. He threatened me, rather, with dire consequences if I kept seeing his wife.

I : Did you ever propose marriage to Mrs Tirthankar?

SM : No.

I : Did you ever propose that you should move in together?

SM : No.

I : Was there any tender feeling of romance from your side?

SM : No.

Interrogator's comments

The subject was calm and collected throughout the interview. He never hesitated to answer a question. He sat erect in his chair, with his hands on the table, fingers curled into fists. He wore a deep-set frown, and every once in a while there would be a flinch and a grimace. It seemed clear that the incident has bothered him greatly. There was a tone of defiance in his answers.

Is he telling the truth? Probably not in response to every question. If he agrees with Mrs Tirthankar's statement, it will affect his career at the university. At the moment, the most pragmatic thing that he can do is insist that he has been a victim.

Having said that, it doesn't appear that he is lying about everything either. The disgust he displayed towards Mrs Tirthankar's handling of him seemed genuine. His views on things, generally speaking, are logical and well-thought out. He appears to be a balanced, conscious individual.

ANKITA KHANDELWAL

Secretary at Dr Ramya Tirthankar's clinic

I : Tell me a little about your time as Mrs Tirthankar's assistant.

AK : It was good, sir. I am doing my MBA. My father has an illness, and this job paid well.

I : What is the nature of your relationship with Sridhar Mallela?

AK : He was my colleague at the clinic, sir. He helped maintain madam's cases and wrote reports on them.

I : Do you know much about his research at the university?

AK : No, sir.

I : Has there been any other dimension to your relationship with him?

AK : I do not understand, sir...

I : Has he ever asked you out for a coffee, for instance? Or to the movies?

AK : No, sir.

I : Did it ever strike you that he was trying to flirt with you?

AK : No, sir.

I : Did you nurture such ambitions, to perhaps explore a romantic angle with him?

AK : No, sir. He is not my type.

I : What was the nature of Mr Mallela's relationship with Mrs Tirthankar?

AK : As I said, sir, he wrote reports on case studies.

I : Was there a sexual angle to this relationship, do you think?

AK : (After a pause) Yes, sir. They would close the door to the chamber under the pretext of discussing a case, and I would hear - sounds.

I : What kind of sounds?

AK : Sexual sounds.

I : Did Mr Mallela ever allude to these sounds during his conversations with you?

AK : No, sir. Our relationship was quite formal, quite cold.

I : So you never - say - shared a joke or laughed with him?

AK : Oh, that we did, sir. But we never had deep conversations or anything like that, you know. Once or twice I pulled his leg about being madam's pet.

I : And how did he respond to that?

AK : He just laughed, sir. I think he rather enjoyed it.

I : Would you say, then, that the relationship between the two of them was consensual?

AK : Oh, yes, sir. Most certainly. The sounds I heard - well - they left one in no doubt.

I : Did you ever feel uncomfortable about what was happening in the chamber?

AK : No, sir. It was not my place to question what madam did on her premises. She paid me well, and always on time. If I did not like the sounds, I could always plug my ears with earphones, can't I? And I did too, often enough.

I : Have you ever met Mr Abhilash Tirthankar?

AK : Yes, sir, he came to the office on the day madam and Sridhar went to the movies.

I : What did he say to you?

AK : He asked me if I would record the sounds, and I said yes.

I : Did he give you anything in return?

AK : Yes, sir. He got my father admitted into a really good hospital. Didn't help him, of course, but his last days were quite peaceful, thanks to Mr Tirthankar.

Interrogator's comments

The subject comes across as timid and easily influenced. She averted her eyes from the questioner repeatedly throughout the session, and she shifted a lot in her seat. Especially, when asked about Mr Mallela and Mrs Tirthankar, she became more fretful. Kept looking at the clock. Chewed gum. Gulped a lot.

It does not appear as though there is anything romantic between her and Sridhar. Both parties deny it, and both do so convincingly. It seems that at least this part of Mrs Tirthankar's statement was born out of her own imagination. Even if we consider the notion that both Mr Mallela and Miss Khandelwal are lying, the latter did not make any attempt to protect the former. Another possibility is that they were once together, and are now no longer so. That may explain the bitterness.

The other thing that deserves notice is that Miss Khandelwal is positively inclined toward Captain Tirthankar for the good turn he did to her father. Yes, he took payback in the form of evidence of Mrs Tirthankar's sexual activities at the office, but it is likely that Miss Khandelwal still feels indebted.

One understands that there is no such thing as a neutral witness. It therefore pays to be aware of all the possible biases that may enter each statement.

HARITHA KRISHNAMURTHY

Patient and Friend of Dr Ramya Tirthankar

I : Tell me about your relationship with Mrs Ramya Tirthankar.

HK : She was my counsellor for a few months. Our relationship was professional for the first month or so, and then we became friends because we had a few things in common. She and I were rape victims at some time or the other in our lives, and we both have such lonely lives. As you know, I am a widow, and she's suffered greatly at the hands of her husband. And now she has all this other stuff to deal with, so it's quite natural that we turned to each other for support.

I : Has Mrs Tirthankar confided in you about her situation?

HK : Yes, absolutely she has. And I have no doubt in my mind that Nari is guilty. And even that boy, Sridhar. It's very fine of him to come out now and say that none of it was consensual, but of course he would say that. He has his research and his image in the university to protect. No man will admit that he played his part in seducing a woman if he can get away with accusing her of all wrongdoing. Typical men, all of them. And with Nari too, I know the media is going all agog with his age and 'innocence' and all that, but whoever has had teenaged boys will know that they are no longer innocent starting from age thirteen. Anyone who denies this is either extremely delusional or extremely dishonest.

I : Have you met Mr Abhilash Tirthankar?

HK : No, and I am glad I haven't. Any man who beats his wife and rapes her can fall off a cliff and I won't even shed a tear.

Interrogator's comments

Mrs Krishnamurthy is an angry and sure woman. One gets the feeling on speaking with her that she's never uncertain or tentative about anything. Her opinions of Narayana, Sridhar and Captain Tirthankar are already made, and she has no doubt at all that Mrs Tirthankar has been a mere plaything in their hands.

She comes across as a woman who believes deeply that all men are born with an instinctive desire to control women. Her record shows that she has had a traumatic childhood. Throughout the interview, she had her chin set at a firm angle and kept her eyes fixed on the interviewer.

She is not one of the main players of the drama, so most of her views are second-hand, but it should be noted that her frienship with Mrs Tirthankar is a strong one. This makes her antagonism toward the men of Mrs Tirthankar's life a little more understandable.

PALLAVI PRADHAN

Librarian at Narayana's school in Hyderabad

I : What can you tell us about Nari?

PP : Smart boy. Very intelligent. A little rustic, and his English is not as good as it should be, but he picked it up very quickly. A little vulnerable maybe, and has an inferiority complex, due to his background. But overall, very sharp.

I : Has he told you about what occurred at the Tirthankar house?

PP : He has, yes, in quite a lot of detail.

I : Do you believe him?

PP : (Pause.) I don't know what to believe.

I : And yet you have arranged for his bail, and for a lawyer to represent him.

PP : I just think that his side of the story needs to be told.

I : Does it not bother you that you may be sheltering a rapist?

PP : It does not, no. Nari is not a rapist until the court proves that he is one.

Interrogator's comments

It is hard to know why Mrs Pradhan is willing to go to such lengths to defend Nari. There is no record of previous association between them. Neither does a glance at Mrs Pradhan's life reveal anything instructive. She has been a school librarian most of her life. Her late husband was also in the army for some time. Their only child - a daughter - lives in Mumbai.

At least from the outside, Mrs Pradhan has lived a most 'normal' life. It comes as a surprise, therefore, that she has taken such an interest in this matter. One cannot help but take her motivations at face value: that she is driven by a sense of justice, which perhaps is not surprising in a teacher.

YASMIN

Former cook at the Tirthankars' house

I : Do you know Nari well?

Y : Not well, sir. We worked together at Captain sir's house for a week, that's all.

I : Nari says in his account of the incident that it was you who taught him to cook. Is that true?

Y : Yes, sir.

I : He also says that he was in the habit of meeting you at the vegetable market on a few mornings.

Y : No, sir. I used to see him, is all, from a distance. Never spoke to him once.

I : You didn't know, then, about what was going on in the house?

Y : No, sir.

I : He didn't tell you about the incidents of Mrs Tirthankar abusing him?

Y : No, sir. Mrs Tirthankar is a nice woman. She would not do such a thing to anybody.

I : You never met Nari in front of the Radha Krishna temple at the corner of the street?
Y : No, sir.

I : Do you know what this is?
Y : (Looks at the table.) A voice recorder, sir?

I : Nari says you asked him to buy one so that he could gather evidence against Mrs Tirthankar.
Y : No, sir. I don't even know how these things work.

Interrogator's comments

The subject seemed to be a quiet person. Either that or she was terrified at being questioned. She did not corroborate any of the details in Nari's story, but it could be that she doesn't want to be involved in a drama such as this. It could affect her equation with her other employers in the area.

She may lean under pressure, but it's impossible to know in which direction.

AFTERWORD

It's not easy to write a novel on rape without raising a few eyebrows. No matter how balanced and neutral an author claims to be, the reader is liable to find hidden meanings in the text. The topic is such.

Many of *Nari's* early readers either loved it or hated it. But they all wondered why I wrote a novel such as this, and what I wished to 'say' with it. Now that you've finished the book, you may find similar questions flitting about your head too. If so, here's my answer.

Any author would agree that at least half of the motivation that goes into writing a book is internal. My primary reason for writing Nari was the hope that by the end of it, I will have learnt more about the issues of rape and sexual abuse. In the larger context, I hoped to learn more about human sexual behaviour in general, because it seems to me that we cannot untangle the knot of rape without examining our sexual selves.

There are deep, inherent contradictions in our daily conversations about rape. Let me give you an example. It is commonly agreed that unless the woman gives explicit consent, any advances by a man would amount to sexual harassment. And yet in all the social scripts that govern our sexual behaviour, the woman is meant to say no, play hard to get, give the man something to chase. The whole narrative of the man wooing and charming the woman into liking him is deeply ingrained into our psyches.

Are the two messages contradictory? Undoubtedly. In writing Nari, I hoped to make sense of such contradictions. I hoped to take the narrative of rape out of the vacuum where it is usually viewed and place it as a sub-theme in the wider, vaster subject of how human beings view and have sex.

After all, one cannot hope to learn much about drug or alcohol abuse without first understanding drug or alcohol use. Why should sex be different?

I think this deep understanding – of sexual behaviour in general, and of abuse in particular – can only help us deal with it better. I can't help but wonder whether the deep emotional reaction we reserve for rape incidents in our country is not driven by a certain fear; a fear of not knowing what it is, where it comes from, and most importantly, how to recover from it and how to fight back against it.

Writing Nari has shown me that rape and sexual abuse are not as simple as they appear – bare and stripped to the bone – on television debates. Often in the interests of time and readability we simplify a topic, and in doing so we lose its very essence. My hope with this story is that you have accompanied me on a journey, not of judgement or anger, but of curiosity, of exploration.

Because in any war, the first – and the most critical – step to victory is knowledge of the enemy. If we're to win this war against rape, we must first know it.

On another level, of course, Nari is a story. And just like any other story, it doesn't stand for or mean one thing, or even a bunch of things. It is not my place to tell you what you should take away from it, or even if you should take away anything at all. One of the great joys of fiction – both in reading it and writing it – is the freedom one has to find one's own meanings, to build experiences, to form judgements. I do not wish to rob you of that joy.

So make of it what you will. Your thoughts are as good as mine.